HARBOR

RENZO + LUCIA, BOOK 2

BETHANY-KRIS

Published by Bethany-Kris

www.bethanykris.com

ISBN 13: 978-1-988197-80-7

Cover Art © London Miller

Editor: Elizabeth Peters

For all the ones who have made my life more amazing simply by showing up.

CONTENTS

PROLOGUE

har·bor

/ˈhärbər/

verb
1. keep (a thought or feeling, typically a negative one) in one's mind,
especially secretly.
2. give a home or shelter to.

There's got to be more to life than this.
Even as the old man landlord bitched in the apartment doorway, Renzo
Zulla's mind was on something else entirely. Somewhere that bills weren't a
problem, and rent wasn't due. Somewhere that a newborn didn't cry harder
than other newborns, and he didn't have to stay up all night just to watch
the baby shake in his sleep because the drugs their mother had pumped into
her body during his pregnancy hadn't left his blood yet.

Somewhere that was better than here.

He'd not found it yet.

"Where is your mother?" the landlord demanded.

Renzo came out of his thoughts to stare the man head-on. What should
he say?

I don't know.

She left the night we brought Diego home.

Probably shooting up somewhere.

Renzo figured none of those things would help his case here. If only
because, well, the man might call someone on Renzo. It was just him and
Rose, and two-week-old Diego in the apartment. He wasn't even fucking
seventeen yet, either.

"She's out," Renzo lied.

The bitterness that festered in his chest whenever he lied for his mother
grew each time he had to do it. Mostly because he didn't want to have to lie
for her at all. It wasn't like she deserved it. She couldn't even do the bare
minimum for the three kids she brought into the world, but here he was
protecting her time and time again.

Even if it wasn't really for her.

Still pissed him off.

"When is she gonna be back?" the landlord demanded.

Renzo swallowed the thickness in his throat, replying, "Later, maybe."

Days was more like it.

If not *weeks*.

Carmen was harder to predict than the weather, and Renzo had stopped trying. Besides, he didn't have the time or patience anymore. He had other things to worry about—the two-week-old in his arms, for example. Diego needed to eat, and Renzo was running low on that powder formula. Or even the girl in the living room trying to get her brush stroke *just right* with paint brushes he'd lifted from an art store, and a canvas her teacher let her take from school.

He couldn't worry about where the fuck his mother was right now, or when she was going to get back. Frankly, a part of him wished she would never come back because honestly, life might be easier.

It would certainly be better.

"Well," the landlord grunted, pushing his heavy body away from the door *finally*, "I am gonna need that rent before the end of the day, Renzo, or a notice is going up on the door. Do you hear me?"

Renzo wished his throat didn't feel so fucking tight, so he could tell this man where he should shove his goddamn rent money. "You'll get your money."

"Make sure of it." The man's beady eyes dropped to the swaddled—the lady next door showed Renzo how to do it for Diego—baby tucked into Renzo's arms. "Cute kid—having them younger and younger, huh?"

The landlord didn't give him a chance to reply and deny that Diego was his son before he turned and left. Not that it would matter, really. Very few people had even known his mother was pregnant with a third child she would never be able to care for because of her drug habit and lack of love for her children. All the drugs she used kept her sickly-skinny, and sickly-looking, too. She'd barely looked pregnant when Diego was finally born, and he barely broke five pounds on the scale, too.

"Ren?"

Closing the apartment door, Renzo turned to face his almost-fifteen-year-old sister with what he hoped seemed like a smile. He couldn't be fucking sure. Even smiling was more difficult than it should be, really.

"Yeah, everything is fine, Rose," he told her.

His sister didn't look like she believed it.

He didn't have time to placate her. Not right now. A quick peek out the window told him they were getting close to the day being over which meant the rent needed to be in that asshole's hand. He didn't have the rent money—all the money he had saved up from doing odd jobs for Vito Christiano—which wasn't very much—went straight into getting them into this place before Diego was born, keeping his mother calm so she didn't ruin the whole damn thing, and making sure Diego had what Renzo assumed a baby needed.

He was deadass *broke*.

He hadn't been able to pick up a job from Vito since Diego was born because he hadn't been able to leave the baby alone. Who the hell else was going to take care of him? His *mother?* Her coked-out ass could barely take care of herself *when* she was around to do that.

"I need you to look after Diego for a couple of hours," Renzo said, passing over the sleeping baby. "*Do not* put him down and walk away from him, Rose. He's still shaking, and he doesn't sleep a lot as it is. It helps when you hold him—he doesn't get as scared or loud."

Really, Renzo thought it didn't hurt the baby as much when someone was holding him. It calmed him. Rose didn't really understand because Renzo never thought to explain to her that drugs plus a pregnancy didn't equal anything good, but as long as she followed his direction with Diego, then that was all he cared about.

Rose peered down at the swaddled baby. "What if he wakes up?"

"Change his diaper, and give him a bottle."

"But he throws up every time he eats, Ren!"

Yeah, that was another thing …

"As long as he doesn't choke, then he's okay. Just pat his back and see if he'll take more. Can you handle it, or what?"

Rose didn't look all that confident, but Renzo didn't have the time to find someone else to watch the baby.

"I need to get out of here—I will be two hours, tops. Okay?"

"Just two hours?" Rose questioned.

Renzo shrugged. "Maybe less."

Unlikely, but if it got him out of that apartment …

"All right," Rose said.

Great.

• • •

Vito Christiano was a terrifying figure on the streets—he always wore black, no matter what. Black shoes, black suits, and a fucking black heart, if you asked anybody. Black was his color. Like his dark eyes, and the color of the Cadillac he drove through the Bronx twice a week just to remind every fucker working on the corner that he *owned their asses*.

Renzo's work with Vito always came down to two simple things— Renzo's availability and willingness to do a job, and Vito's needs at any given moment. He could always be available, and he was willing to do just about any job, but Vito on the other hand, didn't always have work to give Renzo, or … he made it seem that way.

Another thing the guy *didn't* do?

Take requests.

Maybe that was why Renzo was so surprised to see that familiar Cadillac pull up next to the alleyway where he'd been keeping safe from the rain for the last forty-five minutes since he made the call to Vito on the payphone down the block. The passenger side window rolled down, and Vito's cold, dark eyes stared at him from the driver's seat.

"What, are you going to stand in that alley all night, Ren?" the Italian asked. "Because I am not getting my ass out of this car to walk to you, *cafone.*"

It wasn't that getting inside the Cadillac made Renzo scared, but rather … uncomfortable. Mostly because when he was outside of the vehicle, he felt like he had a little more control. He wasn't closed off, and closed in. He could—or he had a chance, rather—to get away if he needed to.

There was nowhere to go inside that car.

And he knew things about Vito … he knew what people said about this man. *Mafioso,* they whispered. *Organized crime*, people said.

Bad fuckin' news.

"I don't have all night," Vito snapped.

Renzo was quick to push off the wall of the alley, and head for the car. It wasn't like he had a choice. The smell of new leather and pine needles filled his lungs the second he sat in the vehicle. Warmth blew from the heaters, and a quiet melody strummed from the speakers—old music Renzo had little to no interest in.

But he wasn't here for the leather, the warmth, or the music.

"Lucky I was in the area," Vito grumbled around the toothpick he'd pulled from behind his ear to stick in the corner of his mouth. "I don't have time to chase boys all around the city, Renzo. What do you need? I thought you had other things to handle. New baby, right?"

Renzo kept one eye on the man in the driver's seat, and one on the road ahead of him. "Need a job. Something to get done and be paid before the day is out."

Vito grunted. "I don't have anything for you at the moment."

Shit.

"At all?"

Vito shook his head, and scrubbed a hand down his throat. "Nothing you would wanna take, anyhow."

"I have a four-hundred-dollar rent bill to pay, and food to buy for my sister and brother. So, I'm not really picky now, Vito."

There, he said it.

Now, he could pretend like he hadn't.

Vito was quiet for a long while, but Renzo still felt the man's eyes burning holes into him from the side. It was easier to act like the guy wasn't sizing him up when he didn't have to look at him. He hated pity—useless emotion, really. It did nothing for him. Pity didn't make money appear, or keep them from going hungry.

Pity just *was*.

"Your Ma's fucked off again, then?" Vito asked.

Renzo stiffened in the seat. He'd *never* told Vito about Carmen, or the constant shit she put her kids through. There wasn't a need to tell the man, really. "How—"

"And I bet your fuck-up of a father ain't been around, either," Vito mumbled.

His head snapped to the side, and he eyed Vito openly, wary, and concerned. They didn't talk personal shit whenever Renzo did a job for the guy, and he wasn't even sure how Vito knew anything about his drug addict mother and deadbeat father.

Vito was about to explain, apparently. "Used to run these streets with your dad, yeah? Me and him, wanted that button like nothing else. Gonna be *made*, we used to say." The man chuckled, and gave Renzo a look from the side as he shrugged with a raised brow, adding, "Made men, you know?"

Yeah, Renzo knew what that meant.

Sort of.

"Sure," he said.

Vito nodded, and laughed in that dry, dark way again. "I think you *know* the words, but not what it is, kid. And that's fine—you don't need to know. Couldn't leave that mother of yours alone, though. Like he couldn't leave the fuckin' bottle alone, too. Or how you couldn't trust him with anything more than a few dollars because he ran it to the casino, or a damn bookie the first chance he could."

Renzo swallowed hard.

None of that was a lie.

"Gotta follow the rules of made men if you're gonna be a made man," Vito mumbled more to himself than Renzo as he patted the pocket of his silk shirt. Soon, he found the cigarette and lighter he was looking for, lighting it up and sticking it in his mouth. Renzo ignored the heavy smoke, and tried to focus on the quiet street ahead of him. "I followed the rules, you know? Got my button, but had to step away from him. Can't be connected to people who make you look bad. Knew about you, though, and your sister. Your ma never got any better; neither did your father."

"Listen—"

Vito coughed on a heavy drag of the cigarette, and rolled down his window a bit to flick the ash outside. "No, you listen. I'll spot you what you need, Ren. I bet you don't like owing somebody money, so I suspect you're gonna do whatever I want you to do to pay me back, and that's good. That's a good thing because you're smart enough and just quick enough to maybe make something of nothing on these streets. We'll get you figured out for that. But it's not that—the money—that you need to worry about, okay?"

Renzo glanced over at the man. "I don't understand."

"There's a book," Vito said, taking another drag from the cigarette and then eyeing the cherry red tip. "A book called *The Angry Christian*. The author—a guy named Bert Ghezzi—says that resentment is akin to taking poison into your body willingly, and hoping it kills the person you're resentful of, or who caused your resentment."

He didn't know how to reply to that, so he just stayed quiet. Vito didn't seem like he minded, really.

"Anger's the same way, you know. Bitterness, too. You harbor enough of that for them, Ren, and it's only going to get worse over the years. It ain't gonna do nothing to them, but it's going to kill you. Like putting a gun to your head, holding it there, and then pulling the trigger hoping it's going to kill *them*. It ain't never gonna kill them, kid … harboring that only hurts you. Learn to let it go."

Renzo blinked.

Vito wasn't wrong.

He hated his parents.

Hated this life they brought him into.

Hated *everything*.

"Yeah," Vito said quietly like he could read Renzo's mind. "Yeah, kid, that right there. Gotta let it go, Ren."

"I don't know how—"

"Do you know what harbor means, yeah?"

Renzo cleared his throat. "I guess."

"Mmm, not the noun, or the usage of the verb I just gave you, the *other* one," Vito said.

"No."

Vito sighed. "If you can't let go of what you're harboring, Ren, then you need to learn to be someone else's harbor. The safe place—the refuge. People are counting on you, right? Don't let them down. Don't let them down by falling into the same rabbit hole of the people who made you, kid. You gotta be better."

Renzo sucked in a sharp breath. "Yeah, all right."

"You gotta *do* better."

With that said, Vito opened the dash on the car to expose *stacks* of money. He gestured at it with one hand, saying to Renzo, "You take what you need, and you pay it back with forty percent interest on the top. You got me?"

That's a lot of money.

"Go ahead," Vito grunted, replacing the cigarette with the toothpick again, "and then we'll talk about what job you're gonna do for me next, kid."

Renzo took the money.

Like Vito said, he had to be that shelter—the safe harbor.

People were counting on him.

He couldn't let them down.

ONE

The world was prettiest when it was dark. Shrouded in silence, all distractions sleeping for the moment, a person could finally reflect on everything. Their life, and what had become of it. Their choices, and why they made them.

Anything.

A person could think about anything when it was dark.

Yet, the only thing Lucia Marcello could think about as she watched the dark highway climb ahead of their vehicle was how long they had been driving. She blinked one too many times, pretty sure that the last time she had stared at the highway, there had been a lot fewer trees and more sunlight. The highway had been far more congested, too.

She peered at the clock on the dash, taking in the time before counting back the hours.

"Twenty," she murmured.

In the driver's seat, Renzo passed her a look. Despite her confusion, she hadn't for one second forgot that he was next to her driving like he had been for the last several hours—*almost an entire day of driving, now.* It was impossible for her to just forget this man was near. Her whole body felt it, like he lit her on fire in the best way possible. All of her little hairs stood on end, and her nerves snapped. Even sitting beside her, he wasn't nearly close enough.

Or, that's how she felt.

Strange how that worked …

His brow quirked up, a silent question without him saying anything to her out loud. He wouldn't want to wake his sleeping brother in the back seat, after all. He'd even turned down the music when it seemed to be making Diego toss and turn more than usual. Always his first concern, Diego took importance.

Lucia didn't mind.

"What are you mumbling about over there?"

Had she been mumbling?

"We've been driving for twenty hours," she told him quietly.

Renzo nodded, and his grip on the SUV's steering wheel tightened. "Yeah, I know."

If he'd been keeping track, too, he hadn't said anything to Lucia about it. Then again, they had just taken off … they were basically on the run in a stolen vehicle after burning another stolen vehicle. She didn't blame him for being distracted, and focusing on the things he needed his attention to be on.

How many hours they had been driving probably wasn't even a blip on his radar. But it was on hers, now. The more she watched Renzo from the side, the easier it was for her to see what he was trying to suppress. His gaze dropped every so often, darting to the clock before going back to the road. His eyes were dimmed with tiredness even if it was hard to see in the low lighting of the vehicle. He kept that tight grip on the steering wheel no matter what, though, but Lucia was wondering how much effort that was taking him to do exactly that.

"Ren?"

"Hmm, what, baby?"

She smiled.

He'd said it so absently, like she wasn't far from his mind now, but he was still worrying about other things. He needed to sleep. They needed to stop and rest, or she needed to drive. Either one would be fine for Lucia as long as it meant Renzo was going to relax for a couple of hours, and close his eyes.

"I can drive," she said.

"I know you can drive."

"So let me do that for a while. Pull over, let me drive."

His gaze drifted to her again, and the edges of his lips quirked up in a smile. "I'm good."

"But—"

"Lucia, I don't even know where I'm going. How are you going to know, huh?"

He did have a good point even if she didn't want to admit it. What good would it do them if she ended up getting lost while he was sleeping?

"Still haven't figured that out, then?" she asked.

"Where we're going?"

"Yeah."

Renzo let out a sigh, and one of his hands finally left the steering wheel to snake across the middle of the seats. His fingers wrapped tightly around her thigh, and squeezed. It wasn't much. He wasn't even looking at her then what with his attention back on the road ahead of them, and the darkness stretching across miles and miles of highway. It didn't have to be a lot, though.

That touch was enough. It sent sparks shooting across her skin, and heated her blood up like nothing else. His touch grounded her. And really, she hadn't realized how much she needed that feeling until he did it.

He was still in that mindset, she realized. The same mindset he'd been thrust into the moment his mother let the threat to take Diego away from him slip out of her dirty mouth. Self-preservation kicked in for Renzo; his need to take care and protect his brother came first before anything else. It

9

was like nothing else mattered to him for the moment.

Just that.

His brother.

He was determined to put as many miles between himself and Diego and the threat as he could. Maybe once he felt like they had gone far enough, that part of his brain would shut off. He would come back—be *Ren* again. Relax, and realize things were as fine as they were going to get. Until he got to that point, though, he was going to be like this. Distracted, and distant. Quiet, and stuck inside his head.

He was still hers like this.

Just a little different.

Lucia blinked at the sign that they passed by in the darkness, lit up only by their headlights. Had she missed an entire state? Because the last time she realized where they were, it had not been Iowa. "I fell asleep?"

Renzo chuckled, and his smile deepened into something sexier. "Might have."

She passed him a look. "What does that mean?"

"Means sometimes you talk in your sleep. Mumble, and go on, you know."

Lucia might have felt embarrassed about that, but it was Renzo, and the last thing he ever did was make her feel ashamed. Oh, he made her feel a hell of a lot of things. Most, she didn't even know what to do with.

The most prominent was *love.*

God, she loved him.

She loved him enough to do this—to get in a vehicle, and just drive. To go without looking back, as long as she was with him while she did it. To say fuck the rest because she was following him.

To forget where she came from because where she was going would always be better.

It would have to be better.

She was going with him, after all.

"I was thinking Vegas, actually," Renzo said, his thumb stroking her inner thigh. "I know somebody there—an old friend, you could say."

"Vegas."

"What do you think?"

The city of sin.

Yet another city that never slept.

Too many people to count. They'd blend in well, the same way everyone else did. Lucia had been to a lot of places in her life, but Las Vegas was not one of them. Her aunt, Kim, came from Vegas and her family tried to keep a healthy distance for the sake of peace. Or, that's what she had always been told.

Some mafia families simply didn't play well together.

"Well?" Renzo asked, giving her another look.

It was still his eyes, she knew. Whatever it was he was feeling or thinking, but especially when it came to her, she could always find the truth shining in his eyes. There, nothing was hidden. At least, not from her.

Like now.

Anticipation.

Fear.

Love.

All that stared back at her, waiting.

"I'm going wherever you go," she said.

Did he need her to keep saying that?

How many times would she say it before he finally believed it?

It was true—no matter what he thought, or how it made him feel, it was still going to be true. She didn't doubt this would cause trouble. Mostly her taking off with him ... everything else was just *everything else*. But couldn't they climb that hill when it came? It wasn't here yet, and so, Lucia didn't want to deal with it yet.

Silly, yes.

Ignorant, sure.

What else could she do?

Lucia was where she wanted to be. Nothing was going to make that any less true.

"All right," Renzo murmured. "We'll stop on the other side of Iowa, grab some food, and switch some shit out."

She didn't know what that meant.

She didn't care, either.

"You should still let me drive for a while," Lucia said. "You could use some sleep, Ren."

Renzo chuckled. "I'll sleep when I'm dead, baby."

Yeah, that's what she was scared of the most.

• • •

Diego sat in the opened hatch of the back of the SUV eating a kid's meal and chattering on in the afternoon light. Lucia opened the toy that came with his meal, and handed it over to the smiling four-year-old. It wasn't like the toy was very much—a small writing pad and a pack of mini pencil crayons to draw with. She supposed that was better than a cheap piece of plastic that would either break before he could play with it, or would get thrown in the garbage when he had no interest in it anymore.

He took the pad and pencil crayons, happy with whatever.

"Thanks, Lucia," Diego said around a half-full mouth of the cheeseburger.

She grinned. "You're welcome. Draw me something pretty, okay?"

"Okay!"

Diego went back to his food—distracted and pleased. Like usual. Lucia took that chance to lean backward on her heels, and peer around the side of the SUV. She found Renzo kneeling against the back of a white car, and just removing the final screw for the license plate. He'd already taken the one off the SUV, too.

He hadn't explained why he was switching license plates yet again. However, they were sitting in a fucking fast food restaurant's parking lot, and while they were parked in the back where no one could see them, it still made her nervous.

"Are you almost done?" she asked.

"Almost. Diego just about finished?"

Lucia gave the boy a look, and found he was still working on his cheeseburger and had half of his fries left. "Almost, but not really."

Renzo chuckled as he stood up, and came around the back of their SUV. He moved to the side of Lucia where he could bend down to the ground, put the license plate on, and still keep out of view with her mostly blocking what he was doing. Diego moved to the edge of the hatch, and watched his older brother with a curious eye.

"What are you doing, Ren?" Diego asked.

"Making us harder to find again, that's all."

"Oh, okay. Like Hide and Seek?"

Renzo glanced up, and smiled at his brother. "Sure, just like that."

Seemingly satisfied with his brother's answer, Diego scooted back inside the hatch and bit into his burger again while scribbling on the notepad with a red pencil crayon. He wasn't paying Lucia and Renzo any attention, now. Renzo quickly finished up his work of switching the license plates on the vehicles—well, he didn't put their original stolen plates on the white car. Instead, he tossed it inside the SUV to keep it before coming to stand next to Lucia. That left the white car with no plate but it was unlikely the owner would even notice that until they got off their shift later in the day.

"You sure you don't want some food?" he asked.

She shook her head. "Not really."

"We're not going to stop for a while."

"I'll be fine."

"If you're—"

"Why did you switch the license plates again?" she asked. "No, sorry … took the license plate from that car and also kept ours."

"I told Diego why."

Turning her back to the hatch, Renzo did the same. Lucia lowered her voice as she replied, "Yeah, but maybe I don't believe that's why."

Renzo snuck an arm around her waist, pulled her in close, and pressed a kiss to the top of her head. Murmuring, he admitted, "You're right. I was thinking it'd be better to switch the plates back to the old one after we cross over into Nebraska."

"But why—"

"We need more money."

Lucia stilled. "We have money, Ren."

"Not enough. Not enough for Vegas." His hand tightened on her waist, squeezing just hard enough to take her breath away but ground her all over again. Without a word, he tugged her around the SUV where Diego couldn't see them. Renzo backed Lucia against the SUV, and came close enough that his nose brushed against hers. All she could see was him clouding her vision, and for a moment, the rest of the world just disappeared. She sucked in a quick breath a second before his lips grazed hers. "Vegas is the most expensive place to live—and we have to stay underground, so that's going to make it worse. We're gonna need shit, Lucia."

"I know."

"Fake IDs. A place to stay. That's going to eat up a lot of cash all at once right there."

Would it?

Lucia didn't know.

"We need to eat, to sleep, to get dressed every day … *more*. Okay? So let me take care of it. Let me handle getting cash to do something with. You just keep Diego in the car, and keep him down out of sight until I get out of here. Then, we're on the road again. No looking back, baby, right?"

"No looking back."

He let her go then only to pull the gun he'd kept tucked in his waistband out of his jeans. Pulling out the mag, he checked the gun, and then quickly tucked it away once more. Passing the fast food restaurant a look, his attention came back to her in a blink. "I'll hit somewhere as we head out of Nebraska."

She knew, then.

He was going to rob a place.

Not this place, she didn't think. He'd said elsewhere. Plus, it wouldn't be smart for them to be seen going inside a place, and then one of them coming back in to rob it. That felt crazy.

Like all the rest of this wasn't crazy, too.

Lucia could tell him no. She could have stopped him, but she didn't. She only nodded.

Whatever he needed, she was going to do.

That's why she came.

That's why she was here.

For him.

TWO

Renzo kept the SUV running at the corner of a building that allowed it to stay hidden from the gas station across the way. There, it wouldn't get caught on camera like it would if he pulled the vehicle right into the parking lot. The side and back windows were tinted anyway, but not the front. He was trying to be safe.

Because *nothing* about this was sane.

He knew it.

What could he do, though?

In the passenger seat, Lucia stayed quiet as she waited for him to do or say something. Right then, Renzo was still trying to figure another way out of doing this. As it was, he'd already left a mess with each step he took to get further away from New York. Did he really want to leave one more mess behind that could be tied to him?

And on the other side of that, what would one more thing really mean in the grand scheme? Look at all he'd done—what was one more thing going to hurt at the end of the day?

The little devil on Renzo's shoulder was loud.

"Ren?" Lucia asked softly.

His gaze drifted to her.

Sweet smile.

Knowing hazel eyes.

Reaching across the seats, his hand found her cheek. The second his hand touched her skin, her gaze lowered, and her lashes fluttered closed. Like she needed his touch, and he needed to touch her. There was something about this girl that brought him down from the clouds, and at the same time, kept him sky high.

"I'll be five minutes, *at most,*" he murmured. "If I'm not out of there in five minutes, you're to go."

Lucia's eyes flew wide at that statement, and thick panic stared back at him. "But—"

"Get in the driver's seat and go."

Her throat bobbed when she swallowed hard. "I can't just go, Ren. I can't go—"

"That's what you'll do because that's what I need you to do. Got it?"

She still looked like she wanted to argue with him. Renzo didn't know if arguing would do either of them any favors except keep them both right where they were. And fuck, maybe that would be the smarter idea. The two of them and Diego in that vehicle alone was a hell of a better place to be than jail or prison.

But he could do this. He knew he could. Hit the small convenience store, pop out the cameras as soon as he headed inside, and go straight for the counter. When he'd scoped it out by driving past, it didn't look like the place was very busy, and the older gentleman behind the counter wasn't going to be a problem as long as he did what he was told, and handed over the money. Renzo highly doubted anyone wanted to be a hero in the face of a robbery.

It should be simple.

Easy, really.

"Five minutes," he repeated to Lucia.

Her jaw tightened, and her gaze dropped but she nodded. The relief that swept through him at that was good, but fleeting. He couldn't sit here for much longer. It simply meant less time they were on the road and gone after this. He had to prioritize the shit he needed to do and the nonsense going on inside his head.

Like everything else lately.

Deal with one thing now, and something else later.

He passed a look into the backseat where Diego was currently halfway between falling asleep, and trying to finish scratching out what he thought was a cat on his small pad of paper. All it took was food, a few minutes driving, and the kid was ready to sleep again. He'd barely said a word the entire time they were driving. He was simply happy to follow his brother wherever Renzo was going to go, no questions asked.

No matter what, Renzo had to do right by that kid. That was the thing about this whole fucking mess—it wasn't about Renzo, and it was not about Lucia. It had very little to do with them, or this thing of theirs that kept growing out of control like a weed. Oh, it was great, yes. He was going to do his very best to keep this girl at his side where she needed to be.

But the truth was simple—it really wasn't about them.

This was about Diego, and Renzo had to remember that when other shit came in to play that took his focus away from where it needed to be. He needed to remember that regardless of what he was feeling, or the things that distracted him from the end goal, it was still going to be about Diego at the end of the day, and what he needed.

This was Renzo's whole life.

He didn't know how to do anything different.

His attention on Diego wasn't missed, if Lucia's next words were any indication.

"You know I'd look after him no matter what, right?" Lucia muttered, bringing his attention back to her. "I would, Ren."

Renzo's thumb stroked her cheek, and the action brought her gaze back up to meet his again. Russet met hazel, and for a moment, the rest of the world ceased to exist just like that. It was just him and her again. Nothing else could ever possibly matter to him when it was just them looking at one another.

"I know you would, Lucia," he murmured.

Of course, she would.

She loved Diego.

He loved Diego.

He'd be taken care of, and at the end of the day, that's the only thing that really made a difference to Renzo. This was all for his brother, anyway. To keep him safe, happy, and right where he needed to be. *With* Renzo.

"Good," Lucia whispered, "I just wanted to make sure."

"You don't have to. I know."

He'd known it from the moment she left everything behind to jump in a car with him and do something absolutely insane. She could have stayed when he left—New York would have been the easy, smart choice for her. She had money, status, and *people*. Enough money to certainly make her forget about him, if she wanted to use it to do just that. She had status in a world he could only really dream about—status that afforded her privilege and respect he had to earn while she had simply been given it for her last name. A whole family that would probably kill for her, but undoubtedly would give her the entire world simply because she was theirs. They could give her things he would never be able to.

New York would have been easier.

Smarter.

Even Renzo knew that.

And yet, she chose him.

She wanted him.

So yeah, he knew.

Leaning across the seat to get as close to Lucia as he could before he would have to force himself out of that SUV, his hand slid around to the back of her head, and drew her forward. Their lips met in a soft kiss. Her lips worked against his, and as sweet as the kiss had been at first, it quickly turned into something else entirely. Something desperate, and burning. Something harsh, and yet still lovely. Her fist clenched into the neckline of his T-shirt like she wasn't going to let him go, and Renzo dragged the pad of his thumb down her collarbone as he pulled away just enough to let them breathe.

"Five minutes," he repeated to her.

Lucia nodded again. "Okay."

"Love you, Lucia."

She smiled for that.

Of course.

"Love you, Ren."

He knew that, too.

Ride or die.

. . .

Renzo's boots hit the sidewalk lining the small convenience store just before the Nebraska border. A few miles away from here, and they'd be out of Iowa. His fucking heart suddenly felt like it was going to explode inside his chest. He hadn't been cocky enough to think that he wouldn't be nervous at all, but he hadn't expected it to hit at once without any kind of warning, either.

Aching lungs.

Clenched fists.

Sweaty palms.

Fuck.

It wasn't like him to be so overt with his emotions, either. He was typically better at hiding it. Hell, he'd beat a guy to death once for stealing from him, and while he felt like he was going to vomit the whole time, he'd been told his expression hadn't changed from a cold, blank slate even once.

Apparently, this wasn't going to be the same. Renzo didn't know how to feel about that, honestly.

Get in, and get it done, his mind said.

Yeah, that sounded about right.

He'd shrugged on a hoodie before he left the SUV—a baggy, black sweater with a hood just large enough to cover the top of the baseball cap he'd pulled on his head, too. As long as he kept his face tilted down, the brim of the hat would give his face some sort of cover as he looked for any cameras, and the hood would add extra shadows.

Would it be enough?

That was yet to be determined.

Renzo couldn't really think about it for too long. He didn't need to go down that rabbit hole when he was already two steps away from going inside the store, and far too many steps away from heading back to the SUV. Still, he knew the faster he got this done, then the quicker he could get back to where he wanted and needed to be.

It was that simple.

As he rounded the corner of the store, and reached for the entrance doors to pull it open, Renzo tossed one last look over his shoulder. He couldn't see the SUV across the street and parked around the side of the building. But he knew it was there, and for some reason, just looking that way was enough to relax him a bit.

Not a whole lot.

But it helped.

It grounded and solidified his decision. *Get in, and get it done.* Then, he'd be right back there with them, and on the road again. That's all he needed to do.

Renzo tightened his hold on the black duffle bag he'd taken from the back of the SUV after dumping out all of his clothes. As he swung the door open to the store, he stepped inside and reached in the bag to palm the butt of the gun resting at the bottom. Glancing upward, but not turning his head up so that his face could possibly be caught on camera, he eyed the most common spots for them and soon enough, found two.

He was aware of the woman at the back of the store digging through the fridges for a soda she wanted. He stepped aside for the man to leave the store with a pack of cigarettes tight in his grasp. He took note of the man behind the counter who was busy watching the game on the small television in the high, right corner.

He was hyperaware of all those things, really. It was like time slowed in his mind as he grabbed tighter to the gun, and readied to pull it out. Like everyone slowed down—everything caught his eye, and he took note of it in his mind—and his mind shifted again, just like that. All those nerves were gone, and that fast beat of his heart that felt like it was going to explode just moments before was now nothing more than a gentle *thump-thump-thump* in his chest.

Not painful, or distracting.

Simply *there.*

Renzo waited until the store door was closed behind him before he decided to move and act. He could have waited for the girl at the back of the store to get the hell out, but as it was, he'd already been standing there far too long. The guy behind the counter was looking his way, and he figured he looked like the stereotypical fucking idiot about to rob a place dressed in black with his face mostly hidden, and a black bag in his grip.

Might as well prove the theory right ...

Pulling the gun from its hiding spot while holding onto the bag at the same time, he raised the weapon and aimed at the first camera he'd seen when he came through the door. The one on the far wall, watching each person that came in and out. He'd already had the gun racked and ready to fire before he even came into the store.

It was good to be prepared.

Renzo pulled back the trigger, and watched that bullet rip through the camera. Several things happened then—the woman at the back screamed, and Renzo couldn't see her anymore when he looked that way. She probably dropped to the floor, but he didn't check. As long as she stayed there, then everything was going to be okay for her and him.

The second thing that happened?

The guy behind the counter fell off his chair.

Maybe Renzo was expecting the older man to come back up with a weapon of his own—Iowa wasn't known for their strict gun laws, after all. But no, the guy didn't come back up with a gun. Rather, he edged higher until his eyes peeked over the counter and landed on Renzo as he aimed and fired for the camera up behind the counter that would catch anyone who approached in its view.

Once that was gone, he put his attention where it needed to be. On the counter, the cash register, and the man who controlled it.

"I really don't wanna fucking hurt you," Renzo muttered, "so let's make this easy on me, okay?"

He stepped closer to the cash, and tossed the bag to the counter at the same time. Tipping the gun sideways, he gestured at the bag, and then at the wide-eyed, terrified man.

"Fill it with whatever's in the cash drawer, and I'm gone. Any trackers in your cash?"

Some stores kept those just in case of a robbery to make it easier on police. Banks usually had them, too, as well as dye packs.

The guy shook his head, and swallowed hard. "We're just a small store, we don't—"

"Good. Hurry up, I'm running out of time."

He wasn't lying.

Already, he'd been in there two and a half minutes. Yeah, Renzo had been keeping count even with all the other shit running through his head and keeping him feeling like he was about to go insane. Counting down time made him feel slightly better, after all.

"Stop wasting time!"

Renzo never lowered his gun, or tipped up his head to give the guy a good view of his face. The man stopped fucking around then, and hit a button on the cash register that caused it to pop open.

It took thirty seconds to fill the bag.

Maybe a little more.

Renzo just kept counting down until he could finally get the fuck out of there. Back to who mattered.

• • •

The engine of the SUV was already running and warm when Renzo slipped into the driver's seat. He threw the black duffle of money into the back seat—it couldn't be much just based on what he'd seen the guy pull from the cash register, and he wasn't willing to wait longer to make him open the safe in the back. Maybe three thousand, give or take a couple of hundred dollars. But add it to the money they already had, and they might be able to do something with it.

That's what mattered.

He knew why the engine was still running, warm, and ready for him when Lucia was still moving from the driver's seat into the passenger seat as he threw the SUV into drive, cut the wheel hard, and put the gas pedal to the floor. She didn't even get the chance to buckle her seat belt as they burned rubber against the pavement.

"Thanks," he said.

Lucia didn't even ask for what. "Figured that was a few extra seconds we could afford to keep, you know."

She wasn't wrong.

Renzo kept darting to the rearview mirror, trying to see if anyone was following them, or if blue and red lights were going to start flashing in the background. They had maybe ten minutes to put as much distance between them and the store as they could manage before the cops would surround the place, and send out cars looking for him.

Speaking of which …

He grabbed the burner phone from the dashboard, and tossed it over to Lucia. "Find us another route. Not the highway."

He didn't explain more, and she didn't ask. Renzo was grateful because the last thing he wanted to do was talk. While he'd went back to that calm state of his inside the store, he didn't stay that way. The second he stepped back outside of the store, he was slammed into reality once again, raging heart, overacting nerves, and all.

"What about this?" Lucia asked, turning the phone for him to peek at what she'd found on the phone's built in GPS. "Could that work?"

Possibly.

"Yeah, better than nothing, baby."

Lucia smiled. "Next left, then."

Renzo took a hard left, and instead of heading toward the highway again, he went for a rural road that would take them twice as long to cross over into the next state, but would make them harder to find. If anything, it gave them a bit more legroom to move and figure something out.

He'd not realized how bad his paranoia still was when even ten minutes later, with trees surrounding them on the left and right, Renzo still kept peering into the rearview mirror. At the same time, Lucia hadn't once peeked over her shoulder to check if someone was following them.

He felt out of control.

She was cool, and calm.

Jesus.

You go, I go.

Her words kept ringing in his head. It was the only thing making him feel even remotely better at the moment. Still, his paranoia raged on like it wasn't going to simmer at all.

What if the SUV had been caught on cameras from another building?

What if the license plate they'd stolen from the first car lot had been put out by now?

"I think we should switch vehicles again," he said quietly.

Lucia didn't even question him. "We'll have to wait until it's dark again. Seems safer."

She wasn't wrong.

In the backseat, it seemed like Diego had finally woken up. "I like trucks."

It was random as hell. Then again, if he'd been listening to them, it wasn't random at all. If it was a truck the kid wanted next …

"We'll find you a truck, buddy," Renzo said.

THREE

"Where are we?" Diego asked.

Lucia passed Renzo a smile. It was the first time the kid had asked them anything in a while. He didn't seem to care what was happening, really.

"Just outside Norfolk, Nebraska," Renzo said, turning to rest his arm over the seat so he could stare at his brother in the backseat of the king cab Dodge truck. Yeah, they managed to *find* Diego the truck he wanted. How long they would keep it was anyone's guess, though. More switched license plates, though this time they managed to grab an older truck out of a secondhand lot. "We're going to stay the night, and drive some more."

Diego peered out the window, and then promptly yawned. "Here?"

It wasn't dark yet—dusk was more like it. The time between day and night when the sun was just beginning to dip below the horizon, and the sky was bright with burnt oranges, reds, and yellows as it promised night was coming soon. Night with a black backdrop and bright stars dotted across the inky canvas.

Lately, Lucia seemed to like night a lot more.

Diego and Renzo continued their conversation, but Lucia's attention was on the window, and the place outside of their vehicle. The parking lot of the motel they had picked for the night, after checking GPS and making sure they were far enough off the beaten path, didn't look like much. A standard three-star motel, according to the sign in the window, and thankfully, given the office was lit up, it seemed like they were still open to accept someone for check-in.

That didn't make the place look any better, really.

It wasn't even two floors, but rather, an L-shaped building with a front step entrance to each hotel room, and white siding that was starting to turn a little yellow. It certainly didn't feel like a great vacation spot, but rather, a stopping point in the night for people like them who had been driving far too long and didn't have any other choice. A sign attached to the entrance of the office said there was an in-ground pool in the back. Not that Lucia figured that was any good for them considering it was September, and they planned on getting back on the road before it was even light out again. The lights on the big sign mostly worked except for a few on the part of the sign that flashed a constant message of *vacancy*.

Which was funny because you know, the place was empty. It didn't look like they had *anyone* staying there at the moment. Lucia figured that was good for them. Less people who might notice them, and all that.

But what did it say for the hotel?

Not very much.

"Hey," Renzo murmured.

Turning away from the window to face him, she smiled. "Hey."

He nodded his chin toward the offices about twenty feet away from where they'd parked. "You're going to need to go in and get the room, just in case."

Lucia frowned. "Just in case of what?"

"My face has been plastered on the news, or something."

For the first time since she realized what Renzo had been planning to do, those nerves and worries that Lucia had managed to suppress came rising fast and harsh in her throat. It felt like a thick ball had come to rest right in her esophagus, and she couldn't swallow. How silly she could be at times ... or naive, really. She'd not even considered how easily Renzo's face could have been caught on camera, and then plastered all over the place for people to be on the lookout for him.

And because they'd be looking for him, they might also be looking for *her.*

Not that she was worried about that, really. More the fact that at the moment, Renzo's face could be widely known. On every news station who felt like the robbery was a big enough story to play it. That made her think—*had they driven far enough to stop; were they really safe right now?*

Her paranoia picked right up like it was an old friend who had come to hold her hand, and keep her extra cold for the rest of the night. She wanted to ignore it, but it was fucking impossible. She had done so well, too. Ignoring her anxiety like it didn't exist in the first place. Maybe God was having a good laugh at her while He reminded her that she couldn't ignore anything forever.

Reality was always right around the corner.

"Lucia."

It was the smooth, dark tenor of Renzo's voice that drew Lucia out of her thoughts. She was grateful for that, really. There was something about the way his voice washed over her senses that just ... relaxed her like nothing else did. It was like an entirely different reminder. One that said if he was there with her, everything was just fine.

"Yeah?"

Renzo reached out and stroked her cheek with the pads of his fingers. They drifted down to her jawline, and then over her lower lip, too. Soft, and slow. It caused her skin heat up under the path his fingers took and made her smile for him.

"Don't panic," he told her like he had been reading her mind the entire time, "we're going to be fine. Just have to be careful."

Oh, was that all?

Lucia didn't entirely believe that, but right then, she didn't think pointing it out would be a good thing. The last thing she wanted was to be upset, or to distress him. They could figure this shit out later.

Right now ...

"Give me some money," she said, "and I'll go get the room."

Renzo grinned, and gave her a wink that made her stupid in her head. Sexy, and playful just like that. Like their whole world hadn't just changed, and they weren't running from the things they had done. Like it might never catch up to them if they just kept moving fast enough.

Who knew?

Maybe it wouldn't catch up to them.

"That's my girl," he said.

Once Lucia had the money in her hand, she stepped out of the stolen truck and headed for the office to get the room. The first thing she noticed about the office when she stepped inside was the fact that it seemed as though she had been thrown back in time about twenty years. The second? Someone liked their tobacco.

The balding man who sat behind the counter didn't even look up from the news he was watching as the daily highlights played through. The bell over the door had jangled to welcome Lucia inside, but he didn't seem to care. Maybe that wasn't a bad thing—if he was distracted by his television, then he wasn't paying attention to her, or who was waiting outside.

Lucia approached the counter, and simply said, "Could I get a room for the night? Two beds, if you have one. But one bed is fine, too, as long as it's a queen or bigger."

The guy didn't even glance away from the television as he muttered, "One-seventy-five a night, and I'm gonna need your ID in case you trash the room."

Fuck.

She had her ID, but she couldn't give it to him. She was not going to put her real name down on anything that might be traced back to her.

"Or," the guy added after a moment, "you can put a credit card on file, so I can charge it if you trash the room instead."

Lucia raised a brow, kind of annoyed. "You just assume everyone is going to trash the room, then?"

"I prepare, not assume."

Right.

"What is the cost if someone trashes a room?"

"A thousand, usually."

Lucia made quick work of counting out the thousand dollars, and the cost of the room for the night, before putting the stack of money on the counter. "There—cost of the room, and the deposit for you to have in case we trash it. We won't, by the way."

That got the guy's attention. He turned away from his television for the first time, and took his time looking her over. Those beady, dark eyes of his traveled over her features, and then took in the simple clothes she wore, too. It wasn't much. A cheap wrap dress she'd picked up at a Walmart when they had a chance to stop. She had grabbed a few pairs of leggings and yoga pants, too, plus some shirts, underwear, and things they all needed to clean up when they did stop somewhere. It wasn't a lot, but rather, just enough.

"You need to be eighteen to rent a room," the guy said.

Lucia's jaw ticked. "I am."

"If you are, you are *barely* eighteen, girl."

Sucking in a sharp breath, Lucia tried to keep her tone and mood calm enough to get the fuck out of there as she dug in her wallet for her ID. She flashed it to the man, just long enough for him to see her birthdate, before she shoved it back in her wallet. "Is that good enough for you, or …?"

The guy still didn't look as though he liked this very much, or her, for that matter. He dug for a key under the desk before slapping it to the top, and pushing it across to her. Lucia was quick to snatch it up because she really just wanted to get the hell out of there. "I suppose. Room nine, third from the far left end."

"Great, I'll grab the money for the deposit in the morning before we head out."

Lucia had just reached the door when the man called out behind her to ask, "We—how many is *we?*"

She didn't answer.

What did it matter now?

• • •

Lucia leaned over the bed while taking extra care not to wake Diego as she checked to make sure that he was, in fact, still sleeping. She'd asked for two beds, but the guy had given her the key to a room with only a queen bed. Which was fine, really. Like Renzo said when they first came in, Diego was more likely to sleep better in a strange place when he was closer to his big brother, anyway.

The boy's breaths came out slow, and steady. His eyes moved under closed lids, telling Lucia that Diego must have been dreaming about something good considering he was smiling a little in his sleep, too.

Standing straight, she wrapped her damp hair into a messy bun and glanced around the room. Renzo had stepped out—for what she figured was a smoke—before she headed in to use the shower. That was a half hour ago considering she'd been towel-drying her hair and she got dressed. Or rather, she threw on one of Renzo's T-shirts and pulled on a pair of tight cotton sleep shorts. But apparently, he hadn't come back in yet.

Knowing Diego was fine for the moment, and the front door to the hotel room was locked so no one was getting in, she decided to go in search of Renzo.

They'd figured out after settling in that the room had a door leading to the back of the hotel, too. Where, apparently, the in-ground pool happened to be surrounded by a high fence. Probably for safety reasons.

Lucia slipped out the back, but found Renzo wasn't anywhere to be found. He wasn't sitting under the small enclave where the back door led to, but his pack of cigarettes and lighter rested on the table like he'd just walked away from it. Lucia's heart picked up its pace a bit as she walked further out into the night, and glanced down the hotel rooms.

Still empty.

Still lonely.

It was a splash behind the tall fence surrounding the pool that drew her in that direction. The locked gate to the pool wasn't really *locked*. It was simply a latch that was too high for most kids to open, Lucia found. She pushed it open to find a pile of familiar clothes sitting at the edge of the lit up pool.

Renzo's clothes.

The smell of chlorine assaulted her senses as she edged closer to the side of the pool. That's where she found him. Not swimming, no, but rather, resting at the bottom of what she could only assume was *very* cold water considering the temperature outside. His eyes were closed, and his arms were spread wide as he floated, suspended, at the very bottom of the deep end of the pool in nothing but boxer-briefs.

For a second, Lucia's heart stopped.

Just the sight of him like that was enough to make her chest hurt, but she didn't entirely know why. Maybe it was the idea that he wasn't going to come back up. That he looked like deadweight down there. Maybe it was just that he was too far away from her.

"Ren!"

She highly doubted that he could hear her, but that didn't stop her from calling out to him a second and third time. The racing of her heart didn't slow until all at once, Renzo opened his eyes under the water, and righted his body before pushing up from the bottom of the pool. He broke the surface of the water with a deep breath, and one hand sluicing the droplets from his face.

"What are you *doing*?" she asked, trying not to let the edge in her voice show.

Renzo blinked for a second before his gaze landed on her. "Thinking."

"At the bottom of a pool?"

He grinned, entirely unbothered and unknowing that she'd pretty much just had a panic attack. *Fucking man.* She hated that he looked entirely too good skimming the water as he came closer to the edge of the pool where she was waiting for him. His arms rested along the edge to hold him steady as he peered up at her.

"Why not?" he asked. "Looked like a pretty good place to think to me."

Lucia bent down and pushed the palm of her hand against his forehead, causing him to float backward in the water with a laugh. "Nearly gave me a heart attack, Ren. Isn't that water freezing?"

"A little. It's not bad once you're all in."

"I'll just take your word—"

"No, you won't." He swam fast to the edge, and before she could properly respond, he'd grabbed her wrist and yanked her into the pool with him. She was right—it was cold as *fuck*. But there wasn't anything Lucia could do about it once her entire body was submerged in the water, and she was shivering all over. He stopped the chattering of her teeth with a kiss—a fierce, hungry kiss that lit her body on fire in an instant. Pulling away just enough to speak, though his lips still grazed hers all the while, he murmured, "See, not too bad."

Well, not when she had other things on her mind.

After all, she didn't care to think about anything else other than the way Renzo's hands were skimming her sides. His fingertips edged along the hem of the shirt she'd thrown on, grazing her cooled skin at the same time. *Fuck yeah*—all she could focus on then was the way heat followed his fingertips. How could she be cold when he made her hot with nothing more than a *touch?*

"You're shivering," Renzo said, his hand dipping under her shirt so his palm could lay flat to her toned stomach. His lips curved in the sexiest way as her tremors kicked up a notch as his hand moved higher, between the valley of her breasts to rest overtop her racing heart. He could feel that beat the same as she could feel her heart kicking in her chest, she bet. Like just his touch alone was enough to make her heart kickstart into overdrive. She *loved* it. "We can go in, if you're too cold."

"No fucking way."

Renzo's laughter filled up the cool air. A dark, heady sound that rumbled in the water, and vibrated all the way through Lucia. She thought, like this, his laughter sounded sinful. Way too sexy. If she wasn't already soaked from being dragged into the pool, she'd be wet from just that sound alone.

He probably knew it, too.

He had to.

His gaze drifted over her face as he edged closer to her in the water. His palm cupped her breast, fingers tightening around the hard peak of her nipple at the same time. The shock of pain from the action quickly melted into a hum of pleasure as it cut right down her middle, and felt like it radiated over her already-clenching pussy.

Dark eyes watched her.

Silent, and glimmering.

Oh, yes.

He most certainly *knew*.

Lucia sucked in a shaky breath as he kept watching her. Like predator and prey, she thought. The intensity in his russet gaze when it was stuck on her was enough to pin her in place, and make her lungs feel like they couldn't possibly drag in enough air. It was a strange feeling, really. Something that should probably terrify her. Except his stare only made her want him more. The last thing she ever felt around this man was fear. He made her feel a lot of things—everything, really.

"Lucia," he murmured.

"Hmm?"

Renzo flashed a grin. "I've got a problem."

She arched a brow. "What's that?"

"I'd like nothing more than to bury my dick between your thighs, but I just realized I don't have any condoms. So, my best bet is to stay right here. If I get any closer—"

They'd slipped up once or twice before and used nothing. She'd never really thought about it—maybe that was because she was young-dumb, or because it was *him*. Either way, it didn't matter.

"I've had the shot since I was fifteen to help regulate my cycles. Never thought to mention it, I guess."

Renzo's tongue peeked out to wet his lips. "Yeah?"

"Yep."

"All right. Just wanna make sure you're good before I get you against the edge of this pool, and fuck you. That's all."

Well, *damn*.

How was she supposed to reply to that?

He was too frank for his own good.

"Perfect," she whispered. "I'm perfect."

"Fucking right you are."

Renzo closed what little bit of distance was between them in the pool all at once. His mouth slammed against hers, and she was a fucking goner just like that. All it took was his kiss—hard, demanding and *rough*. Lips against hers that worked with frenzy and determination to get what he wanted from her. Not that it took long at all for her to respond. She felt the way his tongue struck against the seam of her lips, and already, she was opening up for him.

She liked when he kissed her softly.

Loved when he kissed her deeply.

Lucia *craved* this, though.

This hungry, brutal kiss that left her without air, made her lips numb, and had her aching between her thighs like nothing else ever had. She didn't know how it happened, but in a blink, her back hit the edge of the pool in the shallow end. Renzo was already pushing hard against her body, making the water splash over the echoes of their harsh breaths. His hands were *all over her.* Just when she thought his palms had found one place to focus on driving her insane with their rough touches that she was sure would leave marks, he moved to a new spot altogether.

And then his hands slid down to palm her ass. Firm enough that his fingertips dug into the swell of her backside, and dragged her right up off the soles of her feet. She wrapped her thighs around his waist as he backed her into the edge of the pool again. Pinned like that, the only thing she could think about was how hard this man felt under the water. From the planes of his stomach to the weight of his body pressing against her.

Not to mention, his *cock.*

God.

The full length of his erection ground against her sex through the sleep shorts she had pulled on earlier. But given they were wet, and all he was wearing were thin boxer-briefs, she swore she could feel every teasing inch of his cock sliding along the seam of her sex with each shift and flex of his hips.

Lucia tipped her head back, staring up at the black, inky sky dotted with stars. She released a hard breath as his teeth skimmed over her jaw, drifted down her throat, and then found her collarbone. His hips punched forward at the same time those teeth of his cut into her collarbone, making her whine.

"Shit," she mumbled, finding stability by holding onto his shoulders. She'd lost her self-control, really. That, or she just didn't give a damn when she found herself answering his rolling hips by grinding her own. The rhythm between them was just enough to get her almost to the peak—the orgasm teasing her at the edges of her senses, but not quite crashing down. "Fuck, fuck ... *fuck.*"

"*Look at me.*"

Instantly, she tipped her head back down, and her gaze locked on his at his dark command. Those lips of his twisted in a smirk as his hands tightened even more on her ass, and he pulled her core even harder against his cock. "You like that, huh? Grinding on my dick like that—could you come, Lucia?"

She sucked in another breath.

Why did it feel like she couldn't get enough air?

"Probably," she admitted.

"Too fucking bad for you. I want you on my dick for that, babe."

That sounded way better.

"Please."

The groan that fell from his lips would have been enough to take her to the edge of bliss and throw her over it. She was sure of that, more than anything else. Not that Lucia had time to focus on how sexy and dark Renzo looked groaning when she let that pleading whisper escape her mouth. She didn't.

He moved fast, one of his hands letting go of her backside to fit between them. He had his boxer-briefs tugged down, and his cock freed to his palm. She stared down, watching him fist his length under the water. There was something dangerously sexy about watching a man stroke himself. Something that made her hot in her gut, and aching between her thighs.

"Help me with your shorts," he grunted.

Like he even needed to ask, frankly.

Lucia didn't even bother to take the damn things off all the way. He moved back from her and, she shimmied the wet material down her thighs just enough to give him access. The bunched up shorts bit against her thighs once she had them wrapped around his waist again. If she didn't have bruised along her thighs tomorrow, she'd be lucky.

Not that it mattered.

This was fucking worth it.

So worth it.

The thick head of his cock lined up to the slit of her sex, and Lucia's thoughts drifted away. She locked gazes with him again, and he grinned in that way of his before dropping another kiss to her mouth. His forehead pressed against hers as his hand came up to circle her throat. He grabbed just tight enough to make her gasp, and then his hips flexed forward.

It took one fucking thrust to stretch her open, and fill her full. She swore he hit every fucking nerve ending she had sliding in until he was balls-deep, and she was shaking.

He dropped another kiss to her lips, then. And then pulled out before slamming right back into her. Her shoulders dragged along the edge of the pool, scratching and stinging. She didn't even care.

Not when she had his hand on her throat, his mouth working against hers, and his cock driving into her at a pace fast enough to make her want to scream.

Already, she was going to come.

Already, she was losing control.

"Fucking *come*," he demanded, his tone husky and rough when he finally pulled away from her kiss. "Let me have it—it's all mine, Lucia."

It was.

Only he ever made her feel this way.

The bliss came crashing down only when he leaned in close again, and bit her lip. The shock of pain mixed with her bliss, and she couldn't even remember her own name for a second. Sparks lit up behind her eyes, and heat shot through her body. He quieted her cries with another bruising kiss.

Two deep thrusts of his cock, and she felt him shudder as he emptied inside her pussy. The thick moan that rumbled from his mouth against her own, and the feeling of his cock jerking inside her was enough to make her peak again; to make her crazed again.

She'd ask for more, but she didn't think she could talk.

• • •

Lucia tightened the blanket around her shoulders, and leaned forward on the chair to peer out the window again. She left the curtains closed with just a small slate that she could use to see outside. It was enough. She'd tried to sleep … but something just didn't feel right. She wasn't sure what it was, but after they got out of the pool and came inside to get dry and warm, the uneasy feeling wouldn't leave her alone no matter what she did.

Like a heavy weight on her heart, it kept her awake.

And anxious as hell.

Peering out into the darkness, she found the sign for the hotel was still turned off like it had been for hours. The parking lot was still empty, and down the way, she could see just fine that the office was dark. She didn't have any reason to feel like she did … except it just wouldn't leave her alone.

Maybe that was the Marcello in her.

When something felt off, it was.

Wasn't that what her dad always told her?

Lucia blinked as thoughts of her father filled her mind. It wasn't lost on her that since taking off from New York, her father had only come to her mind a handful of times, and usually, the only thing she felt when she thought of him was the anger and resentment she still harbored in her heart over the things he had done.

Right then, though, she wasn't sure what she felt. Something heavy on her shoulders, definitely, but also something thick in her throat, too. She refused to think on it for long—she couldn't.

Resting back in the chair, Lucia settled on not watching the outside for the moment. If she couldn't sleep, then she didn't need to make her paranoia worse by waiting for something that she wasn't even sure was happening. Instead, she settled on watching the figures sleeping soundly on the bed without her.

Diego had tucked in close to his brother's back under the blankets. Renzo had been turned toward Lucia, and even after she slipped out of the bed, he still stayed facing her in his sleep.

It didn't matter what she felt about her father or family, she decided.

She was still right where she wanted to be. And she needed to be here—who else was going to watch Renzo's back? He only had her to do that, after all.

Lucia was going to keep doing it.

No matter what.

FOUR

Why was the fucking bed shaking?

"Ren, wake up!"

This bed was far more comfortable when he fell asleep in it the night before—he hadn't heard anything from the time his head hit the pillow. He hadn't realized how tired he was from driving nonstop with no time for rest until he finally had the chance to sleep.

Fuck.

He slept like the dead.

"Ren!"

"What?"

His question came out more like a grunt than his actual voice. A husky, exhausted grunt that he wasn't even sure if it made sense or not. He figured it didn't matter; getting back to sleep was what was important to him.

"*Ren, get up!*"

It was only the hint of panic in Lucia's voice that finally broke Renzo out of his sleepy daze. He cracked his eyes open to find her leaning over him in the bed. She was reaching for him again like she was going to grab hold of him, and shake him until he woke up. *Fuck.* Well, that explained why the bed had been shaking, anyway.

He had a good mind to ask her what in the fuck was wrong with her, but it was the fear coloring her eyes that had him sitting up straight in the bed like someone had shoved a rod in his spine. He didn't even speak until he had jumped out of the bed, and was yanking on the pants he'd discarded the night before.

"What's wrong?"

Lucia glanced over her shoulder at the window, but not before Renzo saw the darkness under her eyes. Had she even slept at all the night before? He couldn't be sure because of how quickly he closed his eyes, and the fact he slept like he wasn't going to wake up again. At least, Diego was still out like a light.

"Did you sleep at all?" he asked.

Lucia looked back to him. "That doesn't matter right now."

"Yes, it does. Did you sleep?"

"No." Lucia nodded at the window. "The guy—the one who was in the office last night when I got the room—was walking around this morning. He was trying to look in the truck, and then our window. He had something in his hand—a paper, but it looked like it had a picture on it? And he was talking to someone on the phone, too."

Renzo blinked. "Slow down."

He didn't think she realized it, but he barely understood what she just said. Either his brain was too tired and was struggling to catch up, or nothing she just said made sense.

"Something's wrong," Lucia muttered. "We need to get out of here. Why would he be looking in the truck?"

It was very possible that Lucia was just … nervous. Or rather, paranoid. Who wouldn't be after what happened the day before? But it wasn't like Lucia to panic. That was the thing about her. This whole time, she'd been ridiculously calm. She'd never freaked out even *once*. A part of him knew that, no, she wasn't being paranoid at all right now.

If something felt wrong, then it probably was.

Renzo nodded. "When was he looking around, then?"

"He headed back to the office a couple of minutes ago. I didn't think anything of him walking around at first, but then the second time he was looking at the truck and talking on the phone, so that kind of made me nervous."

Looking at the truck.

"Like what, reading the license plate?"

Lucia shrugged. "Maybe? I'm not sure. What about the money I gave him for the deposit, so I didn't have to put my ID on record, Ren? That was a thousand dollars. Are we just going to leave without *that*?"

He didn't have the time to weigh the pros and cons of trying to get their cash back at the moment. If something bad was happening, like maybe somehow the cops had gotten a bead on them, then they needed to get out of there as fast as they possibly could. Who knew when the police might show up?

"Fuck the money."

"But—"

"Not important. Grab the bags," Renzo told her. "I'll get Diego."

Lucia didn't even question him. "All right."

Diego was not happy to be scooped up from the bed by his big brother before he was even ready to wake up, but Renzo didn't give him a choice. He ignored the boy's grumblings, and slung him over his shoulder still half-asleep. Diego would wake up properly in the truck, or elsewhere for all he gave a damn. As long as he wasn't waking up in some foster home, that's all that mattered to Renzo at the end of the day.

"I wanna sleep," Diego whined as they exited the hotel room. Lucia was fast on his heels, still quiet but doing as he'd said for her to do. "Ren!"

"Sleep in the truck, buddy."

"I don't wanna!"

Renzo juggled his wiggling brother and the screwdriver he'd used to boost the truck the day before. They were lucky really that they'd managed to find two vehicles that were old enough to be boosted simply by shoving a screwdriver in the ignition, twisting it hard and popping two wires together at the same time.

Speaking of which …

"Did the guy look in the driver's window when he was looking around?" Renzo asked Lucia.

She nodded before slipping around the back of the truck to throw the bags onto the bed. All except one—the black duffle that held his gun, and the cash he'd moved into it the night before. She put that in the driver's seat for him. Renzo cursed under his breath, but tried to give Diego a smile at the same time so that his brother didn't think anything was wrong. That wouldn't help them at all. The kid didn't need to be in any sort of panic right now.

But if the guy had looked in the driver's window, there was no doubt in Renzo's mind that he saw the hanging wires under the steering wheel, which was a good fucking indication that the truck was stolen.

Shit.

This was not good.

"Get in the truck," Renzo told Lucia as she came back around the side. "We need to hit the road."

He also didn't want to panic for *her*. Sure, she knew something bad was up, but that didn't mean he was going to fuel her concerns by acting like it, too.

Calm and steady was best.

Right?

"Y'all aren't heading out of here already, are you?"

Lucia was just slipping into the passenger side as the voice drifted over the gravel parking lot. Renzo's shoulders tightened with tension as he turned just enough to look at the guy from the side, but over his shoulder. That way, he wasn't giving the man a good look at his face, not entirely. But he was still able to see him just fine.

"Yeah, thanks for the room," Renzo called out, "have a good day."

He didn't for a second think that would be enough to satisfy the guy, but that also didn't matter. Renzo just needed enough time to circle the truck, get inside, and boost the fucker so they could get on the road. Nothing more, and nothing less. He wasn't about to have a conversation with the man.

"Now, you've got a deposit waiting for you in the office," the man said. "You're not going to leave that, are you? It'll take me a few minutes to go and grab it out of the safe."

Renzo's gaze narrowed.

A few minutes?

A *safe?*

Why in the hell did a shitty little motel in the middle of Nowhere, Nebraska need a fucking *safe*? That screamed *strange* to him in more ways than one. Renzo was not the type to ignore his gut instinct when something felt off to him. Sure, that thousand dollars could do a lot for them once they finally hit Vegas, and they needed as much money as they could get their hands on, but it still wasn't enough to make him feel safe enough to wait.

The guy had come a hell of a lot closer, too.

"No, we're good," Renzo said. "Keep it—a thank you."

He turned to round the front of the truck and jump in the driver's side, but he barely even made it two steps before the guy came up behind him. Had they been back in New York and on Renzo's streets, someone coming up behind him would have meant only one thing—the fucker wanted to get hurt.

But when the man grabbed Renzo's arm, all he could think about was *fuck, don't cause a goddamn scene. Just get out of here, Ren. You need to get the hell out of here now.*

The man's hand tightened on Renzo's forearm. "Now, you wait just a second, young man."

He glanced down at the unwelcomed hand on his body. "Remove your fucking hand before I do, please."

There, he was kind.

He gave the man a warning.

The guy's gaze narrowed on Renzo's face. "I thought something was strange with you two last night, even if you didn't come out of the truck. You think someone wasn't going to see those wires hanging down like that? All I had to do was watch the damn news to hear about the robbery just across the border. Looking for a *dark vehicle*, they said. Likely stolen. You're not going anywhere. The cops will be here soon, so you might as well just give it up."

Oh, was that what he thought?

Renzo had news for him.

"You're going to let me go, or I'm going to make you wish you'd never even seen my face," Renzo murmured. "Last chance, sir."

"I just told you … you're not going—"

"Let him *go*," came a soft, yet still firm, order from the side of the truck.

Renzo really wished Lucia had stayed in the truck, and let him handle this, but she was out now. Out, and *with* his gun in her hand, it seemed. She'd already racked the weapon back by the looks of it, and she had it pointed right at the side of the man's head as she edged closer to them. There was no shake in her hands, and no hesitance in her gaze with each step she took. Just a cold determination leveled on the man still touching Renzo like he had any business doing that at all.

"Babe," Renzo started to say.

"Now, little girl—"

The man had a hand up, as if that was going to stop Lucia or the bullet if she pulled the trigger. Renzo almost wanted to scoff, but somehow, he managed to keep it in. How, though, he didn't have the first fucking clue. If she pulled that trigger, the bullet coming for his head was the last thing the man was ever going to see.

Simple as that.

"You threatening me, girl?" the man asked.

"Looks like it," Lucia returned.

It wasn't much—a couple of seconds where the guy's hand loosened on Renzo while his attention went to the thing he figured was the biggest threat to him at the moment.

Lucia.

And her gun.

No, it wasn't much, but it was enough for Renzo to act. He only needed the chance, and he was the fucking type to take it every time. After all, he'd never know if he didn't *try*. That's what life had taught him, frankly.

Swinging back his free arm at the same time he jerked away from the man, Renzo swung forward fast and hard. His fist connected with the side of the man's face with a sickening crunch. He saw the blood spew from the guy's lips before his body dropped to the ground like a sack of dead weight.

It took Renzo a second, and then two before he realized no, the guy wasn't fucking dead. Just knocked the hell out. Which honestly, worked for him.

The next thing he did was yank that fucking gun out of Lucia's hand before she hurt herself, or somebody else. She just looked startled as he flicked the safety back on, and tucked the gun in the waistband of his pants.

"Stay in the truck," he barked at her.

Okay, maybe that was rude.

Still ...

Lucia blinked. "He grabbed you!"

"I had it handled, Lucia."

"No, you really didn't."

"I did!" Renzo scrubbed a hand down his jaw, and shot her a look he hoped got his point across with his next words. "Don't step in on something like that again. You don't need to do that."

"I will do whatever I want to do for you, Ren. Got it?"

Lucia crossed her arms over her chest, and glowered right back at him. That was probably one of the things he loved best about this woman—she was absolutely willing to go toe to toe with him over whatever she wanted to, even if it was the worst fucking possible time for her to be doing exactly that.

Renzo passed another look at the guy on the ground. The last thing he needed or wanted to do right now was sit here and argue with her. They had more important things to handle.

"We need to get out of here—you heard him," he said.

Lucia frowned. "What about the money—"

"Forget about it. Get in the truck, you can drive. I need to make a call."

• • •

"Yeah, Tuck, hey ..."

Renzo didn't miss the way Lucia's gaze slid in his direction as the guy he'd been calling for a half an hour *finally* picked up the phone. Fuck, it had been years since he talked to Tucker Earl. Far too long, really. The last time the two of them spoke, Tucker had been dealing for a rival on the streets, and they had just about gone to blows over it. But their mutual respect at having known each other since they were kids took over, and they figured something else out.

Shortly after that, Tuck headed to Vegas. He always said if Renzo ever needed anything, to just give him a call and let him know. Well, Renzo was finally making that fucking call. Whether or not Tuck was serious, or if the guy was even in any kind of state to be able to help was another story.

"Renzo?"

"Yeah," Renzo said, laughing. "How the fuck are you, man?"

"Busy. Making coin. Keeping the hustle alive. Shit, it's been ... a year or more since I last talked to you. How the hell are things?"

"Crazy."

Understatement.

"I know that life," Tuck replied.

Highly doubt it, man.

"No, I mean ... crazy as in bad," Renzo muttered, staring out the window. "I need some help. Can you do that—help me, I mean? Just a few things. You know I'm good for it, Tuck."

"Wait, are you in New York, or—"

"No, I'm heading for Vegas right now, actually."

On the other end of the line, Tuck quieted for a second. Renzo waited the man out as he watched the trees passing them on the back roads. Lucia was smart, still staying off the highway. They really needed to get rid of this truck, though. If the guy back at the motel had been talking to the police and trying to keep them there until the cops could show up, he had no doubt he also described the truck, plus likely gave the stolen license plate number.

They had to get rid of it.

Now.

"When you get to Vegas, give me a call and I will see what strings I can pull," Tuck finally said.

Renzo nodded even though his friend couldn't see it. "Great, thanks. Anything you can do for me right now, though? I'm in Nebraska—I need to get rid of this ride I'm in, and take something else. How good are your contacts, huh? You always used to have a whole phone full of people that could get anything done for a price, right? Don't tell me that's changed, Tuck."

His friend chuckled quietly. "Getting right to the point, huh?"

"I'm in a fucking spot, man. Don't fault me."

Putting it mildly, really.

"It might take me a bit," Tuck said, "but I am sure I could pull something together. Are you good to wait, or nah?"

Renzo passed Lucia a look, but she was focused on the road ahead of them. He was grateful for her distraction. In the backseat, Diego was still sitting with his sour face firmly in place. At least, he'd stopped whining. That felt like one battle won, for now. Renzo could deal with his bad mood later.

"I will see what I can do," Tuck muttered. "But so I know, how opposed are you to taking a bus?"

"Like a Greyhound?"

"Yeah, sure."

Renzo wasn't about to be fucking picky, but that wasn't the problem he had with a bus. "I'll need a fucking ID to get a ticket, man." Not to mention, Lucia, too. Diego wouldn't need one if he was traveling with them, though. "Which is something I don't have right now."

Tuck sucked in air through his teeth. "I might be able to pull some strings there, too. Like I said, just need some time. If I get you a ticket, can you get on the bus, Ren?"

"Yeah, man."

"Okay, I'll call you back when I get one—"

"Three," Renzo said quickly. "I need three tickets."

Tuck whistled low under his breath. "Jesus, what are you doing, man?"

Renzo could only laugh. "Right now, trying to get to Vegas."

"What did you leave behind, then?"

"Maybe it's better you don't know, Tuck."

His friend made a noise, but finally muttered, "Yeah, probably not. Listen, we'll talk more when you get here, and get some shit settled. Hang tight, stay out of trouble for a bit, and I will get you tickets for that bus."

Great.

"Thanks."

A quick goodbye later, and Renzo was staring at the blank phone in his hands. Lucia was still quiet in the driver's seat, so he decided to be the first to break the silence.

"We'll get it figured out," he said.

She passed him a look. "Will we?"

Well, they didn't really have a choice, did they?

It was this, or go back.

And he wasn't fucking going back.

Not now.

"Tuck will get us what we need," Renzo said.

Lucia looked his way. "Interesting name."

"His name is Tucker—everybody always called him Tuck, though."

"Huh."

Yeah, that was one way to describe Tuck.

A simple *huh*.

FIVE

Renzo managed to keep a hold on their bags as he hailed a cab at the same time. The noise of the Greyhound station made Diego press tighter against the back of Lucia's legs. His small arms wrapped around her knees, and he was determined not to let go. Lucia might have laughed if she wasn't so damn tired. She understood the boy's desire to hide away from the noise. She wanted to do the exact same thing.

She had never traveled on a Greyhound bus before, and if she could help it, she wouldn't use another one again. Cramped, hot, and uncomfortable, it just wasn't for her. She swore people didn't understand the concept of personal space, either.

"It's all right," Lucia said, reaching back to pat Diego on the top of his head when he squeezed her legs tighter. "We'll be somewhere quiet soon."

Hopefully somewhere with a shower, bed, and food. All things they needed to feel like real, live humans. And despite how tired she was, Lucia couldn't help but feel relieved as she watched the sign across the street light up in bright colors—making a rainbow-like streak of prisms shoot up into the inky sky. She only had to glance down the street to see the same thing over and over again. Bright signs. Huge buildings crawling up toward the sky.

They couldn't see the stars in Vegas, either.

But they were here.

Really here.

That one thing they thought might not happen had finally come true. Here they were.

"That's a sweet sight."

The voice that came far too close to Lucia's right gained her attention. She turned to find a white-haired lady with a face weathered from years gone past and a life well lived smiling down at Diego who was still holding tight to Lucia's legs. The older woman gave Lucia a smile, too.

"Your son is very well behaved," the woman told her. "And loves his mom, like all good boys, it seems."

Lucia laughed. "Thank you, but—"

She was about to say Diego wasn't her son, but she didn't get the chance. Finally, Renzo caught the attention of the cabs driving past the stopping lane. One pulled in quick, and Renzo stepped forward to open the back door. With a nod in her direction, he helped her to get everything in the back of the car before she scooped Diego up, and sat in the back with him. Renzo slipped in with them in the back, muttering an address to the driver who barely even spoke to them except to wave a card reader, *if they needed it.*

They had been driving down unfamiliar streets with lights that were bright enough to make a person think it was daytime when Renzo spoke for the first time.

"We're going to meet up with my friend first, see what he has for us, and then we'll get everything else figured out from there," he said.

Lucia nodded. "Okay."

She had a lot of questions even though she chose to keep them quiet. Like who exactly *was* this friend, how did Renzo know him, and could they trust him? What was going to happen now that they were here?

Instead of asking those things, she simply kept quiet. She trusted Renzo, and that's what mattered. Nothing else factored into it at all if they had a place to sleep, the ability to take care of Diego, and food to eat. The rest, they would figure out in due time.

"Just keep Diego close when we get there," Renzo said, passing her a look. "And stay quiet until everything is figured out. I didn't explain very much about ... all of it."

"What would have happened if you did explain it all?"

Renzo arched a brow, and turned to watch the scenery pass them by again. "I'm not interested in finding out."

Yeah.

She figured.

• • •

"Here to see Tucker," Renzo said to the guy manning the door of a small restaurant that was as empty on the outside as it was on the inside. She suspected the place was closed, but that seemed strange considering Vegas *never* closed anything at night. It was the city that never slept, after all. "He's expecting me—Renzo."

As big as a barrel, the guy narrowed his gaze on Renzo, and then at the people standing right behind him. Lucia and Diego. She shifted in her jogging shoes, holding a little bit tighter to Diego as the man looked him over as well. It took Renzo clearing his throat to bring the man's stare back to him.

"Well?"

Stepping aside to open the door, the man replied, "Tuck's in the back working. He's got shipments coming in tonight, so mind your fucking business when you're in there, huh?"

Renzo nodded, and passed a look back at Lucia. "Understood."

"Good. Follow the back hall as far as it can go, and then turn right. You'll hear Tuck talking by then; follow his voice."

"Thanks."

Renzo gestured at Lucia to follow him, and she stayed close at his back as they stepped into the business. Despite the main floor of the restaurant being dark, the back hallway was lit up. Once they neared the end, they didn't even have to turn right before they could hear a man's voice traveling over the rustle of … something.

"Three kilos in that, then?"

"S'what the boss said, Tuck."

"Good. Bring in the rest from the back while I mark this shit down. And be fucking quick about it. I've got other business to handle tonight, and I do not want to be sitting here all damn night with you."

"Got it."

Without saying anything to Lucia at all, Renzo nodded at her over his shoulder—she understood the action well enough. A silent request for her to stay back in the hallway while he went forward without her. She didn't mind staying where she was with a sleeping Diego in her arms, even if the four-year-old was starting to get a little heavy in her arms. The kid really needed to sleep because as it was, he'd already been up for way too long.

Renzo headed further down the hall, and stopped in the doorway of what she suspected was a back room of some sort. It must have had a door that led out to the back because she could hear the heavy clang of it closing.

"Renzo," the voice from earlier greeted. "Look at you, man. Damn, it's been a minute, huh?"

"Tuck."

All Lucia could see from her position was Renzo's back, and the shadow moving closer to him. She was surprised to find the guy that came to stand in front of Renzo looked no older than he did, and if he was, it might only be by a couple of years. She hadn't known what to expect from this *Tuck* person, but the dark-eyed, blond-haired man wasn't what she pictured in her mind, either. Maybe she figured he would be older … or something. An angular face, sharp eyes, and lips pulled in a smirk, he didn't exactly seem friendly to Lucia, but she didn't really feel settled in his presence, either.

But what did she know?

She hadn't even spoken to the man before.

The two shook hands before Tuck pulled Renzo in with for a quick one-armed hug, and a pat on the shoulder. It was only then that Tuck also seemed to notice Lucia hanging back in the hallway with Diego. The man's gaze drifted over her, and slowed on her face. She thought he had a flash of recognition in his eyes, but she couldn't be sure.

There wasn't any way he knew her. There was nothing about him that seemed familiar to her, as far as that went. She couldn't place his unique features, and his name—Tucker—didn't ring any bells for her, either.

"Just so you know," Tuck said to Renzo, dragging his gaze away from

Lucia, "everything is going to have a price here, man."

Renzo shrugged his shoulders—indifferent and calm. Lucia appreciated that he managed to stay unbothered on the outside even when she knew he was terribly bothered on the inside. It was a lesson to his strength, really. Even if he didn't realize it.

"I figured," Renzo said. "Like everywhere in this fucking life, right?"

Tuck laughed. "You got that right. So what are you gonna need, huh? Give me a list so I can get to work on it, Ren."

Renzo glanced over his shoulder at Lucia and Diego, but when the sound of that door opening and closing resounded again, his attention drifted back to the room. Tucker gave him a look, and waved the clipboard in his hand in explanation.

"Just a sec," he muttered.

Lucia could see just the edge of Tucker's shadow as he moved to the side to deal with whatever had been brought into the back of the restaurant. The sound of something being ripped echoed out from the room before a low whistle cut through the space.

"Damn, that kush is fucking *pretty*," Tucker said. "Look at those colors, huh? What do you think of that, Ren?"

"Looks like a good smoke."

Lucia blinked, realizing what the guy had been talking about earlier now. The business Tucker was doing in the back was not for the restaurant at all, but rather … drugs. He was bringing in a shipment of drugs, and doing an inventory on what he had. She wasn't sure if that made him a drug dealer, or … did he work for one?

Clearly, now was not the time to ask for details.

"Well, do you have that list for me, or what?" Tucker asked.

"I can wait until you're done," Renzo replied.

"I'm not a fucking fool. I can multitask. Speak, I'm listening."

"You always were a shit."

Tucker's laughter rumbled down the hall. "It's done good things for me."

"Looks like it."

"The list, Ren. I don't have all night."

"Immediate things are obvious shit—place to stay, a vehicle, phones, IDs, and if you've got something for me to do, let me know."

Like a job, Lucia realized.

She still kept quiet.

"A place is easy enough," Tucker mumbled. "It's Vegas, man. Look around, there are hundreds of hotels to choose from until you find a reasonable place, or get good cash flow coming in. You know?"

"Or just break into any one of the many empty houses in the 'burbs," a new voice said. "Squatters rule in Vegas, man. They take over a house on the market, and it's almost fucking impossible to get them out of it."

"That's true, too," Tucker added.

Renzo didn't reply to that. "And the vehicle?"

"I've got a couple a few blocks away. They're hot, but the plates are changed, and they've been resprayed, so I don't think that'll be a problem. It will cost you to take one. Every day you take one."

"How much?"

"Hundred a day, say."

Renzo made a noise in the back of his throat. "And the rest?"

"Give me a couple of days. I'll get you what you need. You said *phones* and *IDs*. Meaning, you want one for that girl hiding in the hallway too, huh?"

Lucia didn't miss the way Renzo's back stiffened. "It's me asking, but yes, for her, too."

"Wanna explain to me why you've got a whole little fam—"

"No."

Tucker made a harsh noise. "That could be problematic."

"Not if it's me you're dealing with, right?"

"Doesn't work that way in this life, Ren."

What were they even talking about? Lucia felt like she was entirely out of the loop, but that wasn't anything new, really.

Then, Tucker came back into view of the doorway. She didn't miss the way his gaze drifted to her, but barely passed the sleeping Diego in her arms any attention at all. Yeah, he definitely looked like he recognized her.

All over again, she felt that same sense of discomfort as the guy watched her. There wasn't any reason for her anxiety. He'd not given her a reason to feel unsteady, but there it was. What she wanted to do the very most right then was get the hell out of there. Like Renzo could sense Lucia's discomfort without her even needing to say a word, and without him having looked at her over his shoulder, he inched sideways just enough to block Tucker's view of her.

"I appreciate the help, Tuck. You know that. Where are these cars, then?"

Lucia was glad to have the man's gaze off her.

She still just wanted to leave.

• • •

Lucia's eyes widened as the garage door was lifted to showcase the vehicles safely stored inside. At least three of the vehicles had emblems on the front of them that guaranteed the vehicles cost six-figures, at least.

"I thought he said there were a couple of cars," Lucia said quietly to Renzo. "There's like ten in here."

Renzo chuckled. "Maybe ten is a couple to Tuck now, I don't know."

They kept their conversation quiet so that the man—the same one who had been manning the door of the restaurant—wouldn't hear them. He lingered a little too close as it was, only a few feet behind them as they looked over the vehicles to decide which one they wanted to take.

"Nothing too flashy," Lucia told Renzo as he eyed a particular Corvette. "That draws attention, and we're trying not to do that, remember?"

He grinned at her from the side. "Gutting me, Lucia."

She just winked.

It might not be the right time for their playful banter, but she couldn't help it when it came to Renzo. Things were falling into place, it seemed. It was *good.* Surely, they could enjoy it for a moment.

"I like that one," Diego said softly as he tugged on Lucia's hand to gain her attention. He'd finally woken up on the drive over, and it seemed like that nap did wonders for his mood. He was no longer afraid of all the noise and the bright lights. Instead, it seemed like he couldn't get enough of it all. "That one there, Lucia."

Diego pointed at a black Camaro.

She gave Renzo a look.

He just laughed.

"Kid has good taste," Renzo said like that explained it all.

And maybe it did.

Who was she to say?

"Any car is fine," the guy behind Lucia said. "Pick one; I have all the keys."

Renzo nodded. "The Camaro will do."

"And where are we sleeping?" Lucia asked.

Because now, that felt far more important to her than a car did. They could get a fucking cab anywhere. Take a bus, or something. But where were they going to *sleep?*

"We'll grab a hotel," Renzo said absently, gesturing for Diego to come closer to the car.

Diego left Lucia's side at the same time the man threw a pair of keys across the garage. Renzo caught them easily enough, and hit the unlock button the fob. The car lit up on all four corners.

She said *nothing flashy.*

Sure, the Camaro might not be as flashy as some of the other vehicles in the garage, but it was still going to turn some heads. She still didn't think that was a good thing, but she also didn't want to ruin the moment for Diego who looked like he was having the time of his life as he climbed into the front seat of the Camaro to check it out.

But with them settled on a car, the guy who had brought them seemed ready to leave them be. He stepped away from the garage and pulled a phone out of his pocket. With his attention elsewhere, and Diego distracted by the car, Lucia could focus on Renzo.

"Were they serious?" she asked.

Renzo reached out and slid his palm along hers before weaving their fingers tightly together. He tugged her closer to his side until she was tucked into him. Her favorite place to be, really, but that didn't change the shit on her mind.

"Serious about what?"

"Squatting," she muttered.

Renzo let out a dry laugh. "Yeah, probably."

"We're not—"

He dropped a kiss to her forehead which quieted her. "I said we're going to get a hotel, didn't I?"

"Yeah, but hotels cost money. What about when we run out of money, Ren?"

"Guess we'll figure that out when it happens, Lucia."

How simple that sounded.

She knew it wouldn't be simple at all.

Silently, Renzo's hand tightened on her waist before he turned Lucia so that the two of them were facing one another. Like this, tucked in close to his chest with his hands tight on her body, there was nothing else for Lucia to see or worry about. Just him, and them. They were together, and the rest of the world faded away when she had russet-colored eyes locked on her. The way it should be, she thought. The way she always wanted it to be, no matter what.

"I got us here, right?" he asked.

Lucia nodded.

Renzo smiled sexily. "Exactly. I got us here, and we're getting what we need. That's the important bit. The rest, I will handle as it comes up. That's not the kind of shit I want you to worry about, all right? *You* are what you need to worry about, baby. That's all you need to ever think about, Lucia. Being where you want to be, and doing what you want to do."

"I want to be with you. I want you."

"Then worry about that. Let me take care of the rest."

Yeah, she heard what he didn't say.

Let me take care of you.

And she would take care of him.

That's just how this love thing worked. Even if he didn't realize it yet.

SIX

"It's quiet, though, that probably helped," Lucia told him.

Renzo gave her a shrug. "The hotel isn't bad. I'm sure you've seen better ones in your lifetime."

That comment had Lucia quieting beside him on the loveseat. Renzo glanced over to find her pretty face had lost her usual, soft smile. Instead, she just looked like a blank piece of paper.

"What?" he asked.

"Are you ever going to stop throwing that in my face?"

Renzo blinked. "Throwing what—"

"The fact I grew up with money."

It took Renzo entirely too long to answer, and maybe that was partly because he didn't know how to answer. Was she right? Did he constantly throw that in her face without realizing or meaning to do it? His memories flashed through their conversations since they had met, and he couldn't deny the fact that yes, he did bring it up.

Probably one too many times.

"Lucia—"

"You don't need to throw it in my face. And this place is *fine*. Stop worrying about what I think when it comes to money, what you have, or what you don't. That's never mattered to me. Haven't you figured that out yet?"

The sharpness of her tone told him it was likely this conversation could turn into a fight. That was not at all what he wanted to be doing with Lucia.

She didn't give him a chance to respond, though. Instead, she stood from the loveseat, and headed for a sleeping Diego on the pullout couch. Still, he felt like an ass, so he murmured, "I didn't mean anything. I'm sorry."

That smile was back in a blink. "It's okay, Ren."

She taught him something, then. Sometimes, all it took was a simple apology to make things right. Even if pride was a horrible bitch, simply saying sorry could make all the difference. And he'd try damn hard not to throw that shit in her face again, meaning to or not. She didn't deserve that from him.

Renzo grinned at the way Lucia tried to quietly creep over Diego's sleeping form as the cartoon on the hotel's television continued to flicker with the rest of the show. She quickly grabbed a couple of wrappers and an empty bag of chips tucked into Diego's side. Standing straight, she raised her arms high to show the items as if to silently say, *Ha, I did it.*

A chuckle escaped his lips, but the second Diego shifted on the couch, Renzo went quiet and still all over again. The kid needed to sleep, but he'd fought every second of it once they checked into the hotel. Maybe it was his excitement at all the new things surrounding him, or just the fact that he wanted to explore the hotel room. Who knew?

But Lucia managed to convince Diego to watch one of his favorite cartoons on the television while laying down on the pullout couch, which then led him to cover up with a blanket while he shoved junk food in his mouth. They'd been sitting on the loveseat discussing plans for the next day, turned to check on Diego, and found he was already out.

Hopefully, for the night.

Although, Renzo didn't know what was so interesting to the kid about the hotel room. There wasn't very much to see. Sure, it was clean, the carpet wasn't two decades old, there was a single bedroom and a bathroom separated from the rest of the space. Plus a small sitting area, kitchenette, and a little veranda. A few framed photos of different spots in Vegas and Nevada acted as artwork for the walls, and the curtains on the windows were dark enough to keep the lights from signs out while they slept.

It would do the job.

It wasn't much to look at.

It was still expensive at three-hundred a damn night, though.

"Get over here," Renzo said, chuckling softly. "Before you wake him up again."

Lucia stuck out her tongue at him. "Right, *I'm* the one that wakes him up. It's not like he just hears your voice, and boom, he's up for hours."

Yeah, that was fair.

Not that he was going to admit it.

The second Lucia had dropped the garbage in the small trash bin, and was close enough for Renzo to reach out and grab her, he did just that. It felt like over the last couple of days, this woman was constantly too far away from him for too many reasons. He didn't get to hold her, smell her, or even fucking kiss her nearly as much as he wanted to.

But here they were.

In *Vegas*.

Shit was better—it was finally coming together. And the only thing he really wanted to do in that second was celebrate with Lucia. Quietly, sure. They didn't need to wake up Diego. But he knew *everything* would feel better the second he got her close. Nothing and no one could drag him out of the haze that Lucia put him in every time he was touching her.

Sliding his hands up under her jaw, he tipped her head back so the two of them were staring at one another. Under the dimmed lights of the room, her hazel gaze glittered. The sudden urge that swept through him was unexplainable and undeniable. Like a rope had suddenly been tied around his neck, and then yanked to draw him closer. His mouth dropped to hers, and she met his kiss with a smile. That little grin of hers turned sinful when a kiss just wasn't enough to satisfy either of them. Her tongue stuck out against the seam of his lips, and it felt like *war*.

Everything was second nature, then. Walking her back to the bedroom, never once breaking their kiss the whole way, and then slamming the door shut behind them. Lifting her up so she could wrap her legs around his waist before he dropped her to the bed, and went down with her just as fast.

She arched up from the bed when he fisted her shirt and yanked to hold it taut. Like she was suspended over the bed, waiting for his next move. On his knees, hovering above her, he couldn't help but just *watch her*. There was something about Lucia when she was like this that he found *most* fascinating. How her pupils blew wide, and her lips parted just a little. Soft, tanned skin that begged to be touched and tasted by him. Wavy hair spilling down to the bed. Like a perfect, sexy angel frozen there waiting for him to just *do something*.

"God, I love you," he murmured.

Lucia blinked, and a slow smile spread over those pink lips of hers. "Do you?"

"Way too much."

He'd proven that time and time again, hadn't he? He loved her crazy. Loved her enough to do all the crazy things for her. This love between them wasn't easy to understand or make sense of, really. This love might ruin them, but strangely, that was the thing that scared him the least when it came to this woman.

"I love you, Ren," Lucia whispered. "But I think I might love you more if you got me naked, and loved me while you fucked me senseless, too, you know."

He chuckled. "Demanding girl."

"But you like it."

He did.

He liked that too much, too.

Lucia's hand came up, and her fingertips grazed his lips before drifting over the line of his jaw, too. And then she dragged those fingernails of hers down his throat. Hard enough to leave red lines behind, he was sure of it. The sting was enough to make him hiss, but fuck him if it didn't make his cock hard enough to damn near punch through the zipper of his jeans, too. He was all too aware of the way his heart made the shaft of his dick pulse with each beat.

"So *fuck me*," she breathed.

How was he supposed to refuse?

Renzo let go of her shirt, then, but only to tug his own off, too. She fell back to the bed, but he went with her as soon as he got his pants pulled down, and kicked away. Tugging clothing from her body with rough hands only made her laugh at his impatience. A sexy, high laugh that echoed in the quiet room, and reminded him of the kid in the next room that he *really* didn't want to wake up. He slammed his hand over her mouth as she kicked off her pants, the final piece of clothing on her body except the panties covering her pretty pussy.

Fucking hell.

He wanted a taste of that, too.

More than she could possibly know.

Lucia bit the tips of his fingers, making Renzo cuss low as he pulled his hand away from her mouth. It seemed like she had her own tricks to play on him, really. His momentary distraction was enough for her to grab him by the arms, and pull him to the bed. In the next breath, she had them both flipped over on the bed so that she was straddling him in those black, cotton panties. Her tits caught his attention first as he looked up at her— perky and just big enough to fill his hands.

He stroked her taut nipples between his thumb and forefingers as she ground her hips in circles on his length. Around and around and *around* until a low, rumbling groan forced its way between his lips. He tipped his head back to the pillow, enjoying the way she felt while she teased him just a little too much.

Then, she was slipping down his body. Like a cat with claws already out and ready to drag down his body, her mouth trailed over his chest and across his stomach while her fingernails scored hot lines into his skin. He hissed from her fingernails, but moaned when she freed his cock from the confines of his boxer-briefs, and the head of his cock found the warm wetness of her mouth.

Her palms tightened at the base of his length, and her mouth sucked his tip while her tongue swirled teasing circles against sensitive flesh. He loved the way she moaned with his dick in her mouth—how the vibrations hammered through his cock, and straight down into his balls. He needed something to steady himself; something to make him feel like he had a little bit of control here because she couldn't have it all.

He'd *explode.*

"Fuck, yeah, suck me like that," Renzo grunted.

His hands found the strands of her hair. He used one to gather the curtain her hair made, blocking his view, and piled it on the top of her head so he could see what she was doing to him. Burning hazel slammed into his gaze, and he cursed against at the sight of his thick cock stretching her mouth open. The way her saliva slicked up his dick every time her head bobbed. She grinned, her lips pulled back just enough to flash her white teeth before she dragged them over his length.

"*Shit,*" he choked.

God, yeah.

She was going to kill him.

"Easy, Lucia," he warned.

She just did it again.

Goddamn tease.

Using his free hand, he wrapped his arm around her waist, grabbed tight, and yanked her sideways to get better access to her body. She was just close enough now that he could fit his hand between her thighs. There, he found her slick and hot against his fingertips. Her body shuddered the second his fingers slid along the seam of her sex.

Dripping, really.

Damn, she was wet.

"Does that get you hot?" he asked, sliding two fingers into her clenching pussy. "Sucking my dick—does it get you wet, babe?"

He didn't need her to answer.

Not when he could see it in her eyes.

Yes, it absolutely did.

If anything, his fingers fucking her while she sucked his dick only spurred her on. The harder he fucked her with his fingers, the tighter she sucked on his cock. Lost in the sensation of her tongue dragging along the pulsing vein in his shaft and the sounds of his fingers sliding in and out of her sex, he didn't feel the orgasm coming until it was almost too late to stop it.

"*Jesus Christ,*" he mumbled, yanking her off his cock before he blew his load way too early.

Lucia, wide-eyed and wet-lipped, barely managed to catch herself with her hands when he flipped her over on the bed. He pulled her to the very edge as he stepped off, widening her thighs while his fingers dug into her slicked skin. Because fuck yeah, she was wet enough that just his little bit of playing with her pussy had made her thighs glisten with her juices.

He heard her gasp when he bent down to lick along her inner thigh—he still wanted that taste, after all. His knuckles grazed her sex at the same time, and she let out a *louder* sound.

"Can't have that," Renzo said, plucking those panties up from the floor that he'd discarded from her body earlier. "Can't wake Diego up, Lucia."

She peered over her shoulder at him, and her gaze darkened at the item he held. "Oh, my God."

"Open up."

Lucia grinned. "Seriously?"

"Can you keep quiet?"

"Yeah, probably not."

Sweetly, she opened her mouth and let him stuff those black panties in.

Fuck, he swore nothing looked better than her on her knees with her ass wide, her pussy on display while she watched him over her shoulder, and had panties gagging her quiet. His control was entirely gone, then. The only thing he really cared to think about was getting himself buried as deep into her pussy as he could. He did just that, too. Grabbed her waist with one hand, he lined up his cock against the soft flesh of her sex with the other.

All it took was one hard flex, and he was flying again.

Too close to coming again.

Barely able to breathe again.

There was something about Lucia's pussy that could put him on his knees. She tightened around his length as he stretched her open, and worked his cock in until he couldn't see anything but their bodies tight together when he looked down. Using the tip of his thumb, he dragged it around her sex, stretching those sensitive tissues a little more and loving the way her pussy hugged him tighter because of it.

Those moans of hers were quieter now.

They weren't silent, though.

Pulling out, he slammed right back in again. Her knees slipped on the bed, but he already had an arm around her waist to keep her up. He couldn't seem to fuck her hard enough, then. Like he couldn't pound into her fast enough to satisfy the dark urge clawing at his insides. All the while, she watched him over her shoulder.

Lips curved around those black panties. Hair a wild mess. Eyes glittering.

Goddamn.

She looked good under him.

She always looked good like this.

He kept that pace up, and felt her hand slip between her thighs at the same time. Her hand worked at her clit while he pinned her to the bed by grabbing the back of her neck, and pushing the upper half of her body into the mattress.

Fuck.

"I want you to come," he said, surprised at how hoarse his voice sounded.

Like he was aching from the inside.

Because he was.

He wanted her to come.

Because *he* needed to come.

The only time her gaze left his was when she did finally let go. He felt her back tense, and her hand between her thighs froze. He knew it in the way her pussy clenched even harder around him, and her eyes screwed shut before her teeth bared around those panties. She came hard—shaking and whining. He came harder, leaving streaks of come across her back when he pulled out just in time.

He'd been wrong before. She looked even better spread out on the bed under him with his semen painted on her skin.

She looked like sin, and *his*.

Nothing was better than that.

• • •

"Grab the door, Ren!" Lucia shouted from the bathroom where she was currently brushing Diego's teeth. "It's probably the lunch we ordered."

Hopefully.

He was fucking starved.

Renzo scooped up Diego's handful of cars—he'd gotten to pick one toy when they went shopping, and of course, picked a *pack* of small cars—and tossed them into a pile by the side of the couch. He didn't even bother to check in the peephole before grabbing hold of the door, and swinging it open. The guy waiting on the other side with a paper bag in hand was definitely *not* the food they'd ordered for lunch.

Maybe it was the way the guy carried himself, the aviator shades covering his eyes, or the leather jacket molded to his chest, but he just didn't scream delivery man. He also wasn't recognizable to Renzo, which was a problem. He didn't fucking trust anyone lately.

"What can I do for you?" Renzo asked.

"You Renzo?"

Renzo arched a brow. "Depends on who is asking."

The man grunted in the hallway, shoved his aviators high on his head, and glanced down the empty hallway. "Tuck sent me, actually. Are you gonna make me stand out here in the hallway all afternoon, or what?"

Well, in that case ...

Renzo stepped back, and widened the door. Opening one arm as if to invite the man in, he asked, "Do you have a name?"

"Not for you."

Jesus.

Just who was Tuck messing around with in Vegas, anyway? Renzo had to push that question out of his mind because he couldn't afford to know. If this guy had the shit he needed to move a little easier and breathe a little freer, then nothing else mattered.

The guy headed for the table in the small kitchenette area of the room, and dropped the paper bag down uncaringly. By the time Renzo joined him at the table, he'd already pulled out the items from the bag. Two sleek, black burner phones with cards to activate them. Two IDs.

Renzo picked up the one ID, and looked it over. The brunette on the front looked *nothing* like Lucia, but if she flashed it fast enough and someone didn't really care to look at anything else but the birthdate stamped on the front, then they would be fine. Frankly, the ID that had been brought along for him wasn't in better shape. The guy in the picture didn't even have the same hair color as he did, and he was at least three inches too short according to the height listed. But again, it wouldn't matter, if no one paid too close attention to the ID when it was flashed.

Out of the corner of his eye, Renzo watched Lucia direct a towel-wrapped Diego through the main section and into the bedroom. She shot him a look—a silent, *you good?*—but he only nodded back in response. She didn't need to get involved in his business with Tucker. The more he could keep her away from while they were in Vegas, the better he figured it would be for both of them.

"Well, there you are," the guy muttered, bringing Renzo's attention back to the task at hand. "That's what you asked for, isn't it?"

Renzo nodded, and packed the items away in the brown paper bag once more. "It is. Let Tuck know I appreciate it."

"Can let him know that yourself when he calls one of those two phones. He's gonna have a job for you to do—payback for all of this, if you will," the guy said, gesturing at the bag.

Payback?

Renzo didn't think so.

He wasn't doing shit for free.

"I already paid him for the phones and IDs," Renzo pointed out.

The man grinned, but it wasn't warm at all. In fact, it came off as entirely cold and almost a little patronizing when he nodded, saying, "Yeah, that's not really how Tuck works. Money is a given, but he likes to make sure you really appreciate his willingness to … take care of you, so to speak."

"Is that so?"

"The cost is always doubled with Tuck."

Renzo's jaw tightened with anger, but he managed to keep it in. It seemed that Tuck hadn't changed all that much since he left New York. He was still a fucking prick at the highest level when he wanted to be. Besides, there wasn't very much he could do either way. He didn't need problems here, too. Not when they just arrived.

"Fine," Renzo said.

The guy smiled in that cold way again. "Good. Tuck will call. And when you go for the job, just bring you. No one else. Got it, New York?"

Fuck.

"Yeah, I got it."

Didn't mean he liked it, though.

• • •

"What did he mean?"

Renzo just finished activating the phone Lucia picked between the two—although she was aware Tuck might call either number—and handed it over. She took it, but still looked at him expectantly, clearly waiting for him to answer her question. "About what?"

"That you owe twice … or whatever."

Shaking his head, Renzo muttered, "Nothing, that's just Tuck being a fuck, that's all. He was that way in New York, too. Always liked to have something to hold over someone else, in a way. I guess that's just how he always made sure someone else owed him, and not the other way around. I'll handle this job, and then he'll be happy."

"Except you asked if he had any other work for you, too. So, it's not really going to be over," Lucia pointed out. "Because you still might be doing work for him."

Renzo chuckled, and leaned over to press a kiss to the top of Lucia's head. She really was too smart for her own good. Quick as a whip, maybe. Nothing was getting past her. She grinned up at him like she could read his mind, and winked.

"Doing work for him and getting paid isn't the same thing," he murmured against her hair. "It's kind of equal footing, then. It's when you owe Tuck something that it can be a problem."

Lucia said nothing, and Renzo was grateful. He tapped the phone in her hands.

"Someone you wanna call?"

For a long while, she stared at the blank screen of the phone, clearly thinking his question over. He let her have her moment. He wouldn't blame her if she did want to call her family. For the most part, the phones would be safe. They couldn't be tracked if they didn't stay on them too long, and since they were picked up at basically any convenience store, including the activation cards, that made it twice as hard to track them. Cheap as fuck, easily disposable and replaceable … yeah, it was mostly safe for her to call.

But did she want to?

That was the real question.

"Not really," Lucia finally said. "Not yet, anyway."

Renzo nodded. "All right. I need to call Rose."

Lucia didn't even question him on that. He hadn't said much about Rose since they took off, but his sister wasn't very far from his mind. Sure, Renzo had got her set up for a few months just in case. All those threats from Lucian Marcello had basically guaranteed Renzo would make sure his sister was fine even if he wasn't. At least, for a while. But that didn't mean his sister wouldn't be worried as he hadn't shown up to see her like he did twice a damn week typically. And if she headed down to the Bronx to find him, then she had no doubt gotten the news that he took off with Diego.

At the very least, he owed his sister a call.

Diego came out of the bedroom with a handful of cars. "Lucia, come see what I made!"

Renzo was grateful for the privacy when Lucia slipped into the bedroom with his little brother. Turning the phone on, he dialed a familiar number, and put it to his ear. It took three rings before a familiar voice filled the speaker.

"Hello?"

"Rose …" Renzo cleared his throat. "It's Ren."

A beat of silence passed, and then two. He waited his sister's confusion out.

"*Ren?*"

"Yeah, Rose. Hey."

"*Oh my fucking God, where have you been?*"

Renzo had to pull the phone away just to save his eardrums from the volume of his sister's voice. He listened to her shriek at him even though the phone wasn't anywhere near his head. He could still hear her crystal clear. It might be funny if it wasn't so fucking sad, in a way. Finally, he put the phone back to his ear when he figured his sister had calmed down enough.

"Some shit happened," he started to say.

"I saw Ma," Rose replied just as fast. "She came around bitching about you—saying you hurt her, and took Diego."

Renzo stared hard at the window. "Neither of those things are untrue."

Rose sucked in a sharp breath. "But what *happened?*"

"A lot of shit," Renzo muttered, "and all that's important is that she threatened to take Diego away from me, and I couldn't let her do that. I'm sorry I worried you—that I didn't call when I left, or sooner than now. We're fine, I promise. Once I get some shit straightened out, I will wire you whatever you need to get you through, okay?"

"I don't give a shit about money, Ren! I care about *you.*"

"Hey, everything okay?"

Renzo glanced over his shoulder to see Lucia leaning out of the bedroom doorway. Little Diego poked his head out by her legs, too. He nodded. "Everything is fine, Lucia."

She nodded, and headed back in the room.

"She's there, too?" his sister asked.

Renzo chuckled. "Yeah, she's here, too."

Rose made a noise under her breath. "God, you scared the shit out of me, Ren."

"Sorry."

That's all he could do.

Keep saying sorry.

"Well, where are you?"

Renzo watched the bright lights out the window. Despite it being daylight, Vegas remained lit up like fucking Fort Knox, it seemed. "That's not important right now, all right? I just wanted to make sure you were good, that you knew we were good too, and that you knew I would take care of whatever you needed once I got—"

"I told you—"

"Yeah, yeah. You don't care about the fucking money. But I *do*. I care that you're able to keep going to school, and doing something with yourself, okay? That's the end of it."

Rose sighed heavily. "Well ... could I talk to Diego?"

Renzo laughed. "He'd love that, Rose."

SEVEN

It was the shifting on the bed that made Lucia's eyes fly wide. She wasn't used to sleeping with other people, but more often than not, Diego slipped into bed with her and Renzo. She never found it strange to be tucked into Renzo's warmth throughout the night. If anything, she slept better that way. His arms would lock tight around her waist, pull her in close, and sleep came faster than it ever had before.

But Diego had gotten into the habit of climbing directly in between them when he woke up during the night. Once he slipped under the blankets, he didn't make another noise until the morning.

Lucia turned in the bed to find Diego had rolled over onto Renzo's side of the bed. He'd taken three-quarters of the blankets with him, too. The sight of the kid in his Batman pajamas with his leg hooked over the mound of blankets like he was determined to keep them right there with him would have been a cute picture, if Lucia wasn't so fucking confused about where Renzo was at the moment.

Blinking the sleep out of her eyes, Lucia rolled to her back on the bed, and listened to the hotel room. The quiet thumps from up above told her someone was still awake and walking around. The faint flickering of lights behind the dark curtains said Vegas was still alive and well. It took her a second to recognize the late time staring back at her from the bedside table where the clock rested.

3AM.

Way too fucking early.

Lucia waited another minute, waiting to see if Renzo had simply gone to the bathroom and was now making his way back to the bedroom, but she heard nothing. Convinced Diego was going to stay right where he was, she carefully got out of the bed, and went in search of Renzo. Closing the bedroom door behind her, the first thing she noticed was the fact that the patio door had been slid open a couple of inches, and left just like that.

A quick check told her Renzo wasn't out there. Or at least, not anymore. His pack of cigarettes and lighter still rested on the patio table, safe from any possible rain under the small enclave roof overhead. It wasn't cold outside, and if anything, leaving the door open had allowed a bit of air to circulate in the warm hotel room. Which helped to keep it at a decent temperature. Still, Lucia closed the door and the curtains, too, blocking out the bright lights of a sign across the road advertising a live show with dinner.

Turning around, Lucia finally noticed the bit of light spilling out under the crack of the bathroom door. Closed up tight, she hadn't really paid it much mind before. There wasn't any noise coming from the bathroom—no water running, and no clanging of items, but she had been the one to turn the light off before going to bed. So, it had to be Renzo who turned it back on.

"Ren?" Lucia asked as she came up to the door. She kept her tone quiet, still not wanting to wake Diego up. Listening for a response, she heard nothing coming from inside the bathroom. The next time she spoke, she knocked softly at the same time. "Ren, you in there?"

That time, she did hear a shuffling and a rustle of fabric behind the bathroom door. She still wasn't worried—not really. Of all the things Lucia had come to learn about Renzo, the fact that he was *not* like her in a lot of ways was the most prominent. She was a talker. No matter what. If something happened that upset her, she did not withdraw into her head and deal with shit silently. She needed to talk it out to figure it out.

Renzo was different.

Silent.

Stewing.

Private.

That was how he dealt with everything. Maybe it was because his life had taught him that no one cared to hear about his problems or feelings, and he was simply better off dealing with them quietly and alone. That way, he wasn't going to be reminded time and time again that no, he wasn't that important to the rest of the world. He wasn't even a blip on their radar.

And that was *fine*, too. Perfectly fine if that's what he needed. At the same time, Lucia still needed Renzo to know that he didn't need to do any of that at all when it came to her. He could talk with her, and she wasn't ever going to dismiss him or the things he was feeling. *Ever.*

That's not what people did when they loved someone else.

"Ren?"

One more soft call of his name accompanied by a gentle knock.

Finally, he answered.

"Yeah?"

His gruff reply made Lucia smile. She recognized that tone—not that he was irritated or feeling way about being interrupted, but rather, he'd been sleeping. Or fucking close to it. She loved his voice the best when he was fresh off sleep. All throaty, hoarse, and deep.

Like his face buried between her thighs, it could make her shiver like nothing else. And *damn*, her mind had gone there quick, fast, and in a real hurry, too.

"What are you doing?" she asked, hating that there was a door between them now. "It's three in the morning."

"Is it?" Renzo's words were mumbled that time, like maybe he'd scrubbed his hands down over his face as he spoke. She barely understood his words at all. "The door is open, baby."

Lucia didn't need to be told again. She turned the knob on the door, and pushed it open. Her gaze immediately searched out the man she wanted to see the most. Surprisingly, or maybe it wasn't a surprise considering what he had once told her, she found him resting in the large, empty bathtub.

He wore nothing except his boxer-briefs, while the rest of his clothes rested in a pile beside the tub. Using one of his arms as a pillow, he smiled at her from the other side of the room. The sexy little grin almost came off as a little sheepish as he stretched one leg out in the bathtub, and bent his other at the knee to rest his arm over.

"You know," she half-teased, "there is a bed in this room that you are more than welcome to use. Actually, I like you better *in* that bed with me."

Renzo cleared his throat, and glanced downward. The action made his dark, long lashes fan over his cheeks, but it did nothing to hide his smile. "Oh, is that so?"

"Very much so, yeah."

"I was going to come back to bed. Then, I went outside for a smoke, my head was full of nonsense, and I knew I was going to toss and turn until I did finally sleep again. Didn't want to wake you or Diego up, baby. That's all."

Lucia's smile softened. "There's a couch, Ren. It pulls out into a bed, too."

"I know."

"And yet, you found yourself in a bathtub again."

In fact, she could plainly see that he'd even gone as far as taking out the items in his pockets, and lining them up along the tub's edge. A handful of change, some cash, an extra lighter he kept on hand, a herb grinder, pack of matches, and the face of a watch that he liked to use to check the time, but didn't have a band on it. That all told her he had not simply made a decision to just come in and sleep in the bathtub, but rather, he'd taken time to relax in there and make it more comfortable for himself. How long had he been stuck inside his head in here instead of coming to wake her up?

"Just how long were you in here?"

"Since one," he admitted.

Lucia sighed, and gave him a look.

Renzo only shrugged in response.

She hadn't come further than where she stood in the doorway. Something about Renzo's need to seek out familiar comfort made her feel like she was intruding, even if he didn't give her that impression at all. She still couldn't help but feel exactly that way.

"Lucia."

"Hmm?"

Her head tipped up, and her gaze darted to find his. He was still looking at her the same way he had been before—unbothered, kind of tired, but entirely in love, too. Like no matter what, as long as he was looking at her, then nothing else in his world mattered. Everything was just fine because the two of them were together.

God.

More than anything she needed that to stay the same between them. Lucia could weather any storm that was thrown at her as long as Renzo kept looking at her like he was right then.

She just knew it.

"You're too far away," he told her simply.

Lucia laughed lightly. "I don't want to interrupt your … time, Ren. I didn't mean to wake you up."

He shrugged one shoulder like it didn't matter to him at all. And you know what, it probably didn't. For such an intense man, Renzo was also one of the most laidback, relaxed people Lucia had ever had the fortune of knowing, never mind *loving*. And if shit did bother him, it was hard to tell.

"I said," he murmured, his dark gaze lifting to meet hers, "you are too far away. *Come here.*"

He hooked a finger in her direction, and Lucia had no choice but to follow his silent direction. It was a like a rope had been slung around her waist, and he was pulling on it with every bend of his finger. Before long, she was leaning down over the tub to meet his lips with a kiss that seared her from the inside out. There was something about the harsh lash of his tongue against the seam of her mouth that really made her crazy. The way his hand came up to slide under her throat, and hold tight to her jaw until he had gotten all of her mouth that he wanted.

He kissed her like he was *hungry.*

She loved it.

Grinning against his mouth, she murmured, "Wanna talk, or …?"

Renzo chuckled. "Just have a lot of shit on my mind, Lucia."

"Like what?"

"Vegas. Us. Diego. Tuck—the fact he hasn't called yet. Whatever job I am supposed to do for him tomorrow. *You.*"

"Me?" she asked softly.

Renzo kissed her again—faster and harder the second time. It was enough to take her breath away right then and there. *God*, she loved this man. More than he could possibly know.

"Not you, *you*," he said, as if that was supposed to make sense. "I just don't like leaving you alone, now."

Ah.

She got it.

"Me and Diego will be fine."

"I know," he said, his words whispering along her lips. "That's one thing I can count on with you, huh? You look after him."

She always would.

As long as he wanted her to.

"Ren?"

"Hmm?"

"Stop worrying. At least, about me and him."

Renzo grinned sinfully, and then kissed her again. Only this time, his teeth dragged along her lower lip in the *best fucking way* as he pulled away. "Yeah, not really thinking about that at all right now. Something else sounds—"

She interrupted his teasing by kissing him that time.

Renzo lifted from the tub, never once breaking their kiss the entire time. His tongue warred with hers; his lips worked fast and hard against hers, taking her breath away with each stroke. Their kiss only broke long enough for him to yank her shirt off, and for her to get her hands inside his boxer-briefs. His soft cock quickly hardened under the tugs of her palms against his smooth length. He backed her hard against the counter, his breaths coming out faster with each pull of her hands on his cock.

"Fuck," he grunted against her lips. "Let me get these shorts off you, Lucia. Let me get a taste of you, huh?"

He waited just long enough for her to nod—always good like that; always waiting for her okay—before he grabbed the waistband of her cotton sleep shorts and yanked them down her legs. The fabric bit into her skin from the force of him pulling them off, and even her panties went down with them.

Lucia didn't even care.

All she cared about in those moments was the fact Renzo was on his knees, and his palms felt like hot sin against her inner thighs. He pushed her legs open, and his tongue peeked out to wet his bottom lip when he got the first look at her pussy. She had no doubt she was already wet—just kissing this man could ruin a pair of her panties.

It didn't take very fucking much, honestly.

"Jesus, look at you," he rumbled.

There was something about the tone of his voice when he was turned on that really did it for Lucia. Something about the way it deepened, and roughened. It made her sex clench from just the sound alone.

His hand skimmed higher on her inner thighs, and just the sensation of his knuckles grazing along her bare pussy was enough to make her jerk against the counter. He chuckled at her reaction, stroking her again in the same exact way just to make her do it again.

"You better stop teasing," she warned.

Renzo looked up, and cocked a brow. "Or what?"

Shit.

He had her there.

He knew it, too.

Just the sexy, sinful curve of his lips—wicked in a blink—told her that.

"Ask me, Lucia," he murmured.

She swallowed hard. "Ask what?"

"Ask me to eat you. Ask for my mouth on your pussy. Ask me to bury my fingers in you while I eat this pretty pussy of yours. Open your mouth, and use those words I want to hear you say. Ask me, and I'll give you exactly what you want."

"You're something else."

Renzo licked his lips again, flashing his teeth in a grin. The tips of his fingers glided through the sensitive lips of her pussy, parting them and dragging along the seam of her sex. She felt the slick wetness he found there, and how cool his fingertips felt against the warmth of her pussy. He trailed those wet fingers of his up to her clit where he *pinched* her.

She swore the air was yanked from her lungs.

"*God*," she hissed.

"Ask, baby."

She would if she thought she could speak, but she wasn't sure that she could do that at all. It didn't help that now his fingers were tracing tight, small circles against her clit. Faster, and faster with each one. He watched her all the while, that grin of his deepening as she started to shake from his teasing.

"You're gonna make me come like that," she breathed, her exhale shuddering.

Bliss teased her senses.

It was *almost* there.

"No, I won't," Renzo said huskily, "I can promise you that. Not until you *ask.*"

So he thought.

She knew better.

She could fucking feel it right there.

Almost fucking there.

There was a single second—maybe *two*—before a woman orgasmed where she plateaued. Sensation fled like birds scattering into the sky, her senses honed in on the release that was about to ravage her body, and she sucked in a deep breath in preparation for that blissful feeling.

A single second or two where an orgasm could easily be lost if someone took away the thing that had brought her to that glorious place.

Renzo did just that. It was like he knew—like he could tell by the way her body tensed, and she sucked in her breath in preparation for the orgasm about to drag her under that she had hit her plateau.

And he stopped.

Moved his hands *way too far away* from her clit.

Just like that, Lucia's orgasm was chased away. Her desperation at losing the bliss came out in a harsh noise that clawed its way out of her throat. Her disbelieving—and angry, probably—gaze drifted down to find the man *smiling* at her.

"Told you," he said.

Arrogant.

Knowing.

Entirely too *pleased*.

"That's called *edging*, you know," he murmured, leaning in to kiss her thigh before biting the same spot. His tongue flicked too, tasting her skin and the wetness his fingers left behind to her thigh after being on her sex. "How many times do you think I could edge you before you broke, Lucia?"

She couldn't even talk.

Not that it mattered.

His fingers were back on her sex again—circling and stroking and driving her crazy. It took him even less time during the second round to get her back to that peak. And just like before, he pulled all the way back when she hit the point of no fucking return. He waited for her shaking to simmer before he was back at it again. The third time took a little bit longer to get to the plateau, but she blamed that on the fact he fingered her first, and then teased her clit until she couldn't take it anymore.

That was all it took. Just three times edging her to the precipice, taking it away, and she was ready to *beg*.

"Please make me come with your mouth," she said in a rush, almost fucking sobbing from having a third orgasm pulled away from her. Her hands had come up to grab the edge of the counter behind her, and she swore she was going to break her goddamn fingernails from squeezing it so hard. Renzo grinned in that way of his, and all she could do was whisper, "Please fuck me with your mouth, or I am going to *die*."

"Dramatic."

"And yet, not untrue. Hurry the fuck up."

His palm slapped her inner thigh just hard enough to make her flinch, and then his face was buried between her thighs in the next blink. That mouth of his against her sex was something else. He didn't intend to tease her at all, it seemed. He wasn't going to make her climb higher and higher one slow, agonizing second at a time.

No, he just got to fucking business.

Fingers stuffed up her pussy, and his tongue driving against her clit in a steady beat that took the air right out of her lungs. Fuck the counter. She had to put her hands on him because she swore that if he moved away again, she was going to *kill him*. Her fingers threaded into his hair, and grabbed tight. Renzo stared up at her, a knowing glint reflecting back in his gaze.

She didn't need to hear his voice to know what he was saying.

You want that?

You like that?

Gonna come for me?

Fuck.

"Right there," Lucia mumbled.

That fear he might pull away when she hit the plateau was pointless, it seemed. The second that orgasm started to rush through her body—it came on fast and *hard*—he stayed right there. Never letting up his pace, or how hard his fingers curled against her G-spot with every thrust. His tongue came a beat faster, and then he was sucking on her clit when she let out a shout of his name.

She'd never came harder.

Never appreciated an orgasm more.

And she wanted another the second it was gone.

Renzo kissed a path up her stomach, and only slowed when his wet lips pressed against hers. There was something dangerous and addicting about tasting her own sex on his mouth. Like she could suck the taste of her right off the tip of his tongue, and still wouldn't be able to get enough.

Did she taste better on him, or right from the source?

"My turn," he grunted against her lips.

In a breath, he had her lifted onto the counter, and her thighs spread open wide enough to make her muscles ache. She already had her fingers wrapped around the length of his erection. He couldn't even be bothered to wait long enough to push his boxer-briefs down a little bit more before he was letting her guide him to her pussy.

Fuck, she was wet.

So wet, he just glided right in. The clenching of her inner muscles had him tensing, but he didn't stop. He didn't even give her a chance to breathe or adjust to his size before he was shoving her back against the vanity mirror, his hand found her jaw, and he was pounding into her. She felt the cheap counter and thin vanity mirror shudder from the impact, but it was all secondary to the way his cock felt driving into her over and over.

"Fucking *watch*," he demanded.

It was the tug of his hand against her jaw that made her look down. *Jesus*. It was a beautiful sight, she thought. The length of his cock splitting her open, and slipping out of her soaked in her juices. The way his heartbeat showed in the length of his cock, and the tension pulling every single one of his muscles taut as he slowed just enough to give her a better show while he fucked her.

"Wanna do it again?" he asked.

Lucia's gaze jumped up to meet his, and she dragged in a ragged breath. Her voice felt oh, so faint as she asked, "Do what again?"

"Edge you, baby." Renzo grinned. "Only this time, I'll be fucking you. See how long *I* can take it."

Lucia laughed, breathless and high. "Fuck yeah."

• • •

"Do you think maybe Tuck changed his mind?" Lucia asked as a knock echoed on the hotel door.

Renzo gave a bitter chuckle as he headed for the door to answer it. "Not likely. Something else has caught his attention for the moment, that's all. Or he's just being an ass and making me wait because he thinks it's funny."

Yeah, well ... Lucia was liking Tucker less and less. The more Renzo told her about the guy, the less she liked about him when it came right down to it. She didn't tell Renzo that because she didn't want him to having yet another thing to worry about, but she was thinking it. That was enough for her.

Before she could ask something else, Renzo pulled open the door to reveal the pizza delivery man waiting on the other side with a bright red bag in his hands. It was just their luck that at the same time Renzo was pulling out money to pay the guy, the phone on the table started to ring.

Renzo's phone.

"Shit, maybe that's Tuck," Renzo said over his shoulder, offering nothing else because the delivery man was still standing right there. Diego, on the other hand, was practically trying to climb up his brother's back because the pizza was here, and he'd been asking about it all morning leading into the afternoon. They'd finally broken down and agreed to order him one—*clearly.* "Answer it, Lucia. Just tell him I'll be a second."

Lucia plucked up the phone, and without even checking the caller ID as she didn't know Tuck's number, picked up the call, saying, "Hello?"

For a second, silence answered Lucia back on the other end of the call. It only lasted long enough for her to hear someone let out a heavy breath. An exhale that *echoed* with relief. Lucia blinked, and glanced over in Renzo's direction, but he wasn't paying her any mind. He was too busy handing over the cash for the pizza, and trying to keep a very active Diego out of the way while he did it.

"Just a second, now," he said to his brother. "The pizza's gonna taste the same in two minutes, Diego, damn."

Lucia went back to the call, but there was still a silence on the other end. She pulled the phone away to look at the screen just to check and see if someone had hung up on her, but no. The call was still connected. The stranger part? The caller ID showed *Rose Zulla.* Renzo had put his sister's contact in the night before to make it easier on himself when he called.

But he had not given his sister the private number attached to the burner phone. She was not supposed to be calling him back. He was only supposed to call her.

Putting the phone back to her ear, Lucia said, "Rose?"

"No, it's not Rose, Lucia."

It took her a second.

Then, two, and … three.

John.

It was her brother's voice on the other end of that call.

She had to take those couple of seconds to fully realize the voice that was speaking back to her. She hadn't talked to him in a month or a little more. Not since before he cornered Renzo in an alleyway, and warned him to stay away from Lucia. Oh, sure, he had tried something akin to communication with her. Hundreds of texts—at least fifty missed calls, all accompanied by him leaving her message after message on her voicemail that she simply deleted without even listening to.

John had been her *best friend.* Not just her brother, but the member of her family that she was most close to. He was her big brother, but he had never acted like the stereotypical big brother until Renzo.

Maybe that was why hearing his voice made her heart kickstart for a second. It caused a brief warmth to shoot out from her chest, and travel into the rest of her body. Because her first inclination when she spoke to her brother was to always fill him in on *every single detail* of her life that he might have missed out on since the last time they talked.

Despite her anger, all that bitterness and contempt she felt with John for taking her father's side, she still had a habit of loving her brother simply because he was John, and she was Lucia. The two siblings so far apart in age that they never should have made friends, and yet, they had done just that. More so than the rest of her siblings.

But as quickly as that happy, warm feeling came, it was replaced by something hateful and angry. That just made Lucia so fucking mad. She didn't want to feel that way, but she did.

He did that.

Just like her father.

"You there, Lucy?" she heard her brother ask.

God, she hated that nickname.

Lucia sucked in a sharp breath, noting the fact that Renzo was now closing the door with a pizza in his hand. "How did you get this number, and *why* are you calling from Rose's phone?"

"Those are good questions. None of which I really want to give you the answers for."

"Well, then I have nothing to say to you, John. So, good—"

"Hackers can do anything, Lucia. *Anything.*"

"Babe?"

Renzo's quiet call of her name made her turn to look at him, and it was the concern written heavily on his brow that told her that he knew something was wrong. She waved a hand, not wanting to get distracted before she could end the call.

Especially not after she heard someone in the background say, "Sixty more seconds, John, and we'll have the area code, maybe a full number, and possibly a location. Just keep her there for sixty more seconds."

They were tracking her. It didn't surprise her that they had access to a hacker with a program to get into Rose's phone, and somehow call back a *private* number without having the number. But if they didn't have her location or number yet, then that didn't mean anything.

Right?

Not if they didn't know an exact location.

Surely …

And if they only needed sixty more seconds …

"Where are you?" John asked.

"Happy," Lucia answered simply.

"But are you—are you safe? Do you care how fucking worried we all are? Do you—"

"I'm happy, John. This phone won't answer another call. Goodbye."

Lucia hung up the phone knowing that hadn't been sixty seconds. Renzo was already at her side, and picking up the phone. She could tell by the hardness of his gaze that he had basically gotten the gist of the conversation and what happened.

She was still going to have to explain.

And none of this felt good.

EIGHT

"Ren, open the pizza!"

His attention drifted between his little brother who had no idea the trouble that they just walked into, and Lucia who kept staring at that phone in his hands.

"Just a second," Renzo replied absently.

The kid didn't seem to understand that regardless, the pizza was still going to be as hot and good in five minutes as it was right now. Then again, he'd been asking for it every single hour on the hour since he woke up, too. Once Diego set his mind on something, he was going to get it and that's all there was to it.

"*Ren!*"

He was not the type to lose his patience with Diego. Literally anyone else—except maybe Lucia—and he didn't have time to listen to whining and nonsense. But right then, he was a little too close for comfort when it came to snapping at his little brother. It wasn't even Diego's fault, honestly.

"Here," Lucia said, like she could read his mind or something, "let's get this pizza opened for you, Diego."

Renzo let her do her thing for Diego. It was easier for him to try and figure out how in the fuck her family—he was assuming it was her family only because she'd used her brother's name—had gotten a hold of his sister's phone.

"What did they say?" he asked Lucia as she flipped open the pizza box.

"Not a lot," she returned. "I couldn't stay on the phone too long or they would have been able to track me. That's why I got off as soon as I could."

Renzo's brow dipped. "Track, *how*? I don't understand."

Lucia pulled out two pieces of steaming pizza, and set them on one of the paper plates they had grabbed when they went out to shop the day after arriving in Vegas. She barely even had time to slide the plate in front of Diego, and the kid was already ripping into a piece of pizza like he had never been fed a day in his life. It would have been amusing to Renzo on any other day if he wasn't entirely fucked up over a single phone call.

Funny how something like that could ruin the peace he thought he found here. Even if it had been a short moment of peace, and only an illusion. Renzo hadn't quite been ready to give it up just yet. Someone was determined to rip it out of his hands whether he was ready for them to or not, and now he had to decide what to do about it.

"Lucia," he murmured when she didn't answer him right away.

Lucia took a moment to wipe her hands on a paper towel before she turned her back to Diego. It effectively put her back to the boy so that they could talk quietly, calmly, and without making him think something was wrong. He appreciated her effort, really. He wasn't even in the right frame of mind to consider how Diego might take all of this.

"I heard someone in the background," she explained, shrugging. "They said something about needing another sixty seconds to grab the area code and phone number, and possibly a proper location. When I asked my brother how he had gotten ahold of a private phone number, he said hackers could do anything."

"But they didn't have the phone number," Renzo said.

It wasn't even a question because one of her statements contradicted the other, and he needed to be absolutely *clear* on this. They couldn't afford to fuck around if her family knew where they were. He had no doubt the first thing they would do was come here, and take Lucia away from him. Which was fine if that's what she wanted to do, but he knew it wasn't. Frankly, the only way Renzo could continue to give Lucia what she wanted—to stay with him—was to keep fucking running.

Lucia sighed. "Didn't seem like it, no. That's what they were trying to get, I think, if I can trust what the guy in the background said. Probably the fucking hacker, right? Is …"

"What?"

She glanced away from him. "Rose's phone … could someone grab that, or no?"

"Doubtful," Renzo answered simply.

His sister was every fucking seventeen-year-old girl to a fucking T. Her phone was never very far from her hands. She could wake up at the sound of a social media notification, but wouldn't blink at a damn alarm clock. She had an account for every major social media app that was popular among her age group. Hell, she had taught *him* how to use one or two of them more than once. Unless someone had broken into his sister's place while she was sleeping to grab her phone, there was no fucking way they got it away from her.

Simple as that.

And he seriously doubted the Marcellos went that far.

Then, Renzo had another idea. "But her number isn't private. It's accessible on at least one of her social media accounts to message her, and shit."

"I don't understand what that means," Lucia admitted.

"It means if they have a hacker, all they needed was her phone number and a hotspot, Lucia. A hacker with the means and the mode, so to speak. Be at a hotspot near my sister, have her phone number, hack into her device, use the right code to call the last numbers that had called her phone, and there you are."

She blinked. "*Really?*"

He echoed her brother's words, then. "Hackers can do anything."

If they had the talent, the means, and the mode.

"But then they didn't have the actual phone number for this phone, then," Lucia said, glancing down at the device in his hand.

"That's probably what the code was running which, if they couldn't track out the exact location during the phone call, would have given them an area code for where we were, and possibly the chance to hack into this phone."

Lucia's gaze hardened.

Renzo didn't know what else to say.

Well, no, he did.

"Is this still where you want to be?" he asked quietly.

Her stare darted back up to his to hold on tight. Unquestioningly, she came closer to him until she could fist the collar of his shirt, and pull him down closer to her. In a breath, her lips pressed to his. Not hungry, rough, and demanding, but soft, sure, and sweet. Everything that Lucia Marcello was, really. All the things that made her most amazing to him.

"I will always want to be with you," she whispered.

That was all he needed to know, then.

"I think we're okay," he said, glancing at the phone. "They didn't get what they needed."

But just to be sure …

He turned on the screen of the phone, and made one of the last calls he planned on making with the device. The call rang twice before Rose picked up. Her cheery voice relaxed him almost instantly. No, he hadn't thought the Marcellos would go as far as approaching his sister or doing something to her to get to him. Lucia's family weren't entirely good people, but they didn't seem like fucking monsters, either.

"Hello?"

"Hey, Rose," Renzo said, giving Lucia a small smile and stroking her cheek at the same time. "Just wanted to check in on you."

There was no need to worry his sister with the details. She didn't need to be freaked out over the fact someone had hacked into her phone, or whatever, not when they weren't after her.

"Hey, everything is good," Rose returned. "But I am just heading to—"

"That's okay. I'll let you get back to … whatever."

"All right."

"Love you, Rose."

His sister laughter. "Love you, too, Ren."

The relief Renzo felt as he hung up the phone seemed traitorous, really. Still, he enjoyed the feeling while it lasted. Which wasn't very fucking long before it was gone. He headed for the bathroom with that goddamn phone in his hands—Lucia was close on his heels the entire way. Diego didn't seem to mind them leaving him behind at the small kitchenette table to eat his pizza alone. He had what he wanted, after all.

In the bathroom, Renzo turned the sink on, stuck in the small plug, and waited for it to fill up with water. Once the water level in the sink was high enough to reach the overflow, he dropped the phone in without hesitation. He watched the screen flicker, and then black out. He left the phone in the water for a good minute, all the while, he said nothing. Neither did Lucia.

Once he was satisfied that the phone was ruined, he pulled it out, dried it off with a towel, pulled off the back, ripped out the battery, SIM card, and small board, and threw it all to the floor. He crushed the items under his boot before bending down, sweeping it all up, and throwing it all in the trash can.

Wasted money.

That's what he saw there. A fucking phone they paid for and couldn't use—even if grabbing another one would be easy and cheap—it was still money they couldn't afford to lose at the moment. Not that it mattered.

The phone was tainted.

It had to go.

The silence felt heavier after Renzo finished, but Lucia was there to break it as he felt her hands slide up his back overtop his shirt. Her lips touched down on the back of his neck, and instantly, he relaxed all over again.

"Everything is good," she told him.

Yeah, he hoped so.

• • •

Renzo stuffed his hands in his pockets, and glared at the sight ahead of him. The barber shop looked old as fuck—certainly not anything modern, or whatever. It also looked, guessing by the chipped paint on the sign and the old curtain in the large front window, like it was on its last legs.

And this was the job from Tuck, apparently.

Or rather, the twenty-six-year-old man who ran the place. Renzo had been told by Tuck when the guy finally called—after figuring out the phone he'd been trying to call was no longer working—not to ask any questions about the place, the guy who ran it, or anything else that might come to his mind while he was in there getting the job done.

Just get my fucking money, Tuck had snapped.

That should have been easy enough, and it wouldn't be the first time Renzo had taken a job like this. Although, it had once been Vito who occasionally threw something like this at Renzo. Never Tuck back in New York. But now, as Renzo was standing there looking at the business in front of him, he couldn't help but wonder why a barber who owned a shop that looked like it was about to be closed down would owe a guy like Tuck money in the first place.

Maybe the shop is exactly why, his mind said.

Yeah.

Because that's exactly how people like Tuck worked. They picked on the weakest chain. The struggling and the needy. Those who could use a hand up because all they knew was how to fall over time and time again. People who could easily be kicked while they were already down because that was fucking life in the grand scheme of things.

Nobody was out to help anybody else.

Renzo figured, since Tuck wasn't willing to talk, the barber probably owed him money he'd taken to keep this place afloat. Likely one of Tuck's sharks since the fucker wasn't one to have his own hand in too many pots, but he didn't mind having many different hands in several pots.

As much as that bothered Renzo—this was exactly why he didn't like these kinds of jobs, because he got stuck in his fucking feelings—he shook off the heavy feeling that was keeping him standing on the edge of the street instead of inside that barber shop. *Get the job done. Get the fucking money, and go back to Lucia and Diego*. It was as simple as that. The quicker he was done here, the faster he could deal with Tuck, and go back to where he wanted to be the most.

Renzo read the business hours on the door as he stepped closer—another five minutes, and the business was closing up for the evening. Through the window, he could see a man in his black apron sweeping a checkered floor around swivel chairs. Pushing the door open, a bell rang up above, but Renzo didn't pay it any mind.

Now, he had to focus on the guy who was looking at him.

"Sorry, we're just about ready to close," the guy—Connie, according to Tuck—said.

Renzo nodded. "Yeah, I saw the hours on the door."

Connie frowned. "I don't have time to cut anybody's hair tonight, man."

He wanted to ask why not—if the guy was struggling for money, then it would make sense to Renzo that Connie accepted someone even if the place was closing just to get a bit of extra cash. It couldn't hurt. And then as quickly as he thought that, Renzo had to remind himself that this was not why he was here. He couldn't fucking *sympathize*. He couldn't let his fucking life of hard lessons and constant struggle affect the way he did a job. Or rather, the fact that he had a job to do.

No way.

Reaching back while still keeping one eye on Connie, Renzo flipped the lock on the barber shop door. The gun he never let get too far away from him was tucked into the back of his jeans, and he swore he'd never been more aware of that metal against his skin than he was in those moments. Maybe it was the way Connie's eyes widened like he realized no, Renzo wasn't there for a fucking haircut. Or it could have been the way the man's hand twitched to his left like he was thinking about grabbing the closest thing he could use for a weapon.

What would it be?

The shaving razor on the vanity?

The broom in his grasp?

Nothing that would help him, really.

"I'm not here for a haircut," Renzo said, shrugging. "I came to get Tuck's money. I'm sure you don't need me to explain who that is, considering he's sent at least three guys around here to pass along the message that you're late in repaying your debt. Three weeks late. Says you're lucky he even let you go that long, Connie."

"I-I don't have—"

"So here's the thing," Renzo continued, not able to listen to the guy yammer or beg. As it was, he was already having enough difficulty with this whole fucking thing. He was not going to add to it by letting the man go on and on. He'd sleep with his guilt tonight, and maybe by the morning when he woke up, it wouldn't be as bad. A useless hope, but one he had nonetheless. "Here's the thing, Connie ... I'm gonna take whatever money you have in here, and whatever you might think is worth something to sell to get more money, and then I'm going to have to teach you a little lesson."

The man's face paled.

Yeah, fuck, get it together, Ren.

"Nothing that'll hurt your hands, or arms," Renzo said, keeping a close eye on Connie's hands just in case, "as you're still gonna have to work, right? But no worries, it'll be enough that you'll understand how this is going to work from here on out, Connie. That's all Tuck wants—just for you to understand who is in control."

More so that Ren understood ...

Tuck didn't just want the barber to realize who had control, but Renzo, too.

Fucking prick.

As Renzo expected Connie would do—they always did this same thing in these situations, never failed—he started rambling. It was simply a way to get more time. A way to try and figure something else out. Bargaining, if you will. Not that it was going to work. It never fucking worked.

"I don't have any money here," Connie said quickly, his voice cracking a bit. "A couple of hundred, nothing more. The safe in the back is empty. I can go to the bank, and grab some—"

"How about you show me the safe?" Renzo interjected calmly.

The man blinked.

Renzo knew then that he was lying.

Buying time.

Nothing more.

Nothing less.

The safe might not have the full five-thousand plus interest that Connie owed, but it certainly had *something*. Renzo would get around to checking that in due time. He had a crow bar in the trunk of his car to pry it open because he seriously doubted a man who owed five G's plus had a safe that was worth any kind of good money. Likely something from Walmart that would make due. Probably screwed to the fucking floor, too.

"Y-yeah, okay," Connie mumbled. "Just ... this way."

The guy turned to set his broom aside, and then moved for the doorway that led into what looked like a back hallway or a small room. Renzo couldn't be sure. He wasn't all that interested in the space back there. He was more concerned with the way Connie leaned down as he entered the doorway like he was grabbing something just around the corner.

Tuck was a fucking idiot, Renzo thought. If Tuck honestly believed he could send three people here *before* sending Renzo without Connie deciding to do something to protect himself, he was a fucking fool.

Because that's exactly what Connie had done.

Clearly.

The man spun around with a sawed-off shotgun in his hands, pointed right at Renzo. The problem was—this wasn't the first job like this that Renzo had done. Sadly, it wasn't going to be the last. His life had taught him not to get too comfortable where he could refuse a paying job, even if he didn't like the details of said job.

He expected a fight.

He expected *Connie* to fight.

Renzo already had his gun pulled out from his back, racked the weapon, and his finger pulled tight on the trigger before Connie had properly gotten the threat in his sights. The bullet from Renzo's gun plugged into the man's forehead—a perfect shot, really. The body hit the tiled floor with a morbid *thump*.

He kept staring at the doorway where Connie had just been standing instead of the body on the floor. He didn't look at the body when he needed to step over it to go in search of money, either.

It was easier this way.

• • •

Tuck pushed off the edge of a beat-up desk as the man who had walked Renzo into the warehouse stepped out of the way to showcase him standing just behind him in the doorway. "You got what I wanted, or what?"

Renzo pulled out the wad of cash he'd taken from the barber's shitty safe, and handed it over when Tuck came close enough to grab it. Tuck counted the cash, and didn't even bother to hide the scowl that skipped over his lips when there was only a little over three thousand in his hands.

"Where's the rest?"

Renzo pulled out the few items he'd taken off Connie, and out of the man's small office at his barber shop. A watch, and a wedding ring. Nothing that was going to make up the rest of that two-thousand, anyway.

What could Renzo do?

Nothing.

Money didn't fucking magically appear, after all.

"That's what I've got for you there," Renzo said.

Tuck grumbled under his breath, but took all the items anyway before shoving it on the desk behind him. Folding his arms over his chest, he faced Renzo once more. "No problems, then? He got the point? Because I can always go back for the rest in a couple of weeks when he's … feeling a little better, I suppose."

Yeah, that was the thing …

"There's nothing to go back for," Renzo replied, shrugging. "He tried to come at me with a sawed-off shotgun. He's dead."

Tuck's face hardened.

Renzo kept quiet.

"Shit happens sometimes," the guy in the chair next to the desk muttered out of the corner of his mouth where a lit joint bounced on his lips. "You know how it is, Tuck."

Tuck sucked in air through his tight lips, and his gaze turned on Renzo again. "Yeah, I know how it fucking is. Guess we're gonna call that even, then, Ren. You and me, I mean. You still want some work, or what? I've got a few things coming up."

Renzo wanted to say sure, as long as it wasn't another job like the one he just did. But frankly, at the moment, he couldn't afford to be very picky about what work he did or didn't take. "Yeah, Tuck. Whatever, I'm up for it. Good for it, you know."

The man nodded. "Good, be on call. I'll let you know. By the way …"

He'd already turned to leave the warehouse because he really just wanted to get back to Lucia and Diego, now. This whole night had been a little too much for him. He was ready for it to be over.

Staring at Tuck over his shoulder, Renzo asked, "Yeah, what?"

"Nothing else you wanna tell me, right? You're good and all, yeah? No shit is gonna come my way because of you, right, Ren?"

It was a strange question.

And it wasn't at the same time.

Renzo couldn't give an honest answer either way. He was trying not to bring trouble here, but who fucking knew if it would come nonetheless?

"No, I'm good. It's all good," Renzo echoed.

Tuck nodded. "All right. I'll be seeing you, man."

Yeah.

Probably too soon for comfort.

NINE

One day in Vegas melted into two, and then three. Before Lucia had blinked, they'd been there for almost a week. It felt like they were getting into something akin to a rhythm here. Between taking care of Diego, Renzo heading out to work at all hours of the day and night, and Lucia waiting for when he would have to leave … days melted into one another.

That wasn't a bad thing.

Lucia just didn't know how much longer it was going to keep on like this before something changed. She'd not gotten another call from her family since that one. While she felt like she had to look over her shoulder when she did leave the hotel, she never found that there was a reason to do so. No one was ever following behind, after all.

Everything seemed fine.

Quiet, even.

It felt like the calm before the storm.

Wasn't that how life worked lately?

Diego kept a tight hold on Lucia's hand as they headed into an upscale apartment complex. She glanced up at the high ceiling of the entry, and noted the crystal chandelier hanging low and glittering from the lights. The walls, a soft cream color, felt like it was meant to be warm and welcoming.

She didn't feel warm or welcomed here at all.

Lucia waited to speak until they were standing next to the bank of elevators, asking, "Why did Tuck call you in again?"

Renzo shrugged. "Not sure."

He tried to sound unbothered by that fact, but Lucia could hear the anxiety lingering at the edges of his voice. Sure, he was doing a damn good job of hiding it, but that was the thing about the two of them …. Lucia always heard it. She could *see* it, too. In the way his gaze had hardened as they drove across the city after Tuck called, and how Renzo made an effort to keep his hands tucked into the pockets of his jacket, so she wouldn't see how often he was clenching them into tight balls.

The three of them stepped into the elevator when the door for the middle one opened, and quieted again. Even Diego, but he was always good like that. Probably one of the most well-behaved kids Lucia had ever had the privilege of meeting in her life. Plus, he was more interested in staring at all the new things and trying to take it all in at once instead of causing problems. Not that he ever made an issue for them, really.

"So, this is where Tuck lives, then?" Lucia asked.

Renzo nodded. "Guess so. Little uppity for him, as even when he was making decent cash, he preferred something less ... obvious about it, I guess you could say."

Huh.

Lucia didn't know how to respond to that, so instead, she stayed quiet. She had been to the warehouse where Renzo usually went in to get his details for a job—only once, though. She knew the address of the place and the numbers to call if she needed to get ahold of Renzo for any reason. Tuck didn't like to see her tagging along whenever Renzo had to do a job for the guy. Apparently, he thought she was a problem, or that she might cause one. Despite how much that kind of pissed her off, Lucia could see his point.

But ... it was always Renzo who brought her and Diego along. She never really asked to go—she was fine with staying at the hotel, and looking after Diego until Renzo got back from wherever. However, if he thought she was fine to come along because he wouldn't be doing anything that he didn't want her to see or know, then he brought her along.

Tuck had a problem with that.

She wondered ...

"Did he mention not bringing us along when he called?" she asked.

Renzo kept his gaze forward, but it was the slight curve of his lips edging into a grin that had her shaking her head. "Not really. He didn't say anything about the two of you at all. Mind you, he won't like the fact you're here, but he didn't outright say *not* to bring you two along, either. That sounds like something he'll have to deal with, you know?"

"Ren."

He only shrugged, entirely unbothered. That dark gaze of his darted to her as the elevator climbed higher. There was something about the intensity of his stare that always pinned her in place, and loaded with the heavy weight of all the things he felt and saw when he looked at her.

She loved it the most.

Loved how it made her feel, too.

Crazy, and *his*.

She was his.

"You've been stuck in the hotel all damn day," Renzo muttered, "did you really want to stay there all night alone, too?"

"Not really."

"Exactly, so I brought you along."

Lucia's gaze narrowed. "If you thought I would have to stay there alone all night, then Tuck must have made you think you were coming in to get a job."

Renzo grinned lazily. "I told you no."

"Well—"

"Maybe I just wanted to bring you, Lucia. I like having you close, all right? There doesn't have to be anything else to it. Not when saying that is enough, you know? I wanted to bring you. Simple as that."

Lucia blinked.

Renzo laughed.

"Okay," she whispered.

Diego tugged on Lucia's hand, and his child-like, toothy smile made her heart kickstart when he pointed at the numbers lighting up above the elevator doors. "Fifteen, right?"

This kid was smart, she thought. He knew all his numbers, letters, and colors. He didn't have everything going for him because society was hell on those who had less than someone else. Born to a punishment of being poor and to a constant struggle, it was very likely that things would often seem bleak for this kid's life. And yet, he never seemed to know it. He was too busy loving everything around him and being all too eager to learn about anything that someone else would take the time to teach him.

Lucia loved to teach, too.

"Yeah, that's right, buddy. What comes after fifteen?"

"Sixteen," Diego answered immediately.

"Good job," Renzo said.

"And then seventeen, eighteen, nineteen, and twenty!"

Once he got to the last number, Diego did a fist pump in the air to celebrate his achievement. Their laughter filled up the elevator, too.

And then the elevator jumped a bit as it finally came to a stop on the fifteenth floor, the doors opened to a long hallway with doors on either side, and the three of them quieted again. Even little Diego seemed to know something was going on.

She still didn't know why they were here.

Guess we're gonna find out.

• • •

"You brought them along again, then?"

Lucia rolled her eyes at Tuck's question. He couldn't see it, of course. She and Diego had been directed to stay in the living room area of Tuck's large apartment while he and Renzo headed into the kitchen. There, Tuck could get himself a drink, apparently. Good manners also seemed to be lost on the man because he didn't even attempt to offer anyone else something to drink.

Not that Lucia honestly gave a fuck.

She'd be happy once she was out of this place altogether. She didn't mind coming with Renzo, especially because he wanted her there. But that wouldn't change the fact that since the first day Lucia had met Tuck, something about the guy just never sat right with her. Everybody had that instinct about other people—they simply chose to ignore it. Lucia wasn't the type to ignore hers, but given the fact that Tuck hadn't done anything to make her feel uncomfortable, she mostly kept quiet. That didn't mean she wasn't feeling way about the man—and nothing good, really—because she was.

Deal with it on another day.

"Figured I might take them out to do something after," Renzo said, although he hadn't mentioned that to *her* earlier. She didn't know if he was lying to appease Tuck's bad fucking attitude, or he meant what he said. It could go either way. "It'd be a lot easier for me to bring them along than to drive all the way back across the city to pick them up again. I hate wasting money."

Tuck made a noise under his breath. "Yeah, you always fucking did, huh?"

A cupboard creaked as it was opened before the sound of glass clanging echoed to Lucia's spot as well. Silence answered the noise while liquid was poured. She kept Diego entertained with two small cars he'd brought along. One for him to drive along the floor, and one for her to play with, too. He was the *bad guys*, apparently, and she was the police. Or that's what he explained when they first sat on the rug in the living room to play.

Whatever he wanted.

As long as he was quiet for now.

It was the conversation still happening in the next room that drew Lucia's attention away from Diego and their game. The boy didn't seem to mind considering he used her distraction to escape from the police.

"Remember when I asked you if you were gonna bring me any problems, Ren?" Tuck asked.

Renzo cleared his throat. "Yeah, I suppose."

"You *suppose?*"

"You asked. And I told you no. What about it, Tuck?"

"We've got a problem."

Lucia stiffened on the floor as the words filtered out to her spot. *Calm before the storm.* She'd known it—said it to herself, too, hadn't she? Nothing was ever simple or easy for them. Life had to make sure it came around and kicked them right in the ass to remind them that for every step they took, something was going to come around and knock them back all over again.

Despite the way panic and anxiety swelled in Lucia's chest, wrapping around her heart with a death-like grip to silence her and chill her to the bone, Renzo's voice came out calm and steady in the next beat. Like he wasn't concerned about Tuck's words at all. She knew that couldn't be true—he always worried—but he was damn good at hiding it.

Not like her.

"What kind of problem?" Renzo asked.

Tuck laughed, but the sound didn't come off easy or amused at all. More bitter, and dark. Like he was pissed, and he wasn't even bothering to try and hide it anymore. "Why don't you tell *me*, Renzo? Tell me what you were doing and what happened before you showed up in my city, huh?"

"Thought New York was your city, Tuck."

"New York didn't make me fucking *rich*."

Renzo cleared his throat loudly. "Just tell me what the problem is, yeah? I can't fix it if I don't know what's going on, man."

"That's the thing—you can't fix this. At least, not the way you're probably thinking."

"I don't—"

"Your face is on the fucking *news*, Ren. Guess there's an alert out for your little brother. An Amber Alert. Oh, but that's just the tip of the iceberg with you because somewhere along the lines, you robbed a fucking store, too. Made national news, you fucking idiot. Someone must have connected the Amber Alert to the robbery because they figured the picture they managed to get of half of your face during the robbery was a pretty good match to your last known picture. You know, the fucking picture they're shoving all over the news alongside the Amber Alert for your *brother*."

"What's a ... Amber Lert?" Diego asked.

Lucia's head snapped back, and she found Diego looking up at her with a smile. He didn't know in those moments that their entire plans and all their work had been upended all over again. That without even needing to be told by Renzo, she already knew they were going to have to leave again.

Run again.

It felt like a knife in her heart because she knew this was chaotic and bad. For Diego, this situation wasn't good at all. They couldn't keep settling him down just to turn his whole little life into a mess over and over again.

"What is it, Lucia?" Diego asked.

"An important message for people," she settled on saying.

Jesus.

She didn't want to lie.

Diego seemed happy, and went back to his toys. She was grateful because she was able to focus on the conversation in the next room for the moment. How much she had missed in those few seconds, she didn't know.

"No, you are *way* too recognizable now," Tuck snapped.

Renzo let out a heavy sigh. "You think?"

"Your face is fucking *everywhere*. I can't have that kind of trouble on me here, Ren. I am doing ... some big things. I am involved in more than you know here in Vegas. Those people will not want to see me mixed up in this kind of mess because of a friend from fucking *New York*."

"Yeah, I get that, Tuck."

"No, I don't think you fucking do. And speaking of New York, Ren … when were you going to tell me about *her*, huh?"

Lucia froze in place all over again.

Tuck didn't even give Renzo the chance to respond to his question before he barked out, "Do you even know who she fucking *is?*"

As unbothered as ever, Renzo murmured, "I know exactly who she is."

Tuck cursed loudly before a second later, something that sounded like glass shattered with a thump against the wall. Lucia jumped in place, and even Diego stopped playing to look up at her with wide eyes.

"It's okay," she told him quietly. "It's fine."

He didn't look like he believed it.

Frankly, she didn't believe herself.

"So, you knew," Tuck growled, "that you brought a Marcello daughter to this city—that you took her away from her family? Do you know they're looking for her, too? That they've put the word out across the fucking *country* for her? That they're willing to pay a *huge* fucking price to get her back with them? Do you know any of that, too?"

"No," Renzo replied dryly, "I can't say I did know any of that."

"That family's reach is … this is bigger than you and me. She's bigger than even your face on the fucking news, and the problems that could bring. Shit, I might have been able to overlook that as long as you stayed quiet until the alert blew over and they stopped talking about it so much. But her, man? *Them?* I can't be here for that—you can't be here with her."

"What do you want me to do, then?"

"Get the fuck out of my city tonight," Tuck said sharply. "Get your shit, and go. I don't care how you do it, but you can't stay here for one more night. It is only a matter of time before someone recognizes her face given the way you drag her around everywhere, and then they're gonna pass the message along to her family. They're going to come here to get her, and when they find out *I* was the one helping you out, that's going to come back on me, Renzo. So, no, you need to go. Take the fucking car with you—consider it a parting gift for all I give a damn."

"A parting gift," Renzo said quietly.

"It's the least I can do, considering …"

"Considering what, Tuck?"

The other man made a noise under his breath, and said, "Considering nothing. Just get the hell out of this city ASAP. I am not going to stand around and wait to be killed like a forgotten mutt because you and I go way back, Renzo. That's all there is to it. I'm sure you can understand."

Renzo laughed, then.

A cold, dry laugh.

"Yeah, I fucking got it. We all gotta save ourselves, right?"

"Right. Now go."

It didn't matter that Tuck tried to brush off what he said. Lucia heard it, and she suspected Renzo heard it just fine, too. Like there was something he was holding back from them.

Not that they had time to consider it.

Apparently, they had to go, now.

Run.

Again.

• • •

They didn't talk. Not on the way out of Tuck's apartment complex, not on the drive back to the hotel, or even while Renzo pulled those familiar black duffle bags out from beneath the bed. They didn't talk until Diego climbed up on the bed when Lucia hauled an armful of clothes over to drop it into one of the bags, and he looked at her with a sad understanding that no four-year-old should ever have, but especially not this one.

"We're leaving again?" he asked softly.

Lucia glanced at Renzo.

His shoulders dropped a bit, but he forced a smile on his face as he looked his brother's way. "Yeah, buddy ... we're going to head out again. We've got somewhere else to be. It'll be fun."

Diego frowned. "But why?"

Yeah, that answer was not as easy or simple.

Renzo didn't look like he had the right one to give his brother, either. "Because we have to, Diego. That's why."

It wasn't a lie.

Looking more defeated than ever, Diego gave a loud sigh before climbing off the bed. Without needing to be asked or told, he started picking up his toys and bringing them over to shove in the duffle bags as well. Lucia thought the scene was a little heartbreaking, but right then, she didn't have the time to dwell over it.

They had to move.

"I'm sorry," she murmured.

Renzo's hands froze as he shoved a pair of dirty jeans in the bag. "For *what?*"

Wasn't it obvious?

She thought it was.

"If not for me being here, you wouldn't have to up and go again, right? We're going now because it's my family coming, Ren. Or they're looking for me—*whatever.* If they had me, then they wouldn't—"

"Stop."

Lucia stiffened as he quickly came closer to her. Close enough that all she could smell was his unique scent—a mixture of heady smoke, leather, and *man*. Close enough that all she could see was the golden flakes in his russet gaze, and the way his pupils dilated when his eyes locked on hers.

"Stop," he murmured again, "because it doesn't matter. Are you still where you want to be, Lucia?"

He didn't tell her she was.

He *asked*.

"Yes," she replied honestly.

Instantly.

Renzo dropped a kiss to her mouth before just as fast as he closed in on her, he went back to the bags and the work of packing them up. "That's what counts, then. Nothing else matters. We'll figure it out. Just like we got it figured out to get to here, Lucia. All right?"

"Yeah, Ren, okay."

They were caught up in packing the bags when the one good cell phone they still had—and mostly Renzo used to take calls from Tuck—started to ring across the room where it was charging on the table. Renzo should have answered it, but Lucia was closer to the damn thing and maybe it was just the habit of a phone ringing that caused her to go and grab the call.

"Wait," Renzo said, a hand lifting to her.

It was too late.

She'd already picked up the call.

"Hello?"

"Lucia, sweetheart, it's time to come home."

It was like ice had been dropped down her spine. It felt like it had been months since she last heard her father's voice even if it had only been a couple of weeks. She had that same reaction to hearing her father's voice that she did when it had been her brother that called—like she wanted to be *happy*, but it was quickly replaced by her bitterness and contempt that just wouldn't leave her alone because of the things he had done.

"Daddy?" she whispered.

The silence on the other end of the call only lasted a moment before her father said, "John is coming to get you, Lucia. Please, make it easy on your brother. Know that I'm doing this because I love you, *mia cara*. I know it doesn't feel like it right now, but—"

"Doing what, Daddy?"

"Lucia—"

"What are you doing?"

"John is coming. Don't run again."

Renzo grabbed the phone from Lucia's hand. When he put it to his ear and went to speak, the hardness in his gaze and the cuss that left his lips told her the call had been disconnected. He threw the phone to the table hard enough to crack the screen, but Lucia couldn't do anything except stare at it.

He pointed at the phone, and shook his head wildly. "Fucking *Tuck*. Fucking liar."

Lucia still felt like she couldn't move. "What?"

"Tuck." His words came out in a pained growl. His hands fisted into his hair like he was at his last rope. She waited for him to explain what he was trying to say, but he went back to packing. Lucia followed behind him to help, and it was only then that he started talking again. "Tuck's the only one with that number, Lucia. No one else was called with that phone. No one that they could hack like they did my sister's phone. We called a pizza place once or twice with it, but they don't know that. The only person who knows it is fucking *Tucker*."

It took Lucia entirely too long to realize what he was saying to her. To understand what he was trying to explain to her.

"Tuck sold us out? Is that what you're saying?"

Her heart raced.

Her lungs *ached*.

How long did they have now?

Not long, she bet. There was no way her father would give her a warning like that about her brother coming unless John was practically already there.

"Is that what you're telling me?" Lucia demanded. "It was Tuck that told them where we are?"

Renzo's movements slowed to a stop altogether, and his eyes darted to hers. "It had to be. No one else knows."

"But he told us to leave. He gave us the car. He—"

"The least he could do for us, remember?" Renzo spat out a bitter laugh. "It was the least he could fucking do because he already fucked us over, Lucia."

TEN

"Here."

Renzo didn't miss the confusion that lit up Lucia's eyes as he shoved the keys to the car into her hand, but he didn't really have time to deal with it in that moment. He had other things to focus on like getting her and Diego in the vehicle, and on the road. He needed her to put some miles between the trouble coming their way as fast as she possibly could. He'd figure out the rest later.

Story of his fucking life lately.

"Wait, what—"

"You're driving," he said simply.

Opening the trunk of the car, he dropped the duffle bags inside. He was sure they didn't grab everything from the hotel room. They'd only took a few minutes to pack, and it wasn't nearly enough. They hadn't even touched the shit in the bathroom except for the couple of toy cars that Diego had ran in to grab. Nothing that belonged to him and Lucia, though.

Slamming the trunk down, he jogged around the car. Lucia was still standing frozen in the same place, but he figured she would get with the program soon enough. The girl was smart and quick like that—she didn't always know or like the entire plan, but she wouldn't fight him on it if she knew it was right.

You haven't even explained the plan to her yet.

He ignored his inner voice.

It just pissed him off.

"There you go, Diego," Renzo grunted, picking his brother up with one arm. Diego wrapped his arms tightly around Renzo's neck, and for a brief second after he opened the back door of the car, he had to wonder if his brother was going to fight him to get inside. He was holding on so tightly that Renzo didn't know if he was going to let go at all. Thankfully, he did as Renzo bent down, and sat Diego on the backseat. His little brother said nothing as he was buckled in. "I'll see you soon, okay? Be good for Lucia."

Water lined Diego's eyes.

How did the kid understand before Lucia?

"When?" Diego asked.

Renzo shrugged. "Not long, I promise."

Or, that was his hope. He couldn't guarantee it, especially depending on how the rest of this night went, but he was going to do his very best to keep his promise to his brother. After all, he'd already done this much and come this far for Diego. He wasn't going to stop until someone put him in a fucking grave.

Tonight, that was a real possibility.

God knew Renzo was mad enough to make it happen, barring the fact that the Marcellos were apparently on their tail. He wasn't even factoring them into his rage right now. He had another fucker to handle before he was even going to think about them on a real level. He was handling them by sending Lucia and Diego away.

No, it was Tuck that Renzo needed to handle. *Wanted* to handle the lying prick, really. It was Tuck that had sent Renzo's rage flaring because *how fucking dare* he put them in this position? Loyalty meant nothing to the asshole, and Renzo needed the guy to answer for selling them out like he had.

Diego blinked, and a single tear made a track down his pink cheek. "Okay, Ren. Love you."

Putting his fist out for his brother, Diego bumped it with his own as he sniffled. "Love you, too, buddy."

He couldn't look at his brother for one more second. He couldn't handle the tears, or the fact that Diego *might* ask him to go with them. Because if he did those things, then Renzo was going to break. In everything else with his life, Renzo was cool, calm, and unbothered. The cold wind in a fucking hurricane. When it came to his brother, though, he was fucking *weak*.

Way too weak.

Slamming the back door shut, Renzo turned to face Lucia who was already holding the keys back out for him to take. "I'm not going without you."

Renzo refused to take the keys. "*You're* driving. I will follow."

Disbelief flashed over Lucia's pretty features, but as quickly as it came, it was replaced by the heat of her anger. It didn't matter what this girl felt, she looked beautiful all the while. Renzo figured this wasn't the right time to tell her that, though. She probably wouldn't appreciate it.

"Ren—"

"I will follow shortly, and we'll meet up somewhere," he said firmly.

They really didn't have time to argue about this. Besides, his decision was already set in stone. Lucia didn't have to like it or want him to do it, but whether she liked it or not, he was fucking going back for Tucker. The two of them, at the very least, were going to have some words about what the asshole did.

Probably more.

Renzo wasn't thinking about that bit right now.

"Get in the car, okay?" he murmured, stepping closer to her.

Lucia took a step back, her anger melting into something hurt and broken. "Not without you. That's the deal, Ren. You go, I go. Remember?

That's *our deal.*"

"I will follow."

"With *what?* This is the only car we have!"

Yes, and even it was probably tainted. He bet Tucker gave the fucking Marcellos the license plate number to try and track it as stolen, if they wanted to go that far. Not that it mattered right then. Those were all things Renzo would deal with at a later time—more changed license plates, or another stolen car. Who fucking cared?

Right now, he had to deal with Lucia.

Get her on the road.

She couldn't be *here.*

Stepping forward before she could put more distance between them, Renzo grabbed Lucia's face in both his palms, pulled her in close, and kissed her hard. She sucked in a sharp breath as his lips came down on hers. This thing they had now felt bigger than him, but he wasn't entirely sure why. He could blame it on love; he could blame it on his stupid heart; he could blame it on *her.* The truth was simpler, really.

They just *were.*

Better together.

Meant to be.

Whatever the fuck someone wanted to call it.

They weren't meant to be apart, so yeah, he got why she wanted to fight him on this. He understood why she wanted him to get in that car with her because he wanted to do that, too. But he couldn't. Not right now. Someone had tried to fuck them over, which as a byproduct, hurt the people he loved the most.

Renzo couldn't have that.

Not without answering it.

His lips worked against hers in a brutal kiss—every time he touched, loved, or tasted this woman, he swore he left a piece of himself behind with her when he was finished.

It didn't even matter.

She could take it *all.*

All of him was hers.

Pulling away, but still letting his lips graze along hers as he spoke, Renzo stroked Lucia's cheeks with his thumbs. He pretended like he didn't see the trail of tears slipping out of the corners of her eyes.

It was easier this way.

"In your bag," he murmured, "you're gonna find an address. I stuffed it in there when you were putting Diego's shoes on him earlier. A place in San Francisco—that's where you're to go, no matter what. I *will* follow. We will either meet up before, or after, but I will follow. That's where you are to go, no turning around or looking back. Do you get me?"

Lucia refused to speak.

Renzo pulled her back, and held her a little tighter. "Lucia, do you *get me?*"

Finally, she nodded. "Yeah, Ren, I got you."

Of course, she did.

Even when she didn't want to.

• • •

"Ren," the muscle who opened Tucker's door greeted, "I thought you were told to get the fuck out of this—"

Renzo didn't even let the man finish his sentence before he reared back, and pistol-whipped the fucker right in the face. Blood painted the wall with a bright red as it spewed from the fool's mouth. His body hit the wall, the surprise from the attack clearly taking him off guard. Renzo might have taken a second to enjoy the satisfaction he felt about *finally* getting some of this violent need out of his system, but he couldn't even be bothered to do that.

He had shit to do.

Things to handle.

Pulling back, he hit the guy once more just to make sure he was out, and staying that way. Stepping over the guy's body in the doorway, Renzo knew he didn't have time to fuck around now. Tuck wasn't a goddamn idiot. He would have heard what just happened, and was likely preparing for it.

That was fine, too.

Closing the door behind him, Renzo readied his gun and headed down the hall. "Tuck!"

"Man, get the fuck out of here," he heard called back. "I gave you a chance, didn't I?"

Renzo laughed, dark and bitter. The taste of *hate* coated his tongue, and it had a tangy bite he didn't like at all. That was the thing about betrayal, even if one should simply expect it to happen in this life, it always tasted sour in the end. Something you didn't want in your mouth at all, but it was going to be there nonetheless.

At the end of the hall, Renzo stayed tucked close to the wall. He listened through the darkness of Tuck's apartment, and heard what he was waiting for. The shuffle of clothes, and the beat of a foot hitting hardwood. The only place in the apartment that had hardwood—from what Renzo noticed—was the goddamn kitchen.

"How much, huh?" Renzo called out.

"What are you going off about—"

"How much money did you take to sell us out to the Marcellos, Tuck? At least give me the respect of letting me know how much you think I'm worth, yeah?"

"Not fucking enough for this."

Yeah, Renzo figured.

Not that it mattered now, right? It was said and done. Tuck did what he did, and now Renzo was here to deal with it. He bet his old friend had hoped Renzo wouldn't figure it out, and if he did at some point, then he would be long gone. There would be no chance of him coming back here for retribution.

Fuck that.

Renzo was here.

He was getting his.

The sound of shoes on hardwood had quieted, making Renzo tense against the wall. He couldn't let Tuck come in on him around the corner—that would give the fucker the upper hand in a way. Tuck probably thought Renzo was going to be easy to take care of, but he had news for him.

Renzo always came swinging.

If he went down, he'd go down swinging, too.

Maybe that was the problem, though. Renzo, stuck in the haze of his rage at being betrayed by someone he considered a friend of sorts, wasn't really thinking clearly. All he wanted to do in those moments was hurt Tuck—end his useless fucking life—for putting Renzo in a situation where the things he loved the most might be taken away from him. Instead of considering every move carefully, like he usually would, he reacted in anger.

That was his mistake.

He didn't fully realize that until he came around the corner with his gun aimed only to see Tuck already there waiting, and swinging a bat his way.

Renzo *barely* ducked the first swing, and in order to get out of the way, he rammed himself into the goddamn wall. The second swing of the bat hit his wrist, sending the gun flying down the hall out of his hand and reach.

"*Fuck*," Renzo snarled.

The pain reverberated in his *bones.*

"Gave you a chance, didn't I?" Tuck said, a laugh edging along with his words. "You should have just *gone*, Ren. Left like I told you to."

Yeah, fuck the pain.

Renzo's adrenaline kicked in, but maybe that was self-preservation, too. Either one would work, he figured. As long as it did the damn job. Tuck was swinging that bat back to hit Renzo again, this time aiming for his head, but he was quicker. His left elbow came up fast, cracked Tuck right under his jaw, sending his head snapping back hard, before Renzo pulled back, and punched him square in the mouth. Tuck's teeth cut his knuckles.

More blood spewed.

This time, Renzo wasn't sure if the blood came from his split, aching knuckles, or Tuck's mouth. He didn't really give a fuck, either. He just wanted to get the man *down*. For good, too.

"Didn't have to fucking *sell us out*," Renzo snarled, going in for a second round.

His fists snapped one after the other against Tuck's face, knocking the man to the floor. That didn't mean Tuck went down easy because he didn't. Not at all. Pain bloomed in Renzo's mouth when Tuck landed a good punch, and then his ears rang when another hit his temple. Oh, he felt it, sure, but it was still just a whisper in the back of his mind where the rage was still *screaming*. He'd never wanted to beat someone to death like he did for Tuck.

Renzo forgot about that goddamn bat, though. At some point in their struggle, it had slipped from Tuck's hand and fell to the floor. Not far enough away, apparently. Tuck managed to grab the tapered end of the handle, and swing it hard enough to make it feel like it cracked Renzo's skull when it landed against the side of his head.

The force knocked him sideways into the wall. It was just those brief, two seconds where Renzo's gaze tunneled, and he couldn't see straight that Tuck got the upper hand. Just a moment of him *fucking up* and Renzo found himself on his back with Tuck on top of him. Tuck shoved that bat hard against Renzo's throat, holding firm and taking away his air as he put all of his weight down into it.

He couldn't breathe.

Couldn't *see* right.

Couldn't fucking *think*.

Renzo's mind screamed for him to *move*, to figure a way out of this one, to get back to having the upper hand again … *anything*. He had to figure out something, for fuck's sake.

POP.

The crack of a gun firing accompanied Renzo's sudden ability to breathe again. He sucked in a painful breath as Tuck fell away from him. Renzo's vision cleared in just enough time for him to see the bullet wound in the middle of Tuck's forehead, blood dribbling a single, small trail down his nose before the guy's body face-planted right into the carpeted hallway.

It took Renzo a second to think.

Another to breathe again.

A third to realize what happened.

There, at the end of the hallway when he tipped his head back to see who had just saved his life, stood Lucia with his gun in her hands. He thought she kind of looked like an angel—hell, she always looked saintly to him, anyway—standing there in her black jeans and his leather jacket. She was still holding that gun out straight like she might have to shoot again—hazel eyes wide, and frozen. Her breaths came out stuttered and short, but her hands didn't shake.

Why, he wanted to ask.

She never should have killed for him.

Was he even worth that?

"Lucia," he mumbled.

Croaked, was more like it.

Damn, his throat hurt.

Her gaze darted from the body on the floor, to him. "I told you—you go, I go."

Yeah, fuck, she had told him that.

"But I told you to *go*," he said, aching throat and all.

Lucia shook her head. "Not without you, Ren."

Had she followed him? He watched her drive away at the hotel, but he looked in the other direction before she had turned the corner at the stoplight. Had she turned back around, and came after him?

She must have.

His heart was going to explode, but that was better than it being dead. His mind was racing, but that was better than being blank. Every breath he took hurt, but that was better than not being able to breathe at all.

All because of her.

Because she came back.

Because she didn't *listen*.

Lucia choked out a sound.

Renzo was still trying to process.

"You crazy fucking *woman*," he breathed. "You were supposed to go."

"You stubborn fucking *man*. I'm not going without you.*"*

Fine.

Fine.

He got it.

He understood.

How much time did they have?

A few minutes, maybe. Not even. Someone would have heard that gunshot. It was way too fucking loud. But if they had a second, he was going to use it.

"Go to the car, and leave the gun," Renzo muttered, forcing himself to roll over before he pushed up on his knees. "I'll be down in a minute."

This time, she didn't argue. She knew he was coming, too. She made sure of that.

Crazy woman.

"And stay out of the fucking lobby—use the stairwells," he shouted at her back.

Fucking cameras everywhere.

This was going to be a mess.

• • •

"Let me look at your face—"

"I'm fine," Renzo grunted.

Lucia's wild gaze still drifted to him even though she really should be focusing on the road ahead of her. He would have told her that, but the last thing he wanted was to get her in a state. She was doing fine right then— calm, and pretty quiet, except for how she kept going on about his bruised face. He was waiting for her to break, to realize what she had done back in Tuck's apartment.

It would come.

It always did.

The first time he killed someone wasn't even an accident—something he was *forced* to do, but also knew he needed to do. And yet, he still found himself keeled over hours later, unable to get another person's death face out of his head as scalding hot water beat down on his back.

Because that was *human*.

It's what they did.

"What did you find in his place?" Lucia asked.

Renzo's gaze drifted to the backseat where Diego was happily sleeping. Lucia had left him sleeping in the backseat as she came up to the apartment earlier, and the kid didn't know anything. He had no clue what happened. Lost to his dreams, he probably wouldn't even wake up until they stopped again.

Who knew when that was going to be?

"Some money," Renzo said. "A gun in his office. Nothing, really."

Lucia nodded. "Your face looks—"

"Lucia, I am *fine*."

Her grip tightened around the steering wheel. So tight, in fact, that her knuckles turned white from the pressure. Maybe he should have just let her keep focusing on him and the bruises he was sporting. Let her bitch about his busted mouth, and black eyes. Let her fret over his fucking bruised temple, and likely concussion.

At least then, she was worrying about him.

Not lost in her head.

In her thoughts …

"What did I do?" she asked softly.

Her voice *ached*.

He didn't miss the clenching of her hands again. The way they trembled from her fingertips up her arms. How her gaze got a little wet, and her breaths came faster and faster until it was one right after the other without a pause.

The panic was coming.

The breakdown was *there*.

"Pull over," Renzo murmured.

Lucia swallowed hard. "I'm fine—I *am*."

"Pull over."

She did, yanking the car onto the shoulder of the highway way too fast. Even the skidding tires and the car being thrown in park didn't wake up Diego. Renzo was grateful because for the moment, he had someone else to handle. Lucia threw off her seatbelt, and slid across the middle of the car to climb into his lap.

Renzo barely felt the pain. Every blink hurt, and each breath made his ribs sting like a motherfucker. None of it mattered as Lucia broke down in his lap with his arms wrapped around her. He buried his face in her hair, and let her cry. There was nothing else he could do, really. Nothing he could say that was going to make this better for her.

A person had to handle that alone.

Deal with it their way.

The only thing he could do was hold her together while she did it.

Yeah, he could do that.

So he did.

ELEVEN

"Lucia, wake up."

In the background of her dreams, a voice was threatening to pull her from the bliss of slumber. She didn't want to wake up, though. Reality was not nearly as nice as what she found in her dreams. Didn't they know that?

"Lucia?"

Something small grabbed her shoulder, and shook. It was just enough to drag her away from the dream that was currently filling her vision. She shifted, trying to get away from whatever it was wanting to wake her up only to immediately realize how uncomfortable she felt. Something dug into her sides, and something else felt too firm against her back.

"Wake up, Lucia," the tiny voice whispered.

Whisper-*yelled* was more like it.

Her eyes flew wide, and the first thing Lucia saw was little Diego leaning over her with his big, toothy smile. He'd pushed himself between the front seats of the car to get next to her. He shook her shoulder again despite the fact she was awake and looking right at his face.

Damn kid.

She loved him, though.

"Do you know where we are?" Diego asked her.

Lucia blinked, still stuck in a state of half-sleep. It took her entirely too long to realize the car had stopped, Renzo was not inside the vehicle driving, and warm light was shining in through the windshield on her face. She squinted at the sun's rays, enjoying the way it made her skin hot, and at the same time, trying to figure out just how long she had been asleep.

It had been dark when she closed her eyes.

Right?

Was it morning now, or the afternoon?

"Where's Renzo?" Lucia asked.

"There."

Diego nodded his head toward the windshield before slipping between the seats to sit in the driver's seat. He played with the steering wheel of the car and chattered on like Lucia was listening and talking right back to him, despite the fact she wasn't doing either of those things. She was still trying to figure out what was going on, after all.

Where were they?

San Francisco, her mind mumbled, still tired with sleep, too. *You killed a guy, remember? That's where you were supposed to go, not back after Renzo. Had you kept going, that never would have happened. But if you didn't follow Renzo, he wouldn't be here either.*

Lucia squeezed her eyes shut to drown out those vicious thoughts. This was why she wanted to stay sleeping, and not wake up to face reality. At least in her dreams, those thoughts and what she had done didn't follow her to taunt her there, too. She had to do it—it was Renzo, or Tuck.

Simple as that.

She had to do it.

That didn't mean she felt good about it, or that the guilt didn't weigh heavily in her gut like a poison that was slowly starting to spread to the rest of her body. Because it did—she was trying not to let it kill her.

Lucia didn't think her father had taught her to use a gun, and spent hours getting her aim *just right* for her to do this with it. Oh, sure, he'd meant for her to learn how to protect herself if she needed to, and the situation came up at some point in her life. But she seriously doubted her father ever considered this would be the first time she needed to use a weapon.

Not that it mattered.

He wasn't here to know.

"Who's that, Lucia?" Diego asked.

Despite the fact that Diego had woken her up, Lucia was grateful for his question right then. It brought her out of her thoughts, and away from things she didn't want to deal with at all. Instead, she had to focus on him.

It was easier.

She followed the direction Diego pointed with his little finger. It was only then that she realized they hadn't just stopped *anywhere*, but rather, in someone's driveway. Her gaze caught the small, cottage-style home first. Some might consider it a bungalow given the single-level design, but Lucia thought with the high eaves and sloped roofs, it felt more cottage-like than anything else. The cedar siding had been painted with a medium blue, and the front had been decorated with a cobblestone pathway and colorful shrubbery. Quaint and tucked away between two much larger homes, she tried to figure out where exactly they were in San Francisco.

She'd come here once on a vacation with her parents, but she had been younger, then. Maybe twelve, if that. And as far as she remembered, they hadn't done a lot of sightseeing.

Then, she noticed what Diego was trying to point out to her. On the front stoop of the home, Renzo stood talking to another man. Wearing jeans and a band Tee with a faded logo, the guy sported hair that touched his broad shoulders. His strong jaw hardened the longer Renzo spoke, and his gaze didn't show any warmth, either.

Lucia thought—maybe—the shape of his face and the color of his skin was like Renzo's in a way. And even the way the two stood with their arms crossed over their chests, and their backs straight was kind of the same. But that could have just been her mind playing tricks on her, too.

"Do you know who it is?" Diego asked again.

Lucia shook her head.

No, she didn't.

She tried pulling anything from her memories, but nothing came. Renzo had never mentioned who they were going to find in San Francisco, honestly, but she sincerely hoped whoever this man was … that he wasn't another *Tucker.*

"I don't know, buddy," Lucia mumbled.

"Yeah, me either."

Diego seemed fine with that, though. Like the kid was learning to go with the motions, regardless of where it brought him to. He went back to playing with the steering wheel, and pretending like he was driving the car. Lucia, on the other hand, shifted in her seat until she was more comfortable, and then rolled down the window a bit to listen to the conversation happening on the stoop between Renzo and the man.

Eavesdropping was a bad habit.

It led to bad things.

Or, that's what she had been taught.

She still wanted to know.

"Listen, Micheal," Renzo said, "I wouldn't come here and ask, if—"

"You shouldn't be here at all. And your brother—he's all of what, *three?*"

Renzo's jaw tightened. "Four."

"Should be with his mother, then."

"Yeah, because she always took care of us, right?"

That time, it was Micheal's turn to stiffen. The man let out a sigh, and scrubbed a hand down his jaw. He eyed the car with a curious eye, his gaze landing on Lucia first. His stare lingered, like he was trying to figure out who she was just by looking at her, but it didn't feel uncomfortable. She stared back, unbothered.

"Listen, Ren, I—"

"I just need a safe spot for a couple of days. Maybe a little longer, but we won't be a bother. Just long enough for me to find something to do—get a job—and a place of our own. I have never asked you for anything."

"I don't want that bitch you call a mother around here. All right? She does nothing but cause fucking problems, kid."

Renzo made a noise under his breath. "What do you think I'm trying to get away from, huh?"

Micheal looked back at Lucia again. "Who's that, anyway?"

"Someone important to me. She's not going to cause problems, either."

The man grunted under his breath. "A few days—that's *it.*"

"Thank you."

Renzo's tone was calm, but even Lucia could hear the relief in his tone.

Then, Micheal looked back to Renzo and asked, "*You're* not in any trouble, right? Last time we talked, I was pretty clear to you, right? Stay out of trouble, do the right thing and all that shit. *Don't* be like your parents, Ren. You're still doing the right thing, aren't you?"

Clearing his throat, Renzo shifted on his feet and stuffed his hands in his pockets as he glanced Lucia's way. "Yeah, I'm staying out of trouble. Of course."

What was another white lie added onto the mountain of a mess they'd already made together?

• • •

"What's up *there*?" Diego asked, pointing at a stairwell leading up into a dark enclave.

Micheal chuckled. "That takes you up to the roof. You can eat up there, get a view of the bay, or whatever."

Diego's eyes widened. "Can I go up there now?"

"How about we grab something to eat first," Renzo suggested.

"But I wanna go up *there*, Ren!"

Lucia bumped Renzo's shoulder with her own. "It's fine, I'll take him up."

He could continue his talk with Micheal, then, without their interruption. Diego could only take so much of sitting in the car before he was ready to get out and explore. Stretch his little legs after having been tucked in a backseat for another long drive. Not that Lucia blamed the kid, really.

She was sick and tired of driving, too.

"I, uh, had some stuff ready to put on the grill," Micheal said, scratching the back of his neck. "I could throw a bit more on, and we can eat. I'm guessing you're all pretty hungry."

Lucia gave Renzo a look, not missing the awkwardness of this entire conversation. She still didn't know who Micheal was to Renzo, or why this was where they came when the man was clearly uncomfortable with them being there. Guessing by his house, the lack of pictures of family or kids, she figured he wasn't used to having young people around. There was no ring on his finger to say he was married—if he ever was—and just as a safe guess, she didn't think he had kids, either.

He was being *kind* to offer them a place to stay, but that didn't mean he wanted them there. Lucia could tell that right from the start. She was grateful he was willing to help—without even details to know why they were there—so she didn't want to make this any worse on Micheal than it already was.

Renzo didn't miss Lucia's look. "Yeah, sure, that sounds great, Micheal."

"You can help, kid," Micheal said, slapping Renzo on the back. "Learn some skills, I guess."

Lucia had to press her lips together to keep from smiling at the way Renzo scowled at being called *kid*. He was quick to fix his face when Micheal looked his way, expectantly.

"Yeah, sure," Renzo replied, "I don't mind helping."

Lucia gave Renzo a wink over her shoulder before she climbed the stairs with Diego. The small, dark enclave at the stop of the stairs led to a tiny door that the adults had to duck through to exit onto the roof. The seating area on the deck was only big enough to hold a small circular table, two chairs, and not much else.

But Micheal was right.

They had a whole view from the back of the roof overlooking San Francisco's bay. With the morning light just beginning to melt into the afternoon, it was quite a sight. The sky, a bright blue with very little clouds overhead, warmed her skin as she pressed her hands against the railings and breathed in salt and air.

All the while, Diego pointed out everything he could see. She was more than happy to listen to him chatter on because for the moment, everything felt okay. Like they didn't have to pack up and go all of the sudden. They were just *fine*.

Lucia wasn't sure how long she stayed up there on the roof with Diego. Long enough to indulge the boy's every question and his constant curiosity, anyway. Before she realized it, Renzo was slipping through the doors, and taking a seat beside her at the table. For a long while, he said nothing as he stared out over the bay like she had done when she first come out, too.

"Who is Micheal?" she asked, breaking the silence first.

Renzo sucked in a deep breath, and glanced her way. "My mother's brother. My uncle."

Oh.

That explained a lot.

Lucia didn't know what she wanted to say, so instead, she simply stayed quiet. Renzo didn't mind, as he seemed like he was the one who wanted to talk, anyway. That was just fine with Lucia. Better for him to get out whatever was on his mind. She figured since she had slept through most of the drive here, he probably had quite a bit going on in his head that he needed to get out.

"I haven't seen him in a few years—he moved here when I was young. Came back to New York to visit once, before Diego was ever born ... Carmen was bad off, then. He never could stand her, and I think he felt bad for me and Rose, but he didn't know what to do. He stayed far away from Carmen's mess. She only causes problems."

Yeah, they'd learned that, hadn't they?

"He's not married, is he?"

"Nope. Never had any kids. He's a musician. Works here in the music district at a bar playing shows five nights week." Renzo shifted on the chair, and reached out to cup Lucia's cheek. She gave him a smile when his thumb stroked her cheekbone in that way she loved. Like he just wanted to feel her—he *needed* it. "And after his show is done, he tends the bar, cleans up, and whatever else. He's kind of made himself comfortable here, and he's never looked back."

"I guess us showing up probably put him off balance, then."

Renzo shrugged. "I didn't know where else to go, Lucia. He's the only family I have."

Something painful cut into her heart. Like a fist coming to clench tight, and squeeze the organ right in half.

He had no family, really. No one to fall back on. No one who would catch him when he stumbled, and needed help to get back up again. And she ... well, she had a whole family who had always done exactly that for her. How had she repaid them for that love and support all these years?

By leaving.

Yet, as quickly as those thoughts came, they were replaced by a glaring truth. *She* was Renzo's family, too. She was all he had ... her, Diego, and Rose.

She couldn't leave him, either.

She didn't want to.

They'd have to pull her away screaming and fighting the whole way.

It was as simple as that.

His thumb stroked her cheek again, and while his brother tried to climb up on his lap, Renzo leaned in closer to Lucia. He pulled Diego onto his knee with one hand, and kissed Lucia all the while.

"We'll figure it out," Renzo murmured against her lips.

He couldn't read her mind.

Sometimes, it felt like he could.

• • •

The bungalow wasn't very big. Three bedrooms, one of which was an office-slash-music space, a single bathroom, kitchen, living room, and not much else. The backyard wasn't very big, but the tall fence gave the place a sense of privacy. And yet, the home was comfortable, and it felt welcoming.

That was what Lucia liked it about it the most.

Renzo entered the bedroom as Lucia slipped one of his T-shirts over her body to wear to bed. A shirt from him and a pair of panties was more than good enough for her. "He's out for the night."

Good.

"Didn't fight you, then?"

Renzo chuckled. "He was just happy he was going to be able to sleep with all the instruments. Which means we'll probably get woken up tomorrow morning to a lot of noise."

Lucia only smiled.

Diego could have slept in Micheal's bedroom. The man offered it to Renzo since he worked nights, and didn't get home until around eight in the morning. Diego didn't want that, though. Not after he figured out the couch in the music room was a futon and with a pillow and blanket, it would make the perfect bed for him.

"Is your uncle gone, too?" she asked.

"Yeah, but not before asking a million and one more questions."

Renzo tugged off his shirt, and tossed it to the top of an empty dresser. It wasn't lost on her how despite being allowed to stay here for a while— just a few days, that was the deal—Renzo wasn't willing to unpack their bags or even pull much out of them other than whatever they might need to wear for the next day. Even though she felt like they were okay for the moment, like they weren't going to have to get up and go all of the sudden, he clearly didn't feel the same.

That kind of broke her heart.

"Questions like what?" she asked, moving closer to him.

Renzo sighed, scrubbing a hand down his jaw. As he undid his pants, pushed them down his legs, and kicked them away, he said, "About my mom, and why we left. I don't want to lie, you know."

But he also didn't have a choice.

Lucia knew that better than anyone.

What she hated most of all, though, was that look in Renzo's eye. All distraught, and fucking tired at the same time. Like life just wasn't giving him a break, and he needed one desperately. She understood that, too. They hadn't stopped moving in far too long. Always looking over their shoulder in wait for the next thing that might send them running.

But they were okay right now.

It was good right now.

They had this second *right now.*

"Hey," she whispered reaching up to drag her fingertips through the longer bits of his hair. Renzo's dark gaze drifted to hers, and she smiled. "I love you."

She didn't say it enough.

Didn't tell him nearly enough.

She felt it all the time, though.

Renzo grinned.

That's what she wanted to see.

"Good thing you love me," he murmured. "Don't know why you'd wanna do this with me, otherwise."

Lucia laughed. "There's nowhere else I would rather be, Ren."

"I know, babe." His grin softened into a smile. "That's why I love you."

Renzo gave her another one of his cocky smiles as he moved to slip past her, and get into the bed. She didn't even think about her next move, really. Just that she knew he was stressed, and she wanted to do *anything* to make him feel better. Something to keep that sexy grin on his face, and his mind far away from the mess that had become their lives.

Things were good.

Right now, it could stay that way.

Lucia grabbed Renzo's wrist, tugging him around to face her before he could drop to the bed, and then she pushed both her hands against his chest. The surprise move took him off guard—he fell back to the bed with a husky chuckle. With his back flat against the mattress, and his hands already reaching to grab her, Lucia slipped her hands in with his, and intertwined their fingers together. Climbing up in his lap, she straddled him, feeling the twitching of his soft cock against the line of her cotton panties.

"You know I love the sight of you in my shirts, right?" he asked.

She nodded. "That's why I wear them to bed."

That, and they were comfy.

"Better than lace and silk, babe."

Lucia winked. "Well, you haven't really seen me in all that, have you? How would you know?"

Renzo chuckled. "Yet. I'm sure you'll prove me wrong."

"Someday." Lucia wet her bottom lip with the tip of her tongue, and shifted on Renzo's lap just to make her cotton-covered sex drag a little firmer against his length. "I like you under me like this."

Renzo cocked a brow, and his hands landed on her hips to grab so tight, her breath caught in her chest. Her movements to tease him hadn't gone unnoticed, it seemed. He pushed and pulled at her hips, flexing his lower half upward at the same time to make her sex push harder against his growing cock.

Fuck.

She loved the feeling of him hard between her thighs.

"You better do something with me while you got me like this, then," he demanded.

Well, he did ask.

His fingers tightened at her hips as she lifted up from his waist just enough to get her hands under his boxer-briefs. The thick vein on the underside of his dick pulsed against her palms when she tightened both hands one on top of the other around his length. He was thick enough that her thumb and forefinger couldn't touch when she circled his length with her hands. Long enough to drive her crazy when he had her pinned against any surface, and was fucking her hard and deep.

Her thumbs roved circles over the head of his cut cock. She pressed a bit on the tip, hearing the hiss leave his lips and enjoying the sight of him under her control for the moment. Back down his length she went with her touch, letting her fingernails drag along the sensitive flesh of his cock until she felt his fingers dig so deep into her hips that she was sure he was going to leave bruises behind.

"*Lucia.*"

That dark tone of his …

Thick with a warning, need, and want all rolled into one. His voice could make her do the dirtiest things, she was sure of it. She wondered if he could make her come just from using that voice of his alone.

The hard lines of his face caught her attention as she stroked him again, tightening her fingers around the head of his cock the way she's watched him do it whenever he touched himself. He was a beautiful man, really. And so much more amazing to look at when pleasure was rippling across his features, and those dark eyes of his reflected a sinful kind of hunger when they landed on her. Those lax lips of his trembled, and his jaw tensed before he grunted her name *again*.

"You better fuck me, woman," he uttered.

"Is that what you want?" she asked, feeling his hands slide around her hips and between her thighs. His knuckles grazed her sex before the tips of his fingers slid under the gusset of her panties. He pulled them aside by hooking his fingers against the cotton, and dragging them sideways. "Look at that—so fucking wet, Lucia. See, baby, all you gotta do is lift up a little bit more, and get on top of me. Don't even have to take your panties off when you're like this."

She dragged in a ragged breath.

God.

She could tease him a little more.

Make him wait a little longer.

"Don't you want that, Lucia?" he rumbled, grinning like he knew he had her caught. "Don't you wanna get my cock between your thighs, baby? Feel it fill you up, and ride me crazy? Huh?"

Goddamn him.

He was using *that voice* again.

She would have teased him more.

She just didn't have self-control.

He laughed as she did exactly what he said she would do—lifted a little higher, shifted forward, and used her hands to guide his cock where she really wanted it between her thighs. The thick head of his dick settled between her folds, and for a second, she hovered above him like that. It only took his soft chuckle, and then the pull of his hands on her hips to make her drop down on his length.

"*Shit*," she mumbled, "yeah, that's what I wanted."

Renzo groaned his approval as she seated her body all the way down his length. "Yeah, me too."

He let her take control, riding him slowly at first with her hands flattened to his chest to give her a sense of stability. It was all an illusion—she had no fucking control or stability where this man was concerned, and certainly not while he was fucking her. But he let her think so. He let her ride him soft and slow, until her body was trembling and she just couldn't take it anymore. Until her thighs ached from trying to hold back taking him harder and faster.

Until her lungs ached.

Her fingernails dug into his chest.

And she was ready to go crazy again.

Crazy with him, that was.

Renzo didn't even need her to say anything—he always seemed to know exactly what she needed without her help. In a smooth movement, he had them flipped over on the bed so that she was on her back. He pulled out of her body, rolled her over to her stomach, and slid right back into her clenching sex.

His fist found her hair, yanking hard and pulling tight until her neck was taut, and he could murmur in her ear as he fucked her hard from behind. Each smack of his hips against her ass took her a little higher. And then, without warning, she felt those fingers of his press into the tight hole of her backside. Just the sensation of his fingertips stretching her ass open a little bit was enough to send Lucia flying over the edge.

He pulled out of her then, and she felt him kneel down at the edge of the bed. His hands spread her ass cheeks open while his mouth found her sex. She came while he ate her out from behind, his nose grazing the *most* sensitive part on her body all the while. That alone was enough to make her come a second time within a minute of the first orgasm.

Then, he was straightening up again, pulling her ass against his body, and shoving his dick in again. She felt like a lake between her thighs—dripping wet and so fucking slick.

She thought ... there was no other way she'd want to spend her night. Nope.

TWELVE

Morning sunlight coming up over San Francisco's bay was certainly a sight to behold. Renzo, tossing and turning from being in yet another new place, couldn't seem to let his need to sleep take over. The exhaustion was present—he could feel how tired he was in his fucking bones—but when he closed his eyes, all his mind did was race. He couldn't seem to shut it off no matter how hard he tried, and God knew he tried. He needed to sleep; knew he had to get some fucking rest, but his body just wouldn't allow it. Not until he got something figured out for them, and he finally felt like they were safe again.

Maybe he was just asking for too much.

Who knew?

Instead of fighting with his desire to fall asleep and waking Lucia up because of his constant movement, he slipped out of bed around three in the morning and climbed to the top of the roof. She was able to sleep, so why should he wake her up just because he couldn't? That didn't seem fair, really. He smoked the last bit of herb he kept stashed in the pocket of his leather jacket because he knew it would settle his mind regardless, and then he watched the sun come up over the bay hours later in the same spot. That was probably the closest he came to falling asleep.

He enjoyed the sight of the colors streaking across the sky—colors he didn't think he'd ever noticed before, really. Pinks, oranges, and yellows on a backdrop of blue. That right there was enough to calm a person, he thought. Just watching the sunrise, and the painting it made on a brand-new canvas every single morning.

He wasn't even sure what time it was now.

It didn't even matter.

"There you are."

Renzo didn't even startle at his uncle's voice coming from behind him. Micheal joined him on the small, rooftop veranda. His uncle didn't look like he had just spent the entire night playing in a bar, and then several more hours cleaning up. Taking the only other seat at the table, Micheal settled into the chair and looked out to take in the scene alongside Renzo. The two were silent for a long while until Micheal decided to break it.

"I dumped the car," his uncle murmured. "I know a guy—it'll be crushed before tonight, so no need to worry on that side of things."

Renzo chewed on his inner cheek, muttering, "Thanks."

Micheal offered to take it the night before but only because Renzo admitted it needed to go. He didn't explain the details, not that it was technically a stolen vehicle or the fact that the guy who gave it to them was now dead. He also didn't bother to tell his uncle that the people looking for them—Lucia's family—probably had all the plate details and whatever other info they needed to track the car. He simply said it would have to go, and he only did that as a way of protecting his uncle.

He was helping them out; he didn't need to get in trouble for it, too.

"How long have you been up?"

"Too long," Renzo admitted.

Micheal chuckled, and rested his left ankle over his right knee before leaning back in the chair. "Fuck, I know all about that. It's what sucks the most about working nights, I think. I like being a night owl, but I feel like I miss too much in the daytime when I sleep, too."

Renzo didn't think it was the same at all, but he chose not to say that to his uncle. What would be the point, really?

"The other two are still asleep," Micheal added, like he was trying to fill the silence between them. Renzo didn't know if that was the case, but right then, he wasn't in the mood to talk, either. He wasn't going to be rude, or anything, but he just had too much shit on his mind to be making small talk about anything. He wasn't the type for small talk, anyway. "Didn't even hear me come in from work."

"Been a long couple of weeks for all of us, I think," Renzo said under his breath. "They sleep hard when they get the chance because who knows when they're going to get another one, you know?"

He didn't bother to mention the fact that Lucia and Diego had probably spent more time sleeping in a car while driving than sleeping in a bed for the last little while, too. That likely didn't help them. A car and a bed was not the same.

Micheal passed a look his way like he was waiting for Renzo to say more. Explain what he meant, or rather, what that statement really meant. Renzo said nothing; he explained nothing at all. This was about all he was going to give his uncle. Even if Micheal wouldn't rat them out or send them running—Renzo didn't believe he would, anyway—he didn't think it was necessary to add one more person to this mess they had made together.

Better for it to be just him, Lucia, and Diego.

Wasn't that bad enough?

He thought so.

"They can put shit out of their mind to be able to sleep," Renzo admitted. "I can't say the same."

There, he'd said too much.

Renzo wasn't saying more.

Micheal sighed. "I know all about that. So, while we're on the topic ..."

Great.

Renzo glanced over at his uncle. "What?"

"Say that with a little less attitude, Ren, huh?"

Had he?

"Sorry, long night."

Micheal shrugged. "Ain't nothing, kid."

"You do know I'm not a kid, right? I'm ..." Renzo blinked, his words coming up short all of the second. It took him a second, and then counting back the days. How many days had it been since they left New York, now? There was no possible way he didn't realize ... Had he ... "I forgot my birthday."

Micheal's gaze drifted over the colors in the sky. "Oh?"

"I turned twenty last week, and I didn't even realize it."

"That happens as you get older, Ren. Things like birthdays and celebrating them become unimportant. They're just another day in the grand scheme of things. Everybody always has something more important to deal with, I suppose."

Well, that was his life on a regular day, anyway. Even if his life had been anything but regular lately. But even so, no matter what was going on in his life, Renzo *never* forgot his own birthday. Sure, he didn't celebrate it and usually, it went by without anyone wishing him a good day except for maybe his sister. But he'd never forgotten it before now.

It was a testament to how chaotic these past weeks had been, really.

Micheal seemed to take note of Renzo's silence, and looked over at him. "What, do you want a party or something?"

Renzo barked out a laugh.

Damn, it felt good.

How long had it been since he really laughed?

"I'm good," he finally said, shaking his head. "Just surprised me for a minute. Stop calling me a kid."

That was the important bit. That's what he had meant to tell him from the start, but then got caught up in the realization that he'd forgotten his birthday somehow.

Micheal smiled. "Always gonna be a kid to me. That's how I remember you best, Ren."

Yeah, if only he knew the truth ...

"Anyway," his uncle said, slapping his hands to his knees before pushing up from the chair, "you three are going to have to find a place soon."

"I know. I didn't forget our deal."

"Actually, I might be able to help with that, and getting you a job, too."

Renzo glanced up. "That so?"

Micheal scrubbed a hand down his unshaven jaw. "Yeah, I asked around. They won't ask too many questions. I stopped in before coming home—if you head over there this morning, they'll take you in and let you look around. Give you an idea about what they would want you to do for work, and show you the place they have for cheap rent."

Well, damn.

"Thanks." Renzo stood up, too, all of the exhaustion he'd been feeling earlier was gone at the idea of getting money coming in and a place to stay. "You got the address?"

"Yeah." Micheal pulled out a small business card, and handed it over. By the looks of it, the restaurant wasn't very far away. Only a couple blocks, or so. "Just give the guy behind the counter my name, and he'll know what to do with you."

"Sure."

"Whatever you need, kid."

Renzo didn't correct him that time.

• • •

"Oh, wow, look at the colors on that," Lucia said.

She dropped Renzo's hand to dart closer to the window of the shop. Bright and colorful, an intricately designed dream catcher sat on display in the shop's window. The reds, blues, purples, and crystal beads glittered in the sunlight shining down on the display. The dream catcher spun from a hook in a slow circle, letting them see all the beautiful angles and the extensive work that had gone into the beading.

"How many hours do you think that took the artist?" Lucia asked over her shoulder.

Renzo shrugged. "More than I would care to do."

Lucia gave him a look.

"I'm just saying."

He did not have the patience for that kind of thing. It was beautiful, and he could see that. He recognized the hard work that must have gone in to making the beautiful piece, but that in no way meant he was interested in doing it, too. Simple as that.

Lucia shook her head, and went back to staring at the dream catcher. He knew they would be standing there for another few minutes before she decided she had enough of looking at the item. If he had to guess, he thought the art district of San Francisco was Lucia's favorite place to be so far. There was always something beautiful waiting to be seen. Something amazing right around the corner. Another talent to be discovered tucked away.

She loved *all* of that.

She had an eye for it, too, he noticed. *Art.* Not like his sister in the way that Rose wanted to create art, but Lucia was different. She *found* art. She could talk about it without missing a beat or needing a breath. The more colorful, the better. Paintings. Beadwork. Carvings. It didn't matter, she liked it all.

At his side, Diego tugged hard on Renzo's hand to gain his big brother's attention. He knelt down to be eye-level with Diego while the boy spoke. "You should buy that for Lucia. She likes it, Ren."

Renzo chuckled, and ran his hand through the boy's already-tousled hair. "Thanks, Diego."

"Well, you *should.*"

Yeah, he definitely should.

He'd come back for the dream catcher on another day. That really wasn't what this day out was supposed to be about today, anyway. He didn't explain that to Diego simply because the boy wouldn't care or understand.

All Diego cared about was the fact as soon as he ate his breakfast, Renzo got him bathed, dressed, and took him out to do something other than watch cartoons and play with his cars. He hadn't been able to do that in way too long. Sure, it might have been safer for the three of them to stay tucked away as much as possible, but Renzo didn't want them all going stir-crazy, either.

Which was a real fucking possibility.

None of them had ever gotten to sightsee San Francisco's most famous districts, so he figured that was the best way to spend their day. Then, he could close their day out with something else that would make them all happy, too.

Soon, Lucia drifted away from the window to join Renzo's side again. Without saying a thing, her palm slid in with his, and their fingers intertwined tightly together. He tugged her closer until she was tucked into his side, and he could drop a kiss to the top of her head. She graced him with one of those smiles he loved the best—all soft, sweet, and *knowing.* He didn't know what it was she knew, but whatever it was, it had his heart kicking a fucking beat or two.

That's what mattered the most to him.

That, and having her close.

With Diego on one side of him, and Lucia on the other, Renzo felt better than he had in days as they continued their walk down the block. Some of the shops had set up vendor tents next to their entrance doors for people to shop outside without even having to go in to pay. He supposed that was for the tourists who overscheduled their days and couldn't take the time to experience each thing one at a time.

That also helped them.

With so many people around, Renzo felt ... safer. If that was even the right word for it. There were enough tourists, distractions, and beauty that the three of them could be anybody walking down the street. They blended in with the mixture of people. It was a melting pot of ethnicities and culture, really. They didn't particularly stand out as people to stare at when they walked by. He didn't feel the need to look over his shoulder every five seconds.

It was great.

And probably a fucking lie, too.

Because that was the thing—being lulled into a sense of safety didn't leave Renzo feeling all that great. He didn't want to get complacent just to have the goddamn rug ripped out from under him. At the same time, he didn't want to voice that anxiety of his just to ruin this day for Lucia and Diego, either.

Christ.

Nothing was ever simple.

It was only the tightening of Lucia's fingers around his that finally dragged Renzo out of his pestering thoughts. He found her smiling at him in that way of hers again—like she just knew his mind was going crazy, and she wanted to bring him back to that moment with them. He was grateful.

"You good?" she asked.

He could have said no.

He grinned instead. "Yeah, babe."

Lucia winked. "Better be. So, what's next?"

That was the question of the hour, wasn't it?

"I thought we should go get this brat something to eat," Renzo said, letting go of Diego's hand just long enough to tickle the boy along the side of his neck. His brother squealed, and tried to dart away from his brother's hand, but Renzo was too quick for him. He bent down to sneak an arm around Diego's waist, and pulled him up to carry him while still holding Lucia's hand at the same time. Diego's laughter drew in several kind gazes and smiles all around them, but the people quickly went back to whatever they had been doing before the interruption. "And I guess we better feed you, too, Lucia."

God knew she wouldn't say a thing otherwise. She wasn't the type to open up her mouth and complain if things weren't going her way. She didn't whine when shit was rough. She just got up, and did what was needed. He loved that about her the most, honestly. Well, that and a whole lot of other things, too.

She gave him a look. "I guess, huh?"

Renzo chuckled, and dropped a kiss to her sweet mouth. "I know a place."

Their second surprise, that was.

Something to make this day even better than it already was.

• • •

Diego practically climbed over the table to get the last quarter of the mini pizza he'd ordered for dinner. He couldn't just ask for it, no. He had to climb over the damn table, and drag it back across the top when he fell back into his chair. All Renzo could do was laugh at his little brother because shit, even correcting him probably wouldn't help.

"This place is busy," Lucia noted.

Renzo nodded, and finished the bite of spaghetti in his mouth. "It is. Seems like everybody likes it."

That was putting it mildly. From the time they had entered Richie's Place, the restaurant was filled to the brim. Even now, an hour after ordering and having their food brought out, the place was still packed. And *loud.* Music pumped out from an old jukebox in the corner, adding to the black and white checkered appeal of the decorations and floor tiles. The patent red leather booths that served as tables for the patrons kept everyone in close quarters. Noise from the kitchen usually came out like laughter, or a chef barking at someone to *get it right, Kenny.*

The servers smiled. The floor was clean. The people were nice.

What more could someone ask for, really?

Having finished his plate, Renzo pushed it aside and grabbed the waiting napkin. Wiping his mouth before tossing it to the plate, he polished off the glass of water and watched Diego tear into the last piece of his mini pizza. Lucia had already finished her plate, and was still enjoying the atmosphere of the restaurant.

"Time for some truth," he told her.

That brought Lucia's attention back to him in an instant. Her hazel eyes glittered with amusement as she looked him over like she knew he had some kind of secret he was hiding from her. "And what's that truth, Ren?"

"I've been here before."

Lucia arched a brow. "You said you've never been in San Fran—"

"No, I meant I came here—to this restaurant—this morning. Micheal came home from work early, and he had some news for me. You all were still sleeping, and I didn't want to wake you up. It took me a little over an hour to come over here, talk to the owner, and then get back to the house. You were in the shower when I got home."

"Why were you running all over the place this morning?"

Renzo chuckled. "Because we need a place to stay, and I need to make money."

Maybe it was that statement that finally clued Lucia in to what Renzo had been hinting at because a smile lit up her features. "Here?"

"Yeah, I guess. The owner—Todd—knows Micheal. I guess he plays the drums some nights for the band if the regular drummer is sick, or whatever. Anyway, Micheal said Todd wouldn't ask questions, he just needed a guy to do some work for him on the side."

Lucia nodded. "Under the table, you mean?"

"Basically. Nothing …" *Illegal*, he wanted to say. Renzo settled on saying, "Just extra work that nobody else has time for, you know. Pay is good, and it gave me an opportunity for something else, too."

The money was good enough for them—more than enough to pay rent, get food, and get them by. Which was really all they needed at the end of the day. Sure, it wasn't going to be enough to continue paying for Rose's schooling and everything else his sister needed. That was something Renzo would have to figure out as he went ahead. They still had a few thousand dollars stuffed away in one of their black duffle bags that he could use to carry Rose once the year was finished, and she ran out of money. But he didn't have to worry about that right now, so he put it aside in his mind.

"Like what else?" Lucia asked.

"Have to wait for Diego to finish his food to find out about that, now."

Lucia gave him a look, but Renzo only laughed in response. He liked teasing her probably more than he should, really. Lucia was always a little sweeter when he got her worked up, after all. Not that he was going to tell her that.

"All done!"

Diego's punctuated his proclamation with a messy smile. Cheese, grease, and pizza sauce stuck to the side of his cheek, and painted his lips red. Laughing, Renzo got him cleaned up with the napkins left on the table with a bit of help from Lucia. It was only after they had paid their tab and were heading out of the restaurant that the owner—the same guy Renzo had seen earlier—noticed them as he loitered at the exit with an employee who seemed to be going out on break.

Todd, the owner, had apparently taken over the business when his father was too sick to continue on with it. Richie, hence the name, didn't mind handing the reins over to his son.

"Ren, are you heading up there, then?" Todd asked, leaving his employee's side to come and shake hands with Renzo.

"We are, yeah. Thought I would surprise them."

Todd grinned at Lucia, and then little Diego, too. Or maybe his gaze just lingered a little too long on Lucia for Renzo's liking. Then again, he hated when *any* fucking man looked at Lucia, even if this particular man was old enough to be her father and she had her arm wrapped around Renzo's waist.

It didn't matter.

Jealousy was a monster.

"And who is this?" Todd asked. "The woman you told me about?"

"Yeah, Lucia. Babe, this is Todd."

Todd grinned. "That's me."

"Nice to meet you," Lucia replied kindly.

"I'm Diego," Renzo's little brother said suddenly, shoving himself between the three to stare up at Todd with a smile. "Hi."

The man laughed. "Hey, there."

Renzo tugged Lucia a little closer to his side, adding, "We're good for everything, right?"

Todd's gaze came back to him.

Thankfully.

"Yeah, Ren. We're great. Start tomorrow morning, huh? Don't worry about the noise—no one will hear you over the restaurant anyway. And hey, say hello to your uncle for me."

"You got it."

"Hey, Todd, you're needed back—"

"Gotta go," Todd said out of the corner of his mouth before dropping Lucia a smile, too. "And it was nice to meet you. I hope to see your face around here more often."

"Probably not," Renzo muttered at the man's back as he headed toward the kitchen.

Lucia smacked Renzo gently on his back. "Stop it, he was being nice."

"Looked at you too long."

"Oh, my God." She smacked him again, a little harder the same time, making Renzo chuckle. "He's old enough to be my dad, quit it."

"Whatever, we have better things to see."

He grabbed Diego's hand, and kept his hold around Lucia as he directed them out of the restaurant. Lucia moved to head down the block again where they had come from, but he was quick to redirect her toward the alley at the side of the restaurant. She gave him a look, but he only winked. In the alleyway, toward the back, a spiral, metal staircase led them up to a painted-tan door.

Renzo finally let her go then to pull a single key out of his pocket. He held it out to her, and Lucia took it, eyeing him at the same time.

"What's this?" she asked.

"Killing two birds with one stone," he replied.

Understanding lit up her eyes. God, yeah. That's what he wanted to see from her.

"An apartment?"

"Maybe. Unlock the door."

Lucia laughed. "That was quick."

It paid to have people who knew people, he supposed. Shit, maybe they should have just come to San Francisco from the jump. Hindsight was always twenty-twenty, as the saying went.

Diego was jumping up and down, excitement radiating from him all the while. He tried to grab the key out of Lucia's hand, but she was too quick for him. She stuck the key in the lock even as he shouted, "Open it up, Lucia!"

Their laughter colored up the alleyway. Lucia finally got the door to the apartment opened, and pushed it wide to give them all the chance to go inside. It wasn't much, a small two-bedroom with one bathroom. All the walls were a dull white. Being it was a small loft overtop of the restaurant that Todd had apparently converted into an apartment over the last year, the windows weren't all that big, either. It was furnished to a point of being comfortable. A couch and chair in the living room. A table set in the kitchen. A double bed in one bedroom, and a twin in another.

There wasn't any artwork on the walls. They would need to go out and grab anything extra they might need like dishes, sheets, and curtains. But that didn't take much work.

It wasn't much to look at, sure.

But it was something.

And it was theirs.

For now.

Diego instantly took off to explore, but Lucia turned to face Renzo with that smile playing at the edges of her lips again. He didn't give her the chance to say anything before he kissed her.

Hard, and fast, and *long*.

Home was where the heart was, right?

That's how the saying went.

As long as he was with Lucia, Renzo figured he was always home.

THIRTEEN

A lot could change in five days.

Lucia wasn't really surprised that she felt that way, but sometimes, a reminder was always good. Peace, calm, and the mundane rituals of life day after day could lull someone into a sense of happiness that little else could provide. Or maybe it was the fact that Renzo seemed slightly calmer after a few days of being settled in San Francisco that allowed Lucia to feel like she too could stop looking over her shoulder every second of the day.

God knew Diego liked it here.

Lucia's gaze drifted between the burner phone in her hands, and then to the sight twenty feet away from her in the park. A couple days after moving into their new apartment, Renzo came back from work saying someone had mentioned a park for Diego to play. It wasn't far from their place—maybe a block of walking, nothing much. But the place was full of different kinds of playground equipment that any kid would love. Slides, swings, jungle gyms, and more. Everything that would get the kid running, and climbing. Burning off all that energy he constantly seemed to have.

Renzo made it his first priority to take Diego to the park every day after work, now. Lucia tried to take him during the day, too, if the weather was good and she didn't have other things to take care of first. Which, frankly, she didn't have very much to do except keep the apartment clean and stay busy while she waited for Renzo to come up from downstairs. Keeping busy was a hell of a lot easier than doing nothing for hours at a time, so she often *made* things for herself to do to pass the time.

The good thing about his job, too, was the fact sometimes, he wasn't needed all the time. He didn't have a set number of hours, really. It was whenever Todd called on him to go downstairs and help with something, or run across the city to grab whatever was needed. In a way, Lucia figured that helped Diego a lot, too. He constantly asked about his brother—he stayed by the small window far too often, looking out and searching for Renzo, wondering when, or if, he was coming back.

That broke Lucia's heart.

For more reasons than she cared to admit.

Sometimes, getting the boy out to the park was literally the only thing that would drag him away from the window, and get his mind focused on something else other than looking for Renzo. So yeah, even if the skies did look a little dreary in the mornings when Renzo headed out for work, she still got Diego away from the window, made him get dressed, and took him down the block to the park.

Today, Renzo had joined them for that morning run to the park. He didn't have to go into work until later in the afternoon, for whatever reason. She didn't ask what he was going to be doing for Todd later. Why should she when she was simply happy that he was there with them while he could be?

God knew Diego was happy about that, too.

Diego's squeals of joy carried over the park as Renzo chased his brother from one side of the park to the other. Renzo darted up a metal slide of one side of the playground equipment, while Diego took the winding metal stairs in an attempt to escape his brother. Not that it worked. Renzo still caught Diego in the middle of the equipment, picked him up with both arms, and swung him around. Diego's laughter picked up even more as Renzo carried him over to the tube slide, and both of them came down to the ground, smiling the whole way.

It made Lucia grin, too.

She was happy on the bench looking after their stuff. Usually, she would be the one joining Diego on the equipment, especially if there were no other children for him to play with and all. She really didn't want to interrupt his time with Renzo, though. She knew how much he looked forward to those times with his brother.

Lucia was content to sit right where she was, and watch them enjoy themselves for now. Besides, she had other things on her mind that felt like it was weighing heavily on her shoulders.

Glancing down at the burner phone in her hands, she twisted it around and around. The black screen almost taunted her, in a way. How easy it would be for her to just … turn it on. Turn the phone on, dial a familiar number that was never far from her mind as she had memorized it when she was a child, and just … tell the truth.

Or rather, tell her father the things she hadn't really taken the time to explain. Because if she could just gain the courage to turn the phone on and dial her father, he might listen to her if he picked up the phone. He loved her, didn't he? Next to Renzo, she didn't think there was another man in her life who loved her as much as her father did.

And maybe over the last little while, since they had settled in San Francisco, her father had been on her mind more than she wanted to admit. When things were quiet, and the apartment was peaceful … when she didn't have anything else to do *but* think, Lucia often went back to her father.

She was still mad at him.

Just not as much.

She was still bitter.

Just not as deep.

But, above all else, she loved him. That was most present, and mostly because she knew he loved her, too. Maybe that was why her mind drifted back to her father whenever she found herself quiet, and *happy*. Because she *was* happy, and if only he understood that—if only he knew this was where she wanted to be, and that she hadn't run off with Renzo because she was forced to, then maybe her father would leave her be.

Let her live.

That's all she wanted, really. Just to live.

She entertained that thought far too often, maybe. That if she could just call him, her wish would come true. He would understand, and let her do the thing she wanted to do the most. He would step back. They wouldn't have to run again when he got too close.

That was why, even as Renzo and Diego's laughter drifted over the park again like an invitation for her to join in on their fun, she was stuck staring at the phone in her hands. She pushed the button on the side again and again. Turning the home screen on, and then off. Over and over until all she could see when she closed her eyes was the home screen and the phone icon taunting her.

How easy it would be …

And yet, she knew it wouldn't be easy at all.

The wishful part of herself that hoped her father would hear her words and listen was delusional. The smart part of Lucia knew her father was never going to stop—he would never back down. The only thing that rivaled his love for his children was the love he had for his wife, her mother. If, for any reason, he thought Lucia was in danger … no matter what she tried to tell him … then that's what he was going to think.

No amount of truth and words would change his mind.

Ever.

For the last time, Lucia looked down at the home screen of the phone, and pressed the button on the side to turn it off again. Calling would be pointless, even if she wished for something entirely different.

This all could have been different, really. But right now, it was what it was. And even if she wanted something different between her and Lucian, that was never going to change the fact that Lucia *was* happy right where she was. That, no matter what, she was where she wanted to be with the people she wanted to be with, and her father didn't have to agree or understand.

Not now, anyway.

"Hey!"

Lucia glanced up from her hands to find Diego and Renzo leaning over the railing at the highest point on the playground equipment. If she didn't know any better, she might say Renzo looked a good five years younger in that moment. Like he was closer to his twenty years—yeah, she felt like shit for missing his birthday even if he said he didn't care—than how he normally seemed decades older.

Right then, life was giving him a moment to relax.

And he looked like he wanted her to join.

So did Diego.

"What are you doing over there?" Renzo called out, grinning. "You're missing out, babe."

"Come play, Lucia," Diego shouted.

She couldn't exactly say no, could she?

Not when love was waiting …

• • •

"So, here's how it works," Renzo explained, rolling over to his stomach to get a better look at the board in front of him. "If you land on a ladder, Diego, then you climb *up*. But if you land on a snake, you—"

"Slide down," Lucia said, coming to sit on the floor with them.

She plucked up the small pink game piece, and put it on the starting point for the board. Diego picked his own color, too—a green piece. Renzo's little blue piece was already sitting on the starting point. '

"Do you get it now?" Renzo asked his brother.

Diego nodded. "Yeah, throw the dice—"

"*Roll* the dice," Renzo muttered, trying to hide his smile.

"Fine, we roll the dice, then I move the same number of squares that's on the dice, right?" Diego looked up from the game board, and when they nodded at him, he said, "If I land on a ladder, I get to climb up, but if I land on a snake, I have to go down."

"That's it, buddy. Let's play."

Lucia leaned back to rest against the couch as the boys took their turns first. Diego got a six, but tried to sneak a seventh square where a ladder was waiting for him to go higher. All it took was a look and a chuckle from Renzo for the boy to sneak his piece back to the correct spot. Renzo went next, landing on the square before Diego's. Lucia rolled a fucking *two*.

Playing with only one dice meant it was going to take them forever to get to the top of the board what with all the snakes sending them back down to a bottom level. She didn't even mind. This little game would keep Diego good and distracted for a while. They all needed that for the time being.

A half hour in to playing the game, and Renzo was the only one on the last line of the top of the board. Diego was back near the middle after landing on yet another snake, and glaring at the dice like it was plotting against him. Lucia had given up even managing to get halfway through the board because each time she did, another snake seemed to be waiting to take her to the bottom level once again. It wasn't really about winning, anyway, but rather giving them something to do until—

Renzo's burner phone rang on the counter in the small kitchen where it had been left to charge. He gave Lucia a look—an *oh, well* sort of thing—before pushing up from the floor to go and grab the call. At that point, Diego was still fine considering it was his turn to roll the dice and see just how close to the top he might be able to get with his turn.

Lucia kept one eye on Diego to make sure he didn't cheat again, and one on Renzo picking up the call. He turned his back to them, but that didn't hide his voice from her.

"Yeah, Ren here." A beat of silence passed, and Renzo nodded. He listened for another few seconds before replying, "Yeah, you got it. I'll be down in two minutes, Todd. Sounds good … Later."

Hanging up the call, Renzo shoved the phone in his pocket and turned to face them again. Although, his gaze only drifted to Lucia since Diego was still busy moving his piece on the game to the correct spot, which just happened to be a ladder that took him right up to the square *after* Renzo's piece.

"Look, I'm winning!"

Renzo laughed. "That's great, buddy. Lucia will keep playing with you, though, okay? I have to head out and do some stuff."

Instantly, Diego's happy expression melted away. Like there was nothing else his brother might have said that could have hurt him worse than those words he just spoke. In a way, Lucia felt like Diego had been two seconds away from a meltdown for *days*. Each time Renzo left to work, the first place he went was that window. And she was damn near convinced that if not for her making him get away from the window, that was where he would happily stay all day until his brother got back home, too.

She heard it in his voice when he talked.

Saw it in his face when he looked at her, or looked for Ren.

He was scared they were going to have to go again. Or worse, he was terrified Renzo wasn't going to come back to him when he left day after day. The fears might be unfounded in a way, considering they had unpacked their bags and didn't even *talk* about the possibility of needing to leave again when Diego was within earshot, but that didn't matter. Diego was a kid, and kids didn't understand or process things the same way adults did.

It was as simple as that.

Renzo, clearly seeing his brother was ready to throw a fit about him leaving for work, decided to try a different route of pleasing the boy to keep him calm. "How about when I get back, I bring you one of those mini pizzas you like from downstairs, huh?"

Diego's wide eyes turned from Renzo, to Lucia. She could already see the water starting to line the boy's eyes. All it took was one blink, and fat tears slid down his cheeks. A sniffle echoed, and then the crying started. All out, ugly crying that echoed in the apartment. Lucia let out a sigh, and slid closer to Diego to wrap an arm around his small shoulders. There wasn't very much else she could do, really.

She'd been waiting for this.

Renzo hadn't gotten to see it at all.

"But we're not done playing," Diego mumbled through his tears. "You have to stay and finish the game, Ren. You said we could play—*you said!*"

"Yeah, but I also have to work, buddy."

Yeah, that didn't help at all. If anything, it just urged Diego's crying to turn up a notch. The wailing started, too. An all-out temper tantrum, really. Lucia didn't blame the kid. She figured it was hard for kids to learn the right way to express their emotions at this age, but especially a kid like Diego who had spent the last several weeks in a constant state of chaos.

San Francisco was his first moment of stability, really. Here, they had something that felt like a home to him. He had a bed that was his, and a room he was allowed to put his things inside. He was starting to get a schedule set for himself day in and day out, but that didn't mean anything. She bet to him, all he saw were things that could be taken away from him again.

He was *terrified* they were going to take all of this away from him.

"It's all right," Lucia murmured, kissing the top of Diego's curly head. "Ren'll be back, and we'll finish our game, then."

"B-but—"

"I gotta go," Renzo said. "I told him two minutes."

"Yeah, it's all right," Lucia told him.

But it wasn't.

Diego was far from all right.

It was just yet another thing they were going to have to deal with later. It seemed like that was happening a lot lately. She didn't blame Renzo, herself, or even little Diego. This was just something else for them to handle when they could.

Renzo slipped out of the apartment with his messenger bag on his shoulder, but not before shooting a look back at them. Lucia tried to give him a smile while she hugged a crying Diego, but she didn't know if it felt true or not.

"I don't want Ren to keep leaving," Diego mumbled when the door shut.

Yeah, she knew.

Lucia hugged him a little tighter with one arm, and wiped his face with the sleeve of her sweater. "He's always gonna come back, Diego. Ren is *always* gonna come back to you."

Diego sniffled again when he stared up at her. "How do you know?"

"Because I just do."

Maybe that was what the kid needed to know more than anything else. More than he needed stability and things that felt like home. Maybe he just needed to know that his brother was always coming back to him.

But what did Lucia know?

• • •

Lucia was sitting on the edge of the bed in the bedroom she and Renzo used when he finally got back a little after twelve. Diego had been in bed for hours, but that didn't mean it was easy to get the kid to lay down. Slipping on the too-big T-shirt that Renzo had left hanging off the side of the bed, she eyed him in the doorway.

He leaned against the doorjamb, rocking back on his heels a bit to stare down the hallway. "How long did it take to calm him down after I left?"

"An hour."

Renzo flinched.

Lucia figured the truth was better than a lie. Besides, it wasn't them that was having trouble right then. It was Diego. He needed to realize that the shit they had done leading up to this point left Diego in a bad place. Emotionally … maybe mentally, too.

"We can't run again," she murmured. "He's scared of that, I think. And he's scared you're going to leave him, maybe. It's just been too much for him, Ren. He doesn't know how to process what's happening. He doesn't understand why we had to leave, and why the little bit of stuff that he had, he had to leave behind. All that he's got left is the things that mean the most to him—*you*, really. He's probably scared the next time we go, he's going to leave you behind, too."

Renzo's gaze lifted and met hers. She thought maybe he was going to come back with a rebuttal for a second—*if we have to, then we have to*, sort of thing. Instead, she found an agreement staring back in his eyes.

"Yeah, I know," he replied just as quietly. "That doesn't change the fact that we might still have to—"

"It's not good for him. It's that simple. Think about him."

"I am!"

Lucia stiffened at the tone of his voice. High, and sharp. Like she didn't fucking understand what he was trying to tell her, even if she did understand exactly what he meant.

"I am thinking about him," Renzo said quieter, and *rougher*. "All I do is think about how to keep him with me all the time, Lucia."

"You have to start thinking about what's best for him, too. Running isn't, Ren. That's all."

He cleared his throat, and rocked back on his heels to stare down the hall again. Diego's door was closed, and the kid wasn't making a noise.

"What if someone comes then," he started to say, "your father, or—"

"We'll handle it. But we don't run. Aren't you fucking tired of running, anyway? I am. He is. Aren't you?"

"It's not that simple."

She could hear the anxiety in his voice, even if he didn't acknowledge it, really. The fear that he felt over someone taking her away from him, or Diego. They'd done so much already—robbed, killed, and run. How long would they have before something or someone finally caught up with them?

That was the real question.

Not that it mattered.

Her feelings remained the same.

"We can't keep running, Ren. It's not good for him."

Renzo nodded, stepped into the bedroom, and closed the door behind him. "No more running."

• • •

"*Fuck ... fuck. Lucia? Lucia!*"

She heard Renzo's voice filtering through her dreams, but it was his hands that woke her up. Reaching for her across the bed, and grabbing tight to her body. One on her arm, and another along the curve of her waist. Her eyes flew open, and found his gaze locked on hers. There was something wild staring back at her from him—something *desperate*, she thought.

"Ren?"

He said nothing, simply dragged her across the bed like he couldn't get her close enough to him. Those arms of his wrapped around her like iron bars, and his lips drifted along her forehead at the same time. He cursed low again, his voice a rumbling ache against her skin. Her heart thundered in her chest even as she tipped her head back to stare at him. Reaching up, she traced his roughened features with her fingertips, trying to calm him.

"You okay?"

"Bad dream."

Lucia blinked. "About what?"

"Doesn't matter."

No, she thought it did.

"*Ren.*"

He sighed, the pulse of his breath whispering along her hairline. "Just ... thought you were gone for a second. Woke up, and you weren't right there, I guess. Just, I—"

"Hey." Lucia pressed her fingertips against his lips, silencing him. "I'm always going to be here. Don't you know that by now? I love you, Ren."

"Yeah, I know. I just panicked."

"Don't."

"I'm fine," he murmured, his arms tightening around her body.

But he wasn't.

She could tell.

Skimming her hands down his bare chest, she leaned in and pressed her lips to his. Even in the darkness of the apartment's bedroom, she could see the anxiety lingering in his eyes. The tension in his jaw hardened his features, and kept his lips from pulling in that familiar, sexy smile she loved so much.

If he couldn't get the dream out of his mind, then she could help him forget.

If only for a moment …

All it really took was her hands drifting lower between them to slip beneath his boxer-briefs, and then her fingers circling around his soft cock. She hooked her leg around his waist, stroked his cock until it was hard, and kissed him all the while. Renzo said nothing, simply answered back her touches and want with his own.

Soon, she found herself turned over on the bed, so her back was pressed into the mattress and he was between her thighs. God. She loved the weight of him against her body. Pinning her into the bed, his hand locked around her wrists to keep her hands high above her head. The shift of his hips against her sex to make her body answer him back with the same movements. A familiar rhythm that was sure to get her wet and hot in the best ways.

He let her wrists go just long enough to pull at her clothes. To shed her of the shirt she wore, and the panties keeping her sex hidden from his view. He wasn't slow, by any means. Fast and rough, really.

Desperate, she thought.

Like that look still glimmering in his eyes.

And then his weight was back on her in a blink, his hand pinned her arms above her head, and his hard cock was between her thighs. Sliding home, and promising to take her to heaven. He didn't have dirty words for her that time. Just the harsh exhale of his breath pulsing in her ear with every thrust of his hips that she met with her own.

A brutal beat between them of skin against skin in the darkness, and the scent of sex clinging to his body. The hard lines of his body tucked against hers, and keeping her pinned to the mattress. She couldn't drag in a breath deep enough, but she loved that ache in her lungs. She couldn't make her lips work to whisper his name, but her cries worked their way out of her throat, anyway.

This man was something else.

Something wonderful, and dangerous, and beautiful.

Something made just for her.

Lucia was sure of it.

She didn't mind this—didn't mind losing herself in him, or letting him forget everything because he was lost in her. Her legs wrapped tightly around his waist, her only way of keeping him as close as she could possibly get him. And yet, it still didn't feel like enough. Her soul was screaming, she thought.

Screaming to find its way out of her body, and sink its way into this man. To tangle with his soul, and live there happily for the rest of her days. He could rip the breath right out of her lungs; take every fucking beat of her heart. He could be the sun to her days, and the water to her ocean.

He already did those things.

He already was those things.

And it still wouldn't be enough.

She was still going to want more.

Lucia wasn't sure that was normal.

She didn't want it to be, either.

FOURTEEN

"Are you ready?" Renzo asked, ruffling Diego's curls with the palm of his hand. "It's almost time."

"I can't see! I can't see it, Ren!"

Chuckling, Renzo bent down to pick up Diego. Grabbing the boy around the waist, he lifted his brother so that Diego could stand on the railing and look out over the bay. He kept a firm hold on Diego's middle to make sure he was safe and steady as he waited for the show to begin. The dark sky overhead lit up by the big, yellow moon was the only light they had to use next to the streetlight behind them that wasn't all that bright.

"Now you can't see," Lucia murmured beside him.

He turned his head to see her flash him a teasing grin. It was nothing more than the sweet, sexy curve of her lips that made him lean in closer. Just for a taste—nothing more, and nothing less. A quick kiss before he put his attention back on the sky and the show that was about to start.

Like usual, the second his lips touched hers for that quick kiss, he found that he didn't want to stop kissing her at all. She tasted like that cherry ChapStick she'd picked up from the store earlier in the day, and just a hint of sour sugar, too, from the candies she'd been sharing with Diego on their walk. There was something comforting in the familiarity of their kiss now—the way her lips worked against his, and how the rest of the world just blinked out when he was kissing her.

He needed it, really.

Craved her.

"Look!" Diego shouted.

It was only his little brother's yell that broke the two of them apart. Renzo might have been annoyed, but he was becoming accustomed to this with Diego. Not that the kid was purposely *trying* to break up Lucia and Renzo's private moments—even if they weren't exactly in private—but that was the thing with little ones.

They didn't care.

They had no sense of personal space, or privacy.

None at all.

Tightening his hold around Diego's middle, Renzo tilted his head to the side, so he could see what had his brother so excited. Across the bay, a light flickered. Green, then white. Green again, and then white again. Over and over. He figured that was the boat's signal for the fireworks to start, and he wasn't wrong.

Less than thirty seconds later, the sky lit up with bursts of sparks and colors. All the colors, really. He hadn't known what to expect of the firework show that was advertised, and while he had seen some of the best shows while back home in New York growing up, this was good, too.

Good for Diego, really.

Each burst that exploded in the air, shattering the black, inky sky with colorful sparks had his brother practically dancing on the railing. Diego pointed at the sky and shouted over and over again, like each new firework that went off was the best thing he had ever seen in his life. Renzo could only laugh, and hold his brother tighter to make sure the kid didn't topple over into the bay from his excitement. That would be a sure-fire way to end their fun.

It was Lucia's light laughter that made Renzo take his attention away from Diego and the sky for a brief second. Just long enough to see her face—shadowed by darkness and yet, her eyes were lit up by the colors—staring up at Diego with a wide smile. He'd been holding onto Diego with one hand, and the railing with the other. But he was quick to drop the railing just so that he could get ahold of Lucia's hand with his own.

Their fingers intertwined tightly, and he squeezed his around hers. Her gaze drifted to him, and her smile softened instantly. Tugging on her hand, Lucia moved close enough to tuck against his side for the remainder of the fireworks show. Renzo liked her there with him better. Closer was always fucking better, as far as he was concerned.

He felt her lips press against his jawline as he looked back up at the sky to watch the last burst of fireworks hit the sky. All bright reds, and blues. Sparks that started out little, and then suddenly grew into large, reaching streaks of color across a black canvas. He saw those colors, felt her kiss, and heard her words all at the same time.

"*Love you forever, Ren.*"

Appropriate, he thought.

Those fireworks kind of felt like them, and his heart, in a way. At first, they had been nothing at all. And then something hit his fuse—*her*. She'd been the match against his fuse that set him on fire. Once they had started, there was no stopping them. They exploded in vibrant, vivid colors. She brought something amazing into his life—letting him see his world in something different than the normal shades he had been living with constantly. And he thought …. he had done the same for her.

They were not the same.

He was the blue, maybe.

She was the *red*, most definitely.

Fire and ice.

And still, they fit.

Renzo was so caught up in his thoughts, and staring at Lucia from the side as she talked to Diego like she didn't realize he was looking at her that he didn't even know the fireworks had stopped. At least, not until Diego started squirming on the railing and reached down to pat his brother's arm with his fat palm.

"Can I get down, Ren?"

Renzo laughed, and easily pulled his brother to the ground. "There you go."

Jumping on the spot, Diego looked back at the now inky sky. It was devoid of the colors, but that didn't seem to matter to the kid. He was still just as excited now without the fireworks as he had been a few moments ago when they were coloring up the sky with all their vibrancy and noise.

Even Renzo, really. When he closed his eyes, he could see those colors.

"Can we get some?" his brother asked. "Can we, Ren?"

Renzo grinned. "Get some of what, buddy?"

"Fireworks!"

Lucia let out a small laugh. "I don't think we can let off fireworks where we live, Diego."

Suddenly, Diego's face darkened with worry as he turned to Lucia. "Because they'll make us leave?"

Yikes.

Renzo had to give it to Lucia, though. She was the one who—lately, anyway—spent the most time with Diego. When the kid was having issues with something, she was the first one to pick up on it. And she *never* fucking complained, either. She never said a bad word about his little brother, or the fact she was his primary caregiver at the moment. She just loved the kid—loved him because Renzo loved him, and because Diego loved her.

That was all.

So yeah, when she noticed something was wrong and brought it up to him a couple of days ago, he sat down and listened. She wasn't wrong about Diego, either. His little brother needed stability, and he didn't need to be scared anymore. Not that he was going to have to leave something—or someone—behind, and not that someone or something was going to be taken from him again.

Renzo was going to do his absolute best to make sure that didn't happen, too. It was the least he could do for this kid. He'd been the one to take Diego away, after all. He was the one who gave Diego his safe harbor from the moment he was born. He needed to keep doing that, even if it seemed impossible to do.

"But maybe Uncle Micheal would let us pop some off in his backyard," Renzo said, kneeling down to turn Diego around to face him. The boy smiled, and Renzo grinned back. "How does that sound? I'll go see him in the morning, and ask, okay?"

Instantly, Diego's happiness was back.

Renzo didn't want it to keep leaving.

"Okay, Ren," Diego said.

Done deal.

"Okay, then."

• • •

Stepping inside the convenience store, Renzo pulled the wallet from his back pocket. He moved into the line already waiting at the cash to pay for their items, and eyed the premade firework packages behind the counter. Despite telling Diego he would *ask* Micheal that morning if they could set off some fireworks at his place, he'd called their uncle the night before to make the request.

Like he thought, Micheal didn't have a problem with it. Renzo figured he could surprise Diego by buying the fireworks, dropping them off at their uncle's place, and then just take Diego over later that night to see what was going to happen. He'd say they were going over to have pizza, and the kid wouldn't know anything different.

Worked for him.

Diego would love it, too.

That sounded like a win-win to Renzo.

Soon enough, he was stepping up to the cash. The red-headed woman behind the register cocked an eyebrow at him. A silent question of, *what can I do for you?* Politeness really was a lost fucking art, but whatever.

Renzo pointed at one of the medium-sized firework kits over her head. "Can I get that middle one there, please? Thanks."

The woman turned to reach for the kit in question, but before setting it on the counter for him, she said, "I'm gonna need to see some ID. Policy, you know."

He might have rolled his eyes on any other day, but mostly, the request just irked him. He still had that fake ID from Tucker, like Lucia still had hers, too, but they'd never had to use them. If the woman cared to look at the picture on the ID, she was going to quickly see the guy wasn't him. At the same time, Renzo didn't want to ruin his plans for Diego and the fireworks.

So, he opened the wallet in his hands, flipped it over to show the ID in the slot, and gave the woman a look. "That good enough for you?"

Already, he had flipped it back around. Her gaze hadn't even drifted from his face to check out the ID. She said *policy*, not law. So maybe the woman didn't really give a damn. He didn't know.

"Fine by me."

She rattled off the price of the kit, and Renzo was quick to pull out the bills needed to pay for it. She offered him a bag to put the kit in, but Renzo waved her off, and grabbed the fireworks off the counter. Tucking it under his arm with one hand, he shoved his wallet back in his pocket with the other.

Stepping back out of the store, Renzo headed down the block, enjoying the morning sunlight and relatively warm air. That was the great thing about California in late September, and even in the later Autumn months and well into winter ... the weather was still great. Never uncomfortable, or too cold.

He didn't have to be back at the apartment for another couple of hours when he would need to take off for work. At least today, Todd had given him a rough schedule of what he was going to be doing which let him make these plans for Diego and the fireworks. His uncle's place was only a couple of blocks away from the store where he'd grabbed the fireworks, so it didn't take him long at all to walk the twenty or so minutes to Micheal's house. He could have called a cab, but Renzo was still used to using his feet to get him where he wanted to go.

Besides, he figured if they were going to be staying here ... he really needed to learn the area. What better way than on foot? That's how he learned the streets back in New York. It was how he knew every fucking alley, and where each escape ladder happened to be on any given building within a ten-block radius around his apartment.

It was good to learn.

Walking up the driveway to his uncle's place, Renzo thought the place seemed quieter than normal. Usually, even if it was the morning and Micheal had just gotten home from work, the man would be doing *something*. Tinkering with the antique car in his garage that he was trying to restore when he had time. Or playing music with the windows open. Sitting on the porch with a smoke in one hand, and a hot coffee in the other.

But the house was never quiet.

Never *this* quiet, anyway.

Renzo eyed the closed garage door, and the empty porch. He took note of the fact all the windows on the house were closed, even the music room's window which was rarely closed when he visited.

In the time that they'd been in San Francisco, he'd made an effort to drop by Micheal's place every couple of days just to see his uncle and talk for a few minutes. The man hadn't needed to help them, but he had. Grateful didn't begin to express the way Renzo felt, so he thought making an effort with Micheal might better express his gratitude than anything else he could say.

Also, he wasn't that good with words. Renzo did better with actions.

He put the eerie silence out of his mind as he stepped up on the porch. At the front door, he raised his hand to knock on the door, but thought of his uncle's words when he called the night before. *Just come right in—I probably won't hear you anyway if I'm playing or in the back of the house.*

Still, he knocked twice and then pushed open the door when he didn't hear Micheal's voice calling out to him. In the entry of the home, Renzo found nothing out of the ordinary. Micheal's shoes still rested on the entrance's mat, and the jacket that he always wore for his sets had been hung up on the hook he seemed to prefer.

But the house was *quiet.*

Deathly so, really.

Renzo felt cold—he didn't know why; there was no particular reason for that chill to seep into his bones like it suddenly had without warning. And still, he practically shivered on the spot. Stilling in place, he listened to the sounds coming from the house. Anything to tell him where his uncle might be inside the bungalow. The only thing he could hear were the normal sounds of a home.

A shuddering pipe—the hot water moving through old pipes always made the strangest noises.

A radio humming—Micheal kept one going on the back porch, rain or shine.

The TV—it sounded like the news, maybe.

"Micheal?" Renzo called out.

Silence answered him back.

Renzo took one step deeper into the house, and then another. He only stopped when he came to the entrance of the kitchen, and it was there that he found his uncle.

Or rather, he caught sight of his uncle's sockless, blue-tinted feet peeking out around the corner of the kitchen island. Renzo froze in place as his gaze seemed to narrow in on the sight in front of him. The package of fireworks under his arm fell to the floor with a light *thud.* It took his mind entirely too long to process the sight he was seeing, and what it meant. In his heart, there he knew. He could tell by the bluish-gray tint to his uncle's feet, and the motionless way they just stuck up from the floor.

That didn't stop him from rushing forward, though. Even though a cold fear sliced through his heart, and fear was reverberating inside his veins with every step he took, Renzo still moved fast to enter the kitchen and cross the space. The slick linoleum of the floor made him slip as he rounded the kitchen island, and he barely caught himself from falling right on top of his uncle's dead body.

Instead, he fell *beside* it.

That was bad enough.

Sickness crawled higher in his throat. His fingers flexed against the cold floor. He stared at dead eyes.

He saw the wire around his uncle's throat, and the way Micheal's mouth was stuck in a soundless, grotesque scream. He saw the note on Micheal's chest second, though. He didn't even need to touch it to read the words written in perfect script across the plain white, torn piece of paper.

He didn't need to touch it, but he still reached out and picked it up. Maybe a stupid part of him thought if he focused on the note, then he wouldn't have to keep staring at his uncle's body. Not that it mattered because even as he held the note between his shaking fingers, his gaze continued to drift between the words on the paper, and his uncle right beside him.

You move fast, it read, *but we move faster. We'll be taking her back now.*

Renzo couldn't get up off that floor fast enough. And even then, he felt like he might be too late.

• • •

Renzo almost threw his cell phone to the ground in desperation when the second call he tried to make to Lucia didn't go through. Somehow, his stupid fucking brain clicked that no, it wouldn't be a good idea to destroy the only way he had to contact her.

Problem was, Renzo had only gotten Lucia a burner phone a couple days ago—she didn't really turn the damn thing on unless he was out working, and then Diego mostly just used it to call him.

She didn't have a reason to use it.

"Come on, pick *up,*" Renzo growled under his breath, redialing and putting the phone to his ear again. "Pick up, Lucia, *fuck.*"

A cab—empty, it looked like—passed him by on the street. Like he would if he was in New York, he tried to hail it as it sped on by. He could get to their apartment a hell of a lot faster by a cab than he could walking the several blocks. Instead of stopping to pick up Renzo, the cab kept going.

He swore under his breath, and flipped the asshole his middle finger. *Fuck you, too.*

His mind was still thick with panic. His heart, pumping beats that echoed *fear.* He didn't even know how he was able to walk without stumbling over each step he took, but somehow, Renzo managed it.

He was closer to Lucia.

Closer to Diego.

That's all his mind cared about in those seconds.

"Pick *up,*" he mumbled into the phone again.

Scrubbing a hand down his jaw, his desperation peaked to an even higher level as he eyed the street and didn't see another cab coming. Was he already too fucking late?

Was that what happened?

The call clicked.

Renzo swore his heart fell right out of his fucking *chest*.

Was that possible?

It felt like it.

"Ren?" Lucia asked.

She sounded out of breath.

He *was*. Just from hearing her voice, he felt like he couldn't breathe. That's not how it was supposed to work, though. Everything was better with Lucia. She made everything so much easier in his life.

Even breathing.

Not right now, though. Not when his worst fears felt like they were about to come to life, and there wasn't a single damn thing he could do to stop it from happening.

He'd never felt so incapable.

So fucking *useless*.

"Lucia," he mumbled.

"Sorry, I was outside with Diego. He was kicking his ball in the alley. I left the phone in the apartment."

"*Lucia.*"

Her sharp intake of breath felt like a knife cutting him right to the bone. "What's wrong?"

Renzo couldn't make his mouth work—not properly, anyway. Not to tell her they were in danger, or what he had found at his uncle's home. Not to explain the note that was still crumpled tightly in his fist even though it felt like it was giving him a million and one little papercuts just by holding onto it.

No, he couldn't seem to tell her any of that.

Instead, he said, "Don't fucking move, Lucia. *Do not move.*"

FIFTEEN

"What are you doing?"

Lucia straightened to her full height at the sound of Renzo's sharp voice behind her. She spun around to find him standing in the doorway of the bathroom. The wild look in his eye was only aided by the fact his hair was a mess. Like he'd been running his fingers through it. Even his jacket was skewed, and undone.

He just looked ... out of it.

His call earlier had only served to freak her out, especially when he wouldn't explain anything to her. But when he hung up, there was nothing Lucia could do except wait for him to get home and get on with her evening. Diego still had a routine that needed to be followed even if Renzo was going through some kind of shit.

Simple as that.

"Getting Diego in the bath," Lucia said. "Like I do every night to get him ready for bed. What is wrong with you?"

Bending over, she turned the taps off. There was more than enough water in the tub. Diego, who was probably still playing on the small veranda with his tiny trucks and cars, didn't need much to get clean. Never mind to make a mess. He could do that with a goddamn inch of water, like all kids.

"He's not having a bath," Renzo said, turning to leave the bathroom. "Let's go."

Lucia didn't move. "What?"

"We don't have time, Lucia. We have to *go*."

No, she didn't think so.

"I'm not going *anywhere*, Ren. What is wrong?"

When he didn't answer her, she followed the path he had taken out of the bathroom. A quick peek at the sliding doors leading out to the small veranda told her Diego was still safe and playing happily. The veranda's railing was too high for him to climb over, and the railings were close enough together that he couldn't slide through them, either. They didn't put any chairs out there just to make sure he wouldn't try to climb up on one and fall over the railing, too.

With the sliding doors closed, he also couldn't hear their conversation.

Renzo headed for the short hallway that led into the two bedrooms. Lucia didn't even think about it, she followed him without question. Standing in the doorway, she watched as he yanked the dresser in their bedroom open without care. Some of the clothes they'd unpacked and put into the drawers spilled onto the floor, but he didn't seem to care.

His mind was on something else.

Lucia felt like hers was just starting to catch up to speed.

"What are you doing?" she demanded.

Renzo didn't even turn to look at her as he replied, "What the fuck does it look like?"

She didn't want to answer.

She didn't want to know.

They'd decided, hadn't they? They said they weren't doing this anymore. They couldn't—it wasn't good for Diego. They'd *said.*

Renzo kept moving inside the room even as Lucia stayed frozen in the doorway. He went to the closet, yanking out the two black duffle bags she didn't want to see again, if *ever.* Throwing them uncaringly to the bed, Renzo finally turned to look at her. He widened his arms, as if silently asking, *What are you doing standing there?*

"Renzo," Lucia said quietly.

He just kept staring.

She refused to move.

"We have to go," he told her.

Lucia shook her head. "No."

"Lucia."

"We're not going anywhere."

"We don't have a fucking choice here, Lucia."

She didn't know what he was talking about. She didn't know what had him so spooked that he looked crazed, but none of it mattered. They'd already had this goddamn conversation, and there was no way she was backing down on it.

She couldn't.

"We're not going anywhere, okay?" Lucia stepped forward, once single step into the room. "If we run again, that's going to make Diego even worse than he already is, Ren. You know this. What in the hell is wrong with you?"

Renzo said nothing as he yanked a crumpled piece of white paper from the pocket of his jacket, and threw it at her. Lucia didn't catch it in time before it fell to the floor, but she was quick to bend down and pick it up. It took entirely too long for her to get the paper flattened out so that she could read the words written on it. By that time, Renzo had already yanked out the clothes in the top two drawers of the dresser, and dropped them inside the bags.

Lucia was still frozen.

Stunned.

Silenced.

She read the words on the paper—three times, actually. She understood what they said perfectly well, and what they meant. She didn't need to take them in over and over to comprehend what the words were telling her. No, she read them over and over because that handwriting … so familiar and careful in its strokes. She'd seen it time and time again in her life.

Her father's handwriting.

Lucia's hands trembled as she stared at the words for longer than she needed to. They left her colder than ever, and yet, she was still firm in what she had told Renzo.

"We're not leaving, Ren. We're not running again."

Just like that, all of his movements stopped. It seemed like everything slowed as he turned to face her with an expression that said he thought she had lost her damn mind.

And maybe she had.

"Do you understand—"

"I understand perfectly fine what this means," she whispered, flipping the note over in her hand. "And I also know what I said, Ren. We can't keep running. They're just going to keep chasing us, anyway. That much is obvious, but they don't even matter. It's not about them. It's about *Diego*. Right now, he panics every time he thinks we're going to have to leave again, or God forbid he somehow convinces himself *you're* going to leave and not come back. We can't keep doing that to him. You know it."

Renzo's shoulders dropped. "Lucia, if we stay here—"

"They find us. I get that."

"And they take you away. Is that what you want?"

"They can't take me," she said, although she wasn't even sure if she believed her own words, to be honest. They absolutely could take her, if they wanted to. Her family could do whatever they fucking wanted to do. God knew the Marcellos had enough power, influence, and money to make the world stop turning if they wanted to. But that didn't change what she felt about it, either. "I'm eighteen. I can make my own choices—they don't have to like them. So what if they come here."

"They already *are here!*"

She stiffened at his tone. "I—"

Renzo crossed the room in a blink, and snatched the note out of her hand. It tore in the process, but neither of them gave a damn, really. He waved the ruined note like she needed to take another look at it, or something. "They're *here!* You know where I found this, huh? On my uncle's *body.* Because he's dead. They got to him—your family did that, Lucia. They wanted me to find him first; that's why they left him where I could find him and this fucking … this fucking note," he snapped, throwing it to the floor at their feet between them. "And you think they won't take you just because you say you're eighteen? Look at all they've done! Look at how they keep chasing us, but they're gonna stop, right? Just because you say so, right?"

Her heart stopped for a second. She was sure it did. Like the shock and the pain of him throwing those words at her like they shouldn't have some kind of impact—though they absolutely did—made her do a double-take of him in that moment. No wonder he hadn't been making sense earlier. No wonder he was so fucking crazed and wild.

"Ren—"

"Lucia, *think about it.*"

She did.

And she understood what he was saying.

She heard him perfectly fine.

"That doesn't change what I said. That doesn't make it any less true, Ren. Diego can't be moved again. It's bad for him."

She was going to keep saying that until he heard her. That was all there was to it.

Lucia wasn't sure what did it—the fact she delivered the truth to him with a cold flatness, or maybe the way she just stood there, entirely unmoved by his panic. Whatever it was, Renzo's tense stance loosened, and his arms dropped to his sides. Like all his fight was gone, and all he could do was stare at her like this was it.

The fight was done.

It was over.

"They're coming for you," he murmured.

"I know," she whispered.

"So you go, then. You go … and we'll meet back up. Right, we can do that, can't we? We could do—"

"No."

"*Lucia.*"

His words had turned desperate almost. Like there was an edge to his voice that he couldn't hide no matter how hard he tried. There was a panic in his gaze when it landed on her.

You go, I go.

That was their thing.

She promised.

"I'm not going, Ren," she said. "I'm not."

Not without him.

She knew it was stupid—she knew he was right. If her family was here for her, then there was really only one way this whole thing was going to end. The rational part of Lucia's brain recognized that for what it was, but her heart was an entirely different story. It was her heart that was keeping her right where she was, calm and steady.

Unmovable.

She wasn't leaving.

Not without him.

And they weren't running because they couldn't keep doing that.

Not anymore.

"*Lucia*, please," Renzo muttered.

It was her turn, now. Her turn to tune out all the things she didn't want to listen to or knew were the truth. Her turn to pretend like she didn't hear what he was trying to tell her, and the fact that she knew he was right, even if that's the very last thing she wanted. It was her turn to be desperate and *wild*.

She shook her head. "Maybe … maybe if they give me a chance to explain, then they'll—"

"Lucia, *fuck*." Renzo closed the small bit of distance between them, not even allowing her to finish what she was trying to say. His hand came up to grab her right under her jaw in a firm grip. He tipped her head back to force her to stare up at him, and there, she found his honest to God fear staring back at her. "*Listen to me.*"

"I am," she breathed. "I know, Ren."

She could feel the tremor working its way through his fingers. Then again, that could have been her own shaking reverberating through to him, too.

"It's not going to matter what I tell you, is it?" he murmured, his sadness thick and clear.

"You go, I go. So, no, I'm not going anywhere."

He swore under his breath. The sound reminded her of heartache and heartbreak. She hated the way it twisted out of his mouth like he didn't want to say it, but he didn't have a choice, either.

All those thoughts drifted away when Renzo closed the last bit of distance between them with a kiss that set her blood on *fire*. His lips against hers were rough and harsh and *lovely*. Demanding enough to drive her crazy, even if she already was entirely insane because of this man. Savage enough to make her numb and take her breath away. For the moment, their problems didn't exist. The fear was gone. All it took was the graze of his lips against hers, and the way his tongue struck out against the seam of her mouth for a taste.

He pulled her closer.

She went happily.

"Lucia?"

It was Diego's quiet, soft voice filtering down the hallway that finally made the two of them break out of their daze. She felt the shuddering exhale of Renzo's breath graze the top of her head as he rested his chin on her forehead, and held her tight with one arm around her shoulders, and his other still holding under her jaw. All she could do was hold him back—fist her hands into his rumpled jacket, and keep him right there.

Keep him *close*.

Closer was always going to be better for them.

"Lucia, who is that?" Diego called down the hallway.

Lucia blinked, not sure she was hearing Diego right.

Renzo cleared his throat, and unlike her, seemed well enough to talk to Diego. "What are you talking about, buddy?"

"There's cars down in the alley, Ren. I saw them, they're coming up the stairs and—"

The comforting, tight hold of Renzo's arms on Lucia let go at the same time the first kick against the apartment door reverberated down the hallway. She heard the sound the door made when it was kicked in, and crashed against the wall. The shout of a man—a familiar voice Lucia hadn't heard in a long time—came right after.

Her brother's—John—demand for her drowned out Diego's cry of fear.

Time was up.

They were there.

SIXTEEN

Diego's cry was all Renzo heard, and he *had* to move. It was like an invisible rope had been tied around his middle, and with just that sound alone, it was pulled taut and dragged him in his brother's direction. He let go of Lucia, and slipped past her in the bedroom to head for the hallway even as she turned to go with him.

It felt like he was floating, in a way. Like everything had suddenly slowed down in time around him. He was running for the hallway, but it seemed like slow motion. He couldn't get out of the bedroom fast enough despite the fact he moved so fast, he slipped on the way out of the doorway and crashed into the hallway wall.

Voices filtered into the apartment.

"Lucy, make this easy on me," John Marcello said clearly.

His voice bounced from wall to wall, it was that loud. Another time, and Renzo might have answered the man back with an equally nasty *fuck you.* Not right then, though. His mind was focused on other things.

Lucia's quiet, broken noise behind him bled through it all.

Didn't matter.

All Renzo could see was Diego at the end of the hall. His brother had turned around—his back faced Renzo now. He had a good view of whoever was coming into the apartment while Renzo couldn't see anything but Diego. His little brother's head was tipped back, so he could look up at whoever was approaching him.

"Diego!"

It still felt like his body was slowed down—like he wasn't moving fast enough. Diego turned, and his big, dark eyes met Renzo's. Wide with fear, and wet with unshed tears. Confusion wrinkled the kid's brow.

"Come to me, Diego," Renzo told his brother.

Did he say it loud enough?

He couldn't tell.

His lungs *ached.*

He outstretched his arms to grab his brother, ready to get him safely away from whoever was coming for him. Was it just John, or had they brought others? Diego had said *cars,* meaning more than one. *Fuck.* Maybe he could handle one person, but not a small goddamn army. And right then, the only thing he needed to get out of harm's way was Diego.

Would John hurt him?

Renzo didn't know.

He didn't know anything at all.

"Diego," Renzo shouted, "come to me!"

Finally, that seemed to snap Diego out of his daze. Renzo was only a couple of feet away from him, then, too. Diego turned on his heels, and took a single step forward like he was coming for Renzo.

It was already too late.

The man who darkened the end of the hallway was quick to snatch Diego around his little waist, and rip him out of Renzo's reach just a half of a second before he would have grabbed his brother. Diego's cry of shock as his little arms reached out for Renzo came like a kick to his goddamn chest.

"*Ren!*" Diego howled. "Help me!"

The air might as well have been sucked right from his lungs. His heart? Yanked right out of his chest in the most brutal way. The pain of having his brother pulled away from him before he could even get to him was painful enough that it might have put him on his knees right then and there.

Except he couldn't focus on that agony for too long. Not when the rage that burst inside his gut was a hot, poisonous beast. All that movement and time that felt like he had slowed down was suddenly back up to speed again. If anything, it moved faster than ever. Everything was painfully clear.

Every step.

Each breath.

All the beats of his heart.

Vivid and vicious.

It was like all the rational thought he had in that moment was gone. He didn't care what he had to do, but he was going to get Diego away from that man. He didn't stop to consider he was just *one* single man—a man with no weapon except his fists because his gun was hidden in the kitchen. One man who couldn't do very much.

He didn't even think about what might be waiting for him just outside the shadows of the hallway when he came out of it, heading right for the asshole that was currently holding Diego. A man he didn't recognize at all, but that was just fine, too. He didn't need to know who the man was to bash his fucking skull in with his bare hands.

Maybe that was the point—maybe that was their plan. To get Renzo so pissed off and blind with his anger that he didn't think clearly. He wasn't like these men, and he could admit that. His life had not been one lesson after another in the rules of mafioso—he only needed to learn how to survive.

He came out of the hallway not thinking about anything except getting Diego back, and that was his mistake. He didn't consider who was waiting around the corner, or how many of them there might be. The first strike hit him in the side of the head—heavy and *hard,* it cracked against his temple, and sent him sprawling to the floor with a cloudy vision and pain radiating through his brain.

His ears rang, but he still heard the aftermath of that first hit.

"Ren!"

Diego.

"*Renzo!*"

Lucia.

Her scream was shriller—*scared,* really. And angry.

God, she sounded so pissed.

Not that it stopped the second hit from coming because it didn't. A boot landed hard to Renzo's ribs, taking his breath away. A third hit him in the back. They came one after the other, surprising and fast. One caught him at the bottom of his jaw, and slipped to crack him in the mouth, too. He tasted the blood spray across his tongue, filling his mouth damn near instantly. The cries around him continued. Diego's, terrified and begging. Lucia's, loud, scared, and oh, so angry.

By the time he realized he should *protect* his fucking head and major organs, the man beating the hell out of him stepped back at a low whistle and a single word.

"Stop."

Renzo rolled to his back, a bitter laugh falling from his lips. He felt the blood slip out of his mouth, and drip down his chin even as he coughed and gagged on it. "Like a fucking dog, huh? You've got commands and everything, asshole."

The guy who'd been beating on him stepped forward like he was going to try and take another shot. At this point, Renzo didn't even know if he cared.

"That's enough, Dev," he heard murmured. "He's down, leave him be."

That voice.

Familiar.

Dark and rough.

It sounded like an empty alley while the sun was still hidden. It sounded like a threat to *stay away* from a girl he loved. It sounded like old money and privilege Renzo would never see in his lifetime.

It sounded like John Marcello.

"Let me *go!*"

Renzo blinked in just enough time to see the man holding Diego let the kid down to the floor with a loud cuss.

"Fucking little bastard *bit* me!"

"Ren ... Renzo ..."

"Stop fighting, Lucy."

"Fuck you, John."

Lucia's voice was a secondary focus to Renzo in those seconds. He couldn't concentrate on too many things at once because it made him want to vomit.

"*Ren.*"

Diego again.

The very last thing Renzo wanted to do was move. The pain stabbing through his body at every little twitch of his muscles was bad enough to tell him he wasn't in good shape. Not to mention, the bleeding in his mouth hadn't stopped and he was pretty sure he had bitten his tongue. His vision swam and was hazy when he tried to look around too fast. Besides all of that, his head was still ringing from that first hit.

Jesus Christ.

Had they used a *baseball bat*?

None of it mattered. At the sound of Diego's call for him and the quiet footsteps coming his way, he rolled over in the direction of his brother. He already had his arms opened, ready to get Diego back where he was safe. He forced himself to blink, begging his vision to become a little sharper as Diego's form came closer.

Too slow, he thought.

The kid was scared.

"It's all right," Renzo mumbled, "come here, Diego."

Why was the fucking apartment so quiet?

Or maybe that was just the ringing in his ears taking over all the noise.

That all stopped, though. Or it faded the second Diego slammed into Renzo. Everything around him came into sharp focus all at once when he had his arms wrapped around his little brother.

Like he could breathe again.

See again.

Hear again.

"No, stop it!" Lucia cried. "I don't want to go, John, fucking *stop!*"

"That's enough, Lucy!"

"*Stop calling me that!*"

"I said make it fucking easy on me, and you didn't. This is what happens, kiddo."

"Fuck you. Fuck *you,* John. I fucking hate you!"

"*Lucia.*"

Lucia's gasping sob came further away than her last words. It felt like a snake slithering across the floor to find Renzo, wrap around his body, and tighten on him like it was about to squeeze him to death. All of that confusion muddying up his mind and making him feel off-balance drifted away when he caught sight of Lucia fighting with her brother in the doorway. The other two men who had come in to help stayed a couple of feet back. Like they didn't dare step in and put their hands on her.

Instead, it was just her brother with his arms locked around her like bars she couldn't get free from, and pulling her closer and closer to the door. Further and further away from him and Diego.

Her wild, hazel gaze found Renzo.

Terrified, and fighting.

Not giving her brother an inch at all.

He let Diego go, then. It wasn't like he felt steady enough to get to his feet, but he did just that. He made it all of two steps across the room when three guns came out, racked back, aimed at him, and ready to fire. One from John, and two from the other men. But if a gun was going to be the thing that took Lucia away from him, he was going to have to be dead on the ground with a fucking bullet in his head.

Simple as that.

Renzo took one more step.

"Move again, and I'll blow your fucking brains out," John murmured coldly.

"*John*," Lucia whispered. "Please …"

"You're going home."

"I don't want—"

John's gaze snapped back to Renzo. "One more fucking step, Renzo. Take it, I dare you."

"John!" Lucia tried to pull away from her brother, but it was useless. He had one hold on her, and another firmly on the gun that Renzo was staring down. "Let me go right *now*."

The man never looked away from Renzo. It was like Lucia's fight and defiance didn't affect him at all. He was bigger than her; stronger, too. Her frustration was his annoyance.

"You had a good run," John told him, "but it's done now. You got me?"

Renzo's jaw clenched.

How the fuck was he going to get Lucia away—

He didn't even get to finish his thought process. The next crack to his head sent him to the floor again, but this time, his vision blacked out altogether. He was so busy staring at John and the love of his life that was too far away from him that he forgot to be mindful of the other two men who had moved to either side of him. He was still dealing with that blinding rage instead of trying to be smart.

As he drifted out of consciousness, he heard Lucia *screaming*. Diego was crying.

He blacked out again. The second time he almost came to, Diego was asking someone to help. And he heard the owner of the place—Todd—say he was calling the cops. The third time, he heard sirens. Renzo knew what that meant.

It was all over, now.

There would be no coming back from this.

Ever.

SEVENTEEN

"I didn't want to do this to you, you know," John said.

Lucia continued staring out the port window of the private jet. She heard her brother, of course, but she just didn't care to *listen*. Therein was the difference. Not that John seemed to understand or anything. He seemed perfectly fine with chatting like she was talking back, even though she clearly wasn't.

In fact, she wasn't even pretending to give a fuck what her brother was telling her. She wished he would get the hint, and fuck off. The last several hours of her life had been … traumatic, to say the least. Nothing she had done with Renzo … none of the things they experienced together, including killing Tuck, came close to the trauma of the last few hours. She was never going to forget the sight of Renzo bleeding and broken with his little brother crawling on top of him as he tried to wake him up while Lucia was dragged away.

She couldn't help.

All she could do was scream, cry, and fight.

It wasn't enough.

Not to help him.

So yeah. Fuck John if he thought Lucia was going to entertain his conversation and apologies. Like they were supposed to mean something to her? They *didn't*.

Not at all.

"You didn't think after the mess you all left behind, that no one would come looking for you, did you?" her brother asked. "Dad wasn't going to let the police catch up to you first, Lucia. You have to understand where he was coming from. At first, he was just worried about you and making sure you were safe. But then we started to find messes that we had to try and clean everywhere you two went. The robbery—then *Vegas*. Stolen cars. The hotel. If *we* could find the problems, then you could bet the police were going to catch on, too. They already started to. You gotta understand where he's—"

Slowly, Lucia turned in her seat to face her brother who was just one aisle over. Dressed in a three-piece suit, with his hair combed back and his hands resting in his lap, John didn't look like someone who only a few hours before had stormed an apartment, watched as a man got the hell beat out of him, and then dragged his sister down a flight of stairs before shoving her into a car.

They were funny that way.

The Marcellos, that was.

They could show the parts of themselves that made them horrible, and in the next breath, be right back to the polite, God-fearing, upper echelon beings that allowed them to get private invitations to charity balls and got their pictures splashed in the society rags. No one truly understood the masks a Marcello wore quite like another Marcello.

"Why are you still talking?" Lucia asked him.

John blinked. "I beg your pardon?"

"I haven't replied to you once since you put me in that car. Wasn't that clear enough for you that I don't want to speak to you right now? If I have my way, John, I won't ever talk to you again."

"You don't mean that, Lucy. You're angry with me right now because of all of this. In a few days, once your head clears and you get some distance between you and that man, you'll come to your senses—"

"And I'll still tell you to fuck off, John."

Her brother stiffened.

Lucia smiled coldly.

But that was the thing about John, a lot like the rest of him. He was quick to bounce back because he had to in this life. Nothing could keep him down for too long.

"Fine, if you don't want to talk to me, then you can *listen*," John said, fixing his jacket and turning his gaze on her again. Instead of spinning back around in her seat to stare out the window once more, Lucia chose to stare right back at her brother. She *hoped* and *prayed* and fucking *wished* all that hate she was feeling shone through in her eyes. She wanted him to see it, and to *know*. Nothing would hurt her brother—once, her best friend—worse. And right then, that's all she wanted to do. Just fucking *hurt* him.

He'd hurt her, after all.

He did this to her.

Took her away.

Took away what she wanted.

Hurt Renzo.

Scared Diego.

Her list could go on and on. That was the problem. Add onto that with the fact John didn't seem to be aware of how he'd hurt Lucia by doing what he did, and she just wasn't interested in having this conversation with him. He thought he was right; she knew he was wrong. It would only led to more heartache for her when she told him again and again what he'd done, and he continued to give her excuse after excuse for it all.

A dead fucking end.

Kind of like her life right now.

John never once thought to listen to her, or cared about what she wanted. All he cared about was doing their father's bidding. That was a whole other problem to deal with at another time. Soon, likely. Probably the moment she stepped off the plane and was faced with her waiting father.

Lucia couldn't say how she was going to react, then. Figure it out when the time came, she supposed.

"Listen," John repeated. "Listen to me, okay? I know that the two of you thought you got off scot-fucking-free, but here's a reality check, Lucia … *you didn't*. His face was on the news. His name is being spread around the fucking country. Do you get that? The police were *coming for him*. What do you think would have happened when they finally caught up with Renzo, and you were there with him, too, huh?"

Lucia said nothing.

John didn't seem to care as he continued on with, "How many steps do you think it would have taken them before they figured out your involvement in his mess, too? Is that what you wanted? We're fucking helping you here. Or … *trying*. I'm not going to say it's a bad thing that I got you away from him, too, because clearly, you don't think about anything when you're with him. You make stupid choices and do equally stupid fucking things. Jesus, are you even listening to me right now?"

Oh, she heard him.

Loud and clear.

Lucia would rather be locked up because she stayed with Renzo than free without him because her family came behind them to clean up any evidence of her involvement with him.

Not that John would understand.

He didn't.

"I don't care about anything you have to say," Lucia said, shrugging. "So, why should I care to listen, John? When I asked you to stop … when I asked you to let me go … you didn't listen to me. Give me one good reason why you think I should give a damn now, and listen to *you.*"

Because she couldn't find one.

Not a single fucking reason to do what he asked.

He did that.

Not her.

"Because I am your brother—your *blood*. Family," John said, like she needed a reminder. "And family loves one another. They protect one another. That's what we're doing here, Lucia. That's why I came."

She kept staring.

Blank.

Cold.

Empty.

Fucking *dead*.

Her reply came out barely above a whisper, but she knew he heard it.

That's what mattered most to her. "If that's how you love me, then you can keep it. I don't want it, John."

"Lucia, you don't mean that, now. You're mad, and not thinking clearly, that's all. Give it some time. We'll come back to this."

No, they wouldn't.

And if they did, it would end the same way.

Better he learned it now.

"Choke on your fucking love for all I give a damn. How about that?"

He tried to talk again.

She just turned away.

She saw the clouds out the port window, but in her mind, she was looking at someone else. Or rather, looking *for* him.

Where was Renzo now?

Was he okay?

What about Diego?

Did Renzo know she was sorry?

God.

She was so fucking sorry for this.

• • •

Lucia was wrong. Her father hadn't been standing there waiting for her when she stepped off the plane in New York. It was a brief moment of relief for her, she supposed. She still hadn't been ready to face him, and she wasn't sure how well she would have reacted if he was standing there waiting.

Instead, Lucian was standing on the front porch of their large home with her mother when John pulled into the driveway. At first, her brother didn't put the car into park when he first pulled in. He kept a tight foot on the brakes to keep the car from going further, but without putting the vehicle into the park, the doors also refused to unlock.

It basically forced her to stay in the car with him.

Lucia didn't want to get out.

Not yet.

She also didn't want to be near John.

What a mess.

"Just tell me why," her brother murmured.

Lucia's gaze drifted from the people waiting for her on the porch to her brother sitting in the driver's seat. "Why, what?"

"Why you ran off with him. Why you ... didn't even think about calling me, Lucia. Or anyone, really. The first chance you got, you took off with him and didn't look back. Like we meant fucking nothing to you. And now, look at you ... pissed off, you won't even talk to me despite the fact I've been running after you for *weeks* now. And why? To save your ass from getting put in jail, or worse. So yeah, the least you could do is tell me why."

"I don't owe you anything. I didn't ask for anything, John."

Her brother sighed. "Lucia—"

"But if you have to know, I went with him because there was no other place I wanted to be than right there with Renzo. I ran because I love him, and I don't think you'll ever be able to understand why. You think I didn't care about you or the rest of them … you're wrong. See, you just don't see it the same way, John. You came after me; chased me down and dragged me back here because *why?* Love, that's why. I went with him for the same reason. It might not be the same to you, but there's no difference for me."

"Then I was right. We don't matter to you. Your family … we never mattered."

Lucia shook her head. "You do … they'd make the same choice, too. Daddy, well, he'd run for Ma. She'd run for him. You don't see it the same way—maybe you can't, I don't know. I can't make you understand, John. Love does that, not me. So, when you do finally get it … when you can look me in the face and *know* what you did, maybe I'll care to listen. Or maybe it'll be too fucking late."

John put the car in park.

The doors unlocked.

Lucia couldn't get out fast enough.

Unfortunately, stepping out of that car into cold, autumn wind only meant one thing. The next people she had to face were her parents. Standing side by side on the porch, her mother and father stared at her with stoic, stony expressions. No smiles—no joy. She imagined that she looked similar staring back at them.

Lead weighed down her feet, but somehow, she made them move. One single step at a time until she was climbing the stairs to her childhood home, and staring her parents right in the face. She wasn't going to apologize. She wasn't going to tell them she was sorry when she wasn't.

Marcellos didn't bow or bend.

Not even to one another.

"Lucia."

Her mother spoke first. Soft, and whispered. Jordyn's words almost got carried away in the light wind, but Lucia heard them nonetheless. She hadn't realized how much she missed her mother until she was looking at Jordyn, and heard her voice. The worry shining back in her mother's gaze, despite the fact she wasn't smiling at Lucia, was as clear as day.

That was the one thing Lucia felt bad for.

The guilt was a killer.

"I'm okay, Ma," Lucia murmured.

Jordyn nodded, and inched a little closer. Closing the distance between them with an outstretched hand, Jordyn brushed back the stray waves of hair that had fallen over Lucia's shoulder. The soft touch reminded her first and foremost that her mother, no matter what … no matter how much pain and worry she caused … was always going to be her mother.

"Scared me to death," Jordyn said thickly. "God, Lucia, you scared me to death."

She still couldn't apologize.

She'd choke on those goddamn words.

"I'm fine, though."

"*Now*," Jordyn said sharply.

Both of her mother's hands came up then to grab Lucia on each side of her face to hold tight. It forced her to look her mother right in the eyes—there was no looking away. She could see the tears shining back, and her own unfeeling expression reflecting in her mother's wet irises. Lucia couldn't help but suck in a sharp inhale.

Not at how terrified her mother looked, or how tightly Jordyn was holding onto her like she was scared Lucia might bolt again … but because of how unaffected she felt in those moments. Dead, almost. There was a part of her that was missing, now. In her heart, it felt empty. Her soul? Entirely gone.

She couldn't *feel* anything.

They took it away.

"Now, baby," Jordyn repeated. "But you might not have been. Don't you understand that?"

Lucia shook her head, but said nothing. Jordyn finally let her go, and like she was defeated, took a step back from Lucia. She might have been grateful for the distance, but she couldn't focus on it long enough to feel anything but *contempt* as her father finally glanced her way. Since she stepped up on the porch, the only thing her father had done was stay quiet and look out over the driveway.

Into the darkness.

The void.

Now, he was looking at her.

"For what, Lucia?" he asked softly. "You did this for what—a man? All for him, hmm?"

"I—"

"For a man who will spend the unforeseeable future stuck in a prison cell," her father continued like she hadn't tried to talk at all. "That's what you did this for. And you have the nerve to stand there without an explanation or an apology for your mother. Fuck me—I don't need anything. But you don't even have anything for her, Lucia. But that's what you did all of this for—a man who is destined for a prison cell. How does that feel?"

If she felt cold, then her father was *ice.*

Lucia's heart crumbled, sure, but not for her father.

Only for Ren.

Instead of replying to Lucian—he didn't really want a response, anyway—Lucia headed past her parents, and disappeared into the house. No one followed behind her. She didn't stop to take off her shoes, or to appreciate the home that had raised her. She simply navigated familiar halls and stairs until she found the room that no longer truly felt like hers.

She closed the door behind her.

She sat on the floor instead of the bed.

Only then did her heart shatter.

Only then did she cry.

And she broke.

All apart.

Into tiny pieces.

Alone.

Without.

And so empty.

She broke.

• • •

The days crawled by before Lucia really understood what was happening. One melted into two, then three, and four. It was like a daze had come to settle over her, and no matter what she tried to do to rid herself it, the bitch clung on. It kept her quiet, and stuck in her head. Replaying moment after moment, making her see mistake after mistake, and the only thing she knew for certain was that Renzo's freedom had been sacrificed for hers.

She knew it more now than ever as she watched a handcuffed, and still bruised Renzo be taken from the back of a Sherriff's van and then dragged past waiting reporters as they did what her family would call a *perp walk.* He looked like hell—like he hadn't showered in days, and he didn't get a wink of sleep, either. His gaze drifted to the camera, and paused for a second before focusing on something else.

She saw it, though.

In his eyes ... he looked dead.

It wasn't like she had anything else to do except watch the goddamn news. Her father took away anything she might use to contact someone— her phone, laptop, and tablets. Her house was on fucking lockdown, now. Enforcers all over the place the second she stepped outside for a breath of fresh air, or just to get away from her dad.

Her mother wasn't so bad. Jordyn mostly left her alone, and let her do her own thing. She didn't attempt conversation because frankly, Lucia wasn't willing to talk to begin with.

Her father was an entirely different story.

Tension didn't begin to describe what was happening between the two of them, honestly. She hadn't spoken one word to her father since that night on the porch. If she could help it, she didn't even look at him. Sometimes, he tried … she would dead stare at nothing until he finally walked away.

Whatever worked, really.

So, yeah.

All she had was the goddamn news.

Lucia had been scouring the news channels for days in search of anything about Renzo. Or even about Diego. But since Diego was still a minor, apparently someone had put a media ban on his name. So other than the information that had been shared about the Amber Alert for the boy, nothing else was being said.

Renzo was another story.

Charged with kidnapping, and robbery. Grand theft auto, too. It seemed some of their mess had gone by unnoticed, like Vegas. Lucia didn't know whether she should be grateful for that … or terrified. According to the reports she had seen, the police were looking for a dark-haired girl who had been reportedly seen with Renzo. They had a first name, they said, but they weren't releasing it to the public just yet. The first public briefing the police chief did let her know that Renzo wasn't saying anything, and denied anyone else had been with him and Diego.

That just made Lucia cold all over.

His freedom for hers.

Lucia felt numb as the news program switched back from showing Renzo to the anchors at the station. They discussed the event, and the fact that the *child* in question was reportedly safe in CPS custody. That made Lucia want to be fucking sick.

"You're quite lucky, seems he isn't talking at all," came a voice behind Lucia.

She didn't even turn to face her father. She hadn't heard him come into the living room, but now that she knew he was there, she certainly wasn't going to acknowledge his presence. Not that it seemed to matter to him. He kept talking regardless.

"See, for all the effort I have had to go through in order to scrub your presence from a lot of this mess … to keep you safe, it would have meant nothing if that young man decided to open his mouth and give you up," Lucian murmured. "Had to wait and see if he would, I suppose. I couldn't be sure."

Lucia *refused* to speak.

She wouldn't.

Even if she did want to tell her father to go fuck himself.

Lucian came around the side of the couch to sit on the arm. He rolled up the sleeve of his dress shirt on the right arm until it was firm around his elbow. He did the same to the left side, never looking at her all the while. Not that she gave a damn. She couldn't stand to be near him, but he didn't seem to understand.

It was easier to say nothing at all.

"See, that is something you seemed to forget," her father said, glancing up to meet her cold gaze. "*You* are my blood—made from half of me, Lucia. And because of that, because you are mine, I will always protect you first. But him … I couldn't have cared less about him. Right now, that doesn't matter. You need to understand that you're staring at his future. He's not getting out."

Her throat tightened.

Lucian nodded. "Still nothing to say to me?"

"Telling you that I hate you doesn't seem to be good enough, really."

And nothing she would say would be enough. That was the problem. She was never going to be able to tell her father all the things she felt. She would never be able to say enough to hurt him the way she was hurting.

It was better not to bother.

Her silence bothered him more.

Her father dragged in a long, heavy breath before standing from the couch. "I see."

"What day is it?"

Lucian arched a brow. "October first, Lucia."

Huh.

"I want to go to California," she said.

"I don't think so."

"Yeah, that wasn't a request." Lucia shrugged, and turned back to stare at the television screen again. "I want to go there for school. I'll be late to the second semester when I was supposed to start anyway, but that doesn't make a difference to me. Anywhere that I am far away from you is where I want to be. I don't need your permission. I have my trust fund to pay for school and whatever else I need. I am already in the program, so I don't need that, either."

Out of the corner of her eye, she saw her father's jaw tense. "If you think getting away from me is going to get you closer to him—"

"He's here. Going to prison. You said it. I'd be there—further away from him. If you think I'm going back to California just for him, then you're wrong. I want to go because I want to get the fuck away from you."

Her contempt burned.

Like bile in her throat.

Like fire in her heart.

Fury in her soul.

This bitterness was never going to go away. The longer she stayed here, the worse it was going to be.

She would kill herself with it.

Lucia already knew that.

"Lucia, I did what I had to in order to protect you," her father said quietly.

Almost *pleadingly.*

She did look at him that time. "And what, sacrificed him to do it?"

Lucia didn't need her father to reply to know his answer.

That was good enough for her.

Bad for him, though.

"Sleep at night knowing that, Daddy," she whispered. "I hope you sleep well at night knowing what you did to me, and to him. I won't ever forget it."

Because she couldn't sleep at all.

The bed felt too empty without Renzo.

Just like her whole fucking soul, too.

Like her heart.

And her life, too.

All gone.

EIGHTEEN

"Hey, Zulla!"

Renzo looked away from the calendar someone had taped on the wall of his cell—likely a damn guard at one point or another, or maybe the last person who used the cell. He had a bunkmate, but the guy was in for petty crimes and looking at a slap on the wrist. He certainly wasn't at the level Renzo was in this fucking hell.

Soon, they were going to move him from the jailhouse to the big house. As the cops liked to point out every single time they passed his cell, a prison wasn't like this shithole. It was *worse*. And he was exactly the kind of fresh meat inmates enjoyed taking a bite out of when a guard's back was turned. Renzo supposed they told him that shit as a way to scare him, but really, it just pissed him off.

"What?" Renzo asked.

The guard who had called his name came into view just beyond the bars of his cell. Leaning against the metal, the man rested his arms along the slot where they shoved in the shit they liked to call food. It was better than nothing, sure, but it was also one step above wet dog food, too. He ate it because he had to, not because he particularly wanted to. Besides, it wasn't like he really had a choice about anything in here.

Even going outside was regulated to one hour a day, supervised. And he wore cuffs and shackles all the way out to the yard before he was finally let off his chain like a dog, only to run around a fenced in yard. Yeah, just like a damned dog. They even told him when he could go to bed considering they turned the lights off at eight sharp every damn night.

It was tiring, really.

"Your bunkmate is coming back from his shower time," the guard said. "Told me you switched out with him for the call this week."

Renzo nodded. "Yeah, sure did."

Didn't cost him too much. Promised to keep an eye on the guy for the remainder of his time here. Made sure to snatch the guy a couple of extra magazines when he was able to get his hands on them from a guard that wasn't too bad. Sometimes, things that seemed simple to those who weren't locked up were fucking treasures to people behind bars.

A stupid trade could mean the greatest gift.

Like an extra phone call.

The guard beyond the bars nodded, and stepped back a foot. "Heard your detective was in again to question you."

Renzo scowled, but hid it well enough by looking away. He didn't understand what the fucking point was with the detective. The guy kept coming up with more questions, hoping to all hell Renzo was going to give him some kind of answers. Renzo never did. He had nothing to say. It didn't matter how many times the man said he had witnesses to the fact there was a woman with Renzo, and that even Diego talked a bit about Lucia—without giving her last name, it seemed—he never confirmed it.

He did it all alone.

That was his story, and he was sticking to it.

Even his lawyer—some shithead that was appointed to him when he was first brought up on charges in New York—tried to convince him that a deal could possibly be made if he was willing to give up his accomplice. Renzo still said nothing. There was nothing to say. They didn't have the evidence to bring her in on their own, and he bet her family was keeping her well protected. Which was fine because that was exactly what he was going to do for her, too. He'd be long dead in a grave before he ever gave up Lucia.

Simple as that.

"You know, you could make this easier on yourself if you were smart about this, and talked to the detective," the guard said.

Renzo laughed. "Yeah, I bet. Can I go make my phone call now, or …?"

The guard rolled his eyes, nodded, and then took another step back. "Hands through the slot, kid."

Here he was, twenty years old, locked up and facing twenty-five to life, and people were still calling him a goddamn kid. Renzo wished he could be surprised, but he really wasn't. Story of his fucking life, it seemed.

Giving the calendar and the date one last look—October fourteenth— he stepped up to the cell door, and put his hands through the slot like he'd been told. The guard locked his wrists into the cuffs he had at the ready, and then gestured for him to step back. Which he did. It was better, and shit was just easier in here, when people followed the rules. Or, that's what he had learned rather quickly. Don't cause problems for other people, and they wouldn't cause problems for you.

Easy enough for Renzo.

Putting his hand up for the camera to see, the guard lifted two fingers. Soon after, a loud ring echoed through the cell, and the sounds of the lock coming undone resounded right after. Once the door was open, and the guard was waiting to take him by the arm with an outstretched hand, Renzo finally stepped out of his cell for the first time all day. If all went well, he'd get his hour of yard time later. Which he would use to run a few laps until he was exhausted and couldn't think.

Then, he wouldn't have to listen to the drunks that were brought in to sleep off their stupor throughout the night. Or the fights that seemed to constantly break out between other cellmates throughout the small block.

Renzo was directed through the long hallway past the row of cells, and beyond a second and then a third set of locked doors before the guard stopped before the corridor where a row of payphones waited. Pulling out a quarter from his pocket, the guard handed it over, then lengthened the chain connecting Renzo's cuffs, so it would be slightly more comfortable when he got to make his phone call.

"Let's hope whoever you're calling today picks up, huh?" the guard half-joked.

Renzo wished he could laugh like the man did. Except he couldn't because that was a sad reality for him. Sometimes, he called people, and nobody picked up. God knew he didn't have a lot of people to call in the first place, but it seemed like rubbing salt in an already sore wound when he waited all week for *one* phone call, and the person on the other end didn't even bother to answer it.

In the grander scheme, he supposed that was yet another way of life showing him that he didn't matter all that much. He wasn't that important. People didn't give a fuck what happened to him in here.

He was just another kid from the Bronx that fucked up his life. He'd been raised on the streets, and the only place people like him went was into a grave, or a prison cell. He was living up to that statistic, nothing more and nothing less. Surprise, surprise. He was going to get what he deserved, and they didn't give a shit one way or the other.

"Yeah, let's hope," Renzo muttered.

Without another word, the guard lifted up his hand for the camera above the doors leading into the corridor for the payphones. Once it was unlocked, he let Renzo go through alone, but made sure to stay on the other side of the door in full view of the glass. It gave Renzo nothing more than a false sense of privacy, really. They were always watching him. Cameras were at every angle. Microphones, too, listening to each and every word he said. Not to mention, each phone call was recorded.

Everything he said could and would be used against him.

He always had to be careful.

Stepping up to the payphone, Renzo plucked it off the cradle, and slid the quarter into the slot. He pressed the numbers he had never forgotten. He'd called it once before since being arrested, but she had been way too angry with him to talk, then. He understood, so he hadn't pushed.

Today was not going to be the same.

Today was *important.*

Renzo didn't want her to think he forgot.

In his ear, the call rang and rang. At the fourth, he closed his eyes, and pinched the spot at the bridge of his nose to ward off the feeling of dread resting across his shoulders. He was sure the voicemail would pick up the call, but to his surprise, she picked up on the fifth ring.

"Hello?"

"Rose," Renzo said, "it's me, Ren."

For a second, his sister said nothing. He kind of expected that, really. This wasn't easy on her, and he didn't think it would be, either. He didn't expect her to like what was happening, or to agree with the things he did. He just loved his sister, and it didn't matter where he was or what he was doing, he was always going to look out for her in whatever way he could.

"Ren?"

"Yeah," he said, clearing his throat. "Happy birthday. Eighteen today, huh?"

"Oh, my God, Ren," his sister mumbled. "I can't believe you called me to tell me that."

Yeah, fuck.

He'd gotten the extra call this week just to do that for Rose. Or rather, hoping she wasn't as angry this time, would pick up his call, and let him talk to her. Last time, she just raged while he stayed quiet and let her. It was the least he could do for the hell he bet she was going through.

"Like I'd forget," Renzo said, shifting from one foot to the other. "Did you do anything today, or—"

"Went to see Diego," Rose said, her voice thick with an emotion he couldn't place. "The couple fostering him are really nice—they live in Queens, so it's a bit of a ways for me to go, but he likes seeing me. Keeps asking about you."

Damn.

That hurt.

It wasn't Rose's fault.

He didn't blame her.

"And her," Rose added softer. "He asks about—"

"Don't," Renzo said quickly.

Rose sucked in a hard breath, and then said, "I watch the news, you know. Keep up on what's happening. It's all about you. Nothing ever gets said about ... well, you know. What's going to happen now, Ren? Do you know that Ma's been around, too? She visits Diego, and they know she's messed up, so they haven't released him to her custody. But she's *trying*. Swears she's gonna get clean; she even tried to say she has a lawyer working on it."

Renzo's throat felt far too tight. Almost enough to keep him from speaking, but he knew better than to shut up. His time was running out for this call; he was only allowed ten minutes, and sometimes less depending on the guard's patience. He couldn't afford to keep quiet when he needed Rose to really *hear him* right now.

This was his greatest fear.

It happened.

Diego was taken away.

He couldn't help him.

Rose was out of reach.

He couldn't save her, either.

"You're eighteen," Renzo told his sister, "so that means it's time for you to step up, Rose. You know what I mean? I've looked after you for your whole life—did whatever you needed, made sure you had whatever to get you where you deserved to go. It's your turn now. He's gonna need you, okay? Because he can't depend on me anymore. You gotta look after him; make sure she can't touch him. Be his harbor, all right? Be that safe place. He's really gonna need it now."

Because yeah, Renzo's fears came true, but he wasn't the only one. Diego had fears, too.

That kid was *living* them.

"He's gonna need someone again, Rose."

It just wouldn't be him.

That killed him.

But did it really matter when he already felt dead?

• • •

The tacky Halloween decorations lining the corridors of the prison felt like a joke to Renzo. Even the jail hadn't had that shit plastered up all over the place. He seriously considered ripping some of it down as he was directed through a body scanner before he would be taken to the meeting with his lawyer, but he knew better.

The guards here were *not* like the guards at the jail. He'd learned that his first night in the prison when a guard who was checking the block stood at the door of Renzo's cell as his new bunkmate tried to beat the shit out of him because he dared to sit on the one stool their cell had attached to the small table.

Here, a guard's loyalty to a prisoner was determined by what that prisoner could do for said guard. It depended on a prisoner's behavior, too, and how much trouble they were on any given day. It depended on a lot of shit, and the only thing Renzo had going for him at the moment with the guards was the fact he was quiet and didn't try to start problems.

Except that caused him a whole other problem.

With the inmates, that was.

They took his quietness and loner nature to mean he was easy prey. They picked up on the fact he was young just by looking at him and figured … there was nothing to him. Every single day in this place was like stepping inside a boxing ring against the best boxer in the world, and hoping he would make it out alive.

He didn't let anyone get away with a single fucking thing, either. He just couldn't afford to. If someone came at him whether it was outside during yard time, or in line at the cafeteria, he had to answer them back twice as hard. Prison was a culture in and of itself, Renzo had come to learn.

That culture had rules, and factors that determined a person's worth or standing in the eyes of the other inmates. If they thought for one second that Renzo was a weak fuck, they could and would eat him up and spit him out because of it.

He couldn't let them do that.

He wouldn't.

"All right," the guard said, stopping in front of the room their block used for private interviews with lawyers. Sometimes, they were held right in the visitation area, but if the lawyer put a request in, they would make a special effort to give them better privacy. Lucky for Renzo that today was his day. "Behave, we'll be watching from the other side of the glass in case you step out of line. You *will* be checked before you're returned to your cell. Do you hear me?"

Renzo nodded. "I hear you."

The cuffs on his wrists were loosened, and he was given a bit more chain. The shackles on his ankles, though? The guard didn't even look at those. The man waved at the camera overhead, and the door to the room opened. Renzo didn't even look inside before heading in—he just wanted to get as far away from his cell and block as he could. If that meant the safety and sanctity of a private chat for an hour or less with his lawyer who couldn't do fuck all for him at the end of the day, then that's what it meant.

It was better than getting the shit beat out of him. Better than eating the crap they tried to call food in the cafeteria. Better than having to watch his back in the showers because he swore it was like a game for some of these fucks to try and rape the new kid on the block. *Never going to happen.* He'd add another kill to his list, first. Hell, he already made a shank out of a toothbrush and a razor he traded for an illegal pack of prison rip—tobacco.

The man sitting at the table facing the doorway made Renzo turn into a block of ice just beyond the doorway. He seriously considered turning around and leaving the room as soon as his gaze met the man's cold, hazel eyes, but he had nowhere to go. The door closed the second he stepped inside, and he heard the loud locks close him in.

Fuck.

"What are you doing here?" Renzo demanded.

Lucian Marcello smiled from his seat. He wore a three-piece, black suit that looked tailored to his form. A shiny watch glittered under the bare bulb hanging overhead, as did the gold wedding band on his finger, and the signet *M* ring on his index finger. He just fucking smelled like old money and privilege sitting there smiling at Renzo like he had the upper hand between them.

In a way, the man had exactly that.

Lucian waved a finger at the window on the other side of Renzo. Really, it looked like a mirror, but he knew better. That's where the guard was watching his meeting, and while there was no speaker to say the guard could listen in, he didn't trust any of them with an inch. "See, I have influence and weight being who I am, Renzo. I can pull strings just about … anywhere, really. If I want something, all I really have to do is name the right price to get it."

Renzo didn't move an inch. "Well, if you want me dead, all you really have to do is pay somebody inside to get the job done. I don't see why you'd make the effort to get in here to do it yourself."

The man *chuckled.*

Actually fucking laughed.

Renzo didn't know what to make of that.

"I'm not here to kill you," Lucian said, sobering quickly. He gestured at the only empty metal seat at the table. "Sit, and chat with me."

"I'd rather not."

"I didn't ask what you wanted to do. Sit."

"You can leave; I think you've done enough to me, Lucian. You don't have to gloat. You don't seem like the type of man who would kick somebody when they're already down."

That smile of Lucian's faded fast. He met Renzo's gaze again, and nodded once. "You're right, I'm not. You should really hear me out right now, though … I am willing to help you, if you care to let me."

Yeah, he didn't believe that for a second.

Lucian didn't seem like he cared.

"I want to apologize for what I said to you about your mother," Lucian murmured.

Renzo's gaze narrowed. "What?"

"At your apartment the first time we met face to face, I called your mother a mess, didn't I? And while she is … I said it with an arrogance meant to hurt you. To embarrass you, even. I intended for you to hear me say it and know that I knew where you came from."

"That I came from trash," Renzo said thickly. "Just like her. Yeah, I heard you."

Lucian cleared his throat. "I was wrong; I apologize."

Renzo didn't know what to say to that.

So, he said nothing.

Lucian didn't seem to mind, as he simply continued talking like he was really the only one who needed to speak between them. And hell, maybe he was. God knew there was nothing that Renzo could say to this man that would be nice. Not at the moment, anyway.

"Seems you cared for your brother from the time he was born, didn't you?" Lucian asked, but not like he expected an answer from Renzo. "You see, I did something I perhaps should have done from the start ... look into you, I mean. Thank Vito Christiano for that, really."

Renzo's head snapped up, and his gaze locked onto Lucian's. "What?"

"Vito—he's still around, doing his thing in this life, but not as much as he used to a couple of years ago. But he's still there with a voice, and occasionally, he opens his mouth for the rest of us so that we have to listen to him. This time, he chose to open his mouth for you. Really, in a way, you owe your life to him, but that's a conversation for another day."

Renzo just blinked.

He didn't know what to say to that.

Lucian continued on, unbothered, "So yes, you looked after the littlest of your siblings from a newborn age. And your sister, too, really. Went out on the streets quite young to hustle, do what you needed to do, and make sure you all survived. While your mother was off shooting up and sleeping with her regular Johns, you were .... running the streets, making sure your siblings didn't go cold or hungry like you had to do a time or two."

"A time or two," Renzo said, scoffing hard. "That's funny."

"I was trying to be sensitive."

"Don't bother. I don't need your sensitivity. I lived my life—I know what's happened to me."

Lucian leaned back in the chair, and stroked a hand down his jaw. Never once did he take his gaze away from Renzo, though. "You know what kind of amazed me is that while you were a kid who grew up poor, though, and even when you were bringing in five-K a month selling drugs and handling your group of guys in the Bronx, you still lived like you were poor, too. Shitty apartment, no vehicle ... secondhand possessions, and hand-to-mouth when you could get it. I wondered why that was, but it didn't take me very long to figure it out. Your sister, huh?"

Renzo said nothing.

"See, I talked to an owner of a shop where your sister frequents to buy her canvases—I guess she prefers oil paint to the others—and you know, she's so fucking proud of you, Renzo. Talks about you all the time. Her brother who used to lift paint brushes and whatever else she needed from the art store just so she had something to practice with. And then you got older, she got lucky with the scholarship, but you knew there was no way you were going to be able to afford the things that the scholarship wouldn't cover, right?"

"She's going to be something great," Renzo said, shrugging. "I promised her she would. I made sure of it."

"She is quite talented, I agree." Lucian fiddled with the watch on his wrist as he straightened in the chair. "And so my point here, is the more I went around to ask about you and learn who this *boy* was who turned my daughter into someone I didn't recognize ... the more I realized I didn't know anything about you at all, despite what I had assumed. I asked the right questions too late. I took too long to give you the chance to prove your worth, and now look where you are."

Renzo blinked, unsure he had heard the man correctly. "What?"

"*Mea culpa*," Lucian said thickly. "My hubris always seems a little more vicious than someone else's but then again, maybe I am biased to it as well."

"I have no idea—"

Lucian waved a hand. "Not important. Are you going to sit yet, or ...? I mean, if I wanted you dead, I would have had you killed in San Francisco while my daughter watched on. You know, before I took the time to ... try to understand why taking you away from my child made her hate me. I had to know, you see, what it was about you that she loved enough that she was willing to leave behind the rest of us for you. Not that it matters—she hates me enough that she had to go to an entirely new state just to get away from me. I love her enough that I had to let her go."

Renzo let out a hard breath, the understanding he had been missing for this whole conversation suddenly dawning on him like a hundred pound weight slamming into his chest. He sat down in that chair because it felt a little more stable than standing up in those moments.

"Surprise," Lucian murmured, smiling sadly, "I found those things I couldn't be bothered to look for before. What is more interesting is the things you taught me without knowing, young man. That I am not perfect—I am fallible. I forgot where I came from for a time, that I was not always Lucian Marcello, powerful with just my name alone. And so, here I am ... doing the thing I never wanted to do again. Look at you."

He stared back at the man on the other side of the table ... unashamed and brazen. Renzo was all too aware that in a way, he had no one to blame for his current position except himself. He made the choice to take Diego. He robbed the store. He stole the vehicles. He made bad choice after bad choice, and they caught up to him in the end. Those choices may have caught up to him because of the actions of the man across from him, but at the end of the day, Renzo would still have twice as many fingers pointing back at him when he tried to place the blame on someone else.

"You know, finding you wasn't so hard after Vegas," Lucian said offhandedly. "Your friend there ... he helped us when you had stopped there, but after that, I knew you were running out of options. You only had so many places you could go, and so narrowing down the list to the people I thought could and would help you was simple."

"You had my uncle killed. He was a *good* man."

Lucian swallowed hard. "John sent in the wrong man ... my instructions were not followed. His death was unnecessary, and the man was appropriately punished for it. That's all I can say."

"That doesn't make it better."

"Nothing ever will. No amount of apologies or spilled blood will ever make it better. I know this better than anyone. So will you, in time."

Renzo barked out a bitter laugh. "*In time?* Take a look around, asshole, this is the time I'm looking at. The walls surrounding this place. So if that's the time you mean, thanks, I already know all about it."

Lucian's face gave away nothing as he replied, "That may not be the case. Depending on a few things." He checked the watch on his wrist, frowning. "Our time is running out. I'm not sure if I will be able to pay enough people to look the other way in order for me to get in here a second time … at least, not before the point where it'll already be too late."

"Too late for *what?*"

"Vegas. Let's go back to that, actually. Tucker—what do you know about him, hmm?"

Renzo's jaw tightened. "We were friends."

"Do you kill all your friends, or was he just a special case?"

The chair he was sitting on felt a hell of a lot more uncomfortable after that question. Renzo wasn't one to lie, so he looked away from Lucian's gaze as he replied, "He deserved what he got, I suppose."

Lucian quieted.

It took a second, then two …

"Did you kill him?" he asked.

"Who else would?"

Renzo still didn't look at the man.

"Why are you lying?" Lucian asked, his voice edging lower with every word. "I can tell, you know. There's no reason for you to lie to me about—"

His words abruptly cut off.

Renzo kept staring at the wall.

Then, in a whisper, Lucian said, "It was her. Lucia killed him."

Nope.

Renzo wasn't going there.

Vegas wasn't even on his list of charges for reasons he didn't know. He never brought it up to police, and they never even asked if he drove through the fucking state. He planned on keeping it that way, including to Lucia's father.

"What about Vegas and Tucker?" Renzo asked.

"I watched, you know … waiting," Lucian said, ignoring his question altogether. "I wanted to see if you were going to give her up. I know it would have been easy. You could have done it, washed your hands, and got a lighter sentence, probably. So, I waited and watched to see if you were going to do it. I had to *know.* Were you that kind of man when shit got bad, or are you the kind of man I was hoping you would be at the end of the day, Renzo."

That did make Renzo glance back at the man—angry and glaring. "I would *never* give her up for anything or anyone. *Ever.*"

Lucian chuckled, adding, "Not even to her own father, hmm? Just now, you were willing to lie for her about Tucker to me. Even now, locked up without the people you've worked your whole life to protect and love … you protect her above all else."

Why did Renzo's lungs ache each time he exhaled?

God, he wished he knew.

"That's why I'm here … in case you were wondering," Lucian said. "Because this was the test. She was the thing I needed to know about before I did anything else. Despite all I knew and the things I found out, I still had to know what you were going to do for her."

"I love her."

"Don't we all." Lucian sighed, and tipped his head down to check his watch again, muttering, "Five minutes left. All right, back to Tucker. He's connected. Did you know that?"

Renzo scowled. "Connected to *what?*"

"The mafia. The Vegas syndicate, specifically."

What?

Lucian nodded. "I can tell by your expression that this is a surprise."

"Was he always connected, or …?"

"No, he gained connections in Vegas. Specifically, he works for a brand of the syndicate there. A company called *The League.*"

"That doesn't ring any bells to me."

Lucian smirked. "Good, then they are doing their job."

"I don't—"

"Listen for a moment instead of speaking. It will do you wonders, I promise." Standing from the table, Lucian fixed his suit jacket and rounded the side to stand closer to Renzo. "You took away someone they considered important to The League. Well, Lucia did, it seems, but they blame you, and by proxy, me, too. And because you could be traced back to *my* family through Lucia, that means I am in their debt, now. A dangerous place to be."

Lucian told him to be quiet, so Renzo chose to do just that because none of this shit was making any sense to him.

"I could help you, that's the thing," Lucian said frankly. "Get you out or break you out between your time here and when they extradite you to Iowa for the robbery charge. I could *like* you … the way my daughter wants me to, and I know how easy it would be. She would forgive me, then, too. Not because she believes I did anything good or right … but simply because I would give you back to her. She doesn't see the problems with that, though."

Then, the man added in the same flat tone, "I could also put you away for the rest of your life, if I wanted to do that. God knows I have the evidence to do it, or I could *pay* to get the evidence to do exactly that."

Renzo blinked.

Lucian chuckled.

"Except I wouldn't do that either, not knowing all that I do now," Lucian muttered, glancing up at the ceiling. "I also can't give you the easy way out, you see. Because you and me, we're a lot alike in some ways."

"How so?"

Because Renzo didn't think they were anything alike.

"We're not the kind of men—given the circumstances of where we come from—to just take things that are handed to us," Lucian explained. "It's too easy—we've not *earned* it. We're not that type of men, let's be honest."

Well, he wasn't wrong.

"What happens if you don't pay back that debt to Vegas?" Renzo asked.

"A war, I imagine. One my family doesn't need. They'd go for her first. Lucia, I mean."

At that, Renzo felt cold all over.

"So, how do you pay them back, then?"

Lucian smiled over at him. "I kill two birds with one stone. I give you everything you want, Renzo, and them, too. All in the same breath, really. You can earn your spot in this world—have everything you want in time, and know it wasn't something simply handed to you. And they get what they want at the same time."

"I don't have any idea what you're talking about."

Lucian smiled grimly. "What is five years of your life worth, Renzo?"

"In here?"

"Being free ... well, as free as they'll let you be."

"Who is *they*?"

"The League."

Renzo shifted in the chair. "And what do they do, exactly?"

"Everything and anything." Lucian glanced at his watch again, and scowled. "Time's up—they'll be knocking soon. Do you want to hear the deal, and the plan, or not?"

To do *what*?

"What's it going to hurt?" Renzo asked.

A lot, he suspected.

It was going to hurt *a lot.*

"Five years of your life will be contracted to The League," Lucian said, "as a repayment for their debt. They have rules about things ... who you can contact, and how you will live in those five years, of course. But that is up to them and how they decide it should happen. They'll train you. *Teach you.* To be something you never even considered before—to be something greater than who you are. Don't we all want to be better, Renzo?"

Do better.

Be better.

He'd been repeating those words all his life.

He also heard *freedom.*

That meant Diego, Rose ... Lucia.

"Five years?" Renzo asked again.

He didn't care about the training. He didn't know what the fuck Lucian was talking about. None of it mattered because the man had just given him a hand out to help him up when all he had ever done was kick Renzo down to the ground. He saw the truth looking back at him—Lucian was trying to *do better.*

He was trying to be better.

"Five years," Lucian echoed. "They make the rules until that time is up."

"How do you get me out of here, then?"

"When you're extradited to Iowa, an event will happen. Let me worry about the details. You just keep yourself alive until then. This place is rough, I know. As for your brother and sister, because I know they're probably on your mind, too ... she now has a lawyer working pro bono on her case to get full custody of Diego. Well, pro bono to her, I guess. I'm the one who pays the bill for it."

Jesus Christ.

Renzo swallowed the thickness forming in his throat. "Should I thank you?"

Lucian shook his head subtly. "Don't thank me for what I am about to do to you.; for what *they* will do to you."

Maybe that should have been Renzo's warning.

He was still hearing the echoes of freedom.

What was five years?

Famous last words.

NINETEEN

Two months later ...

Lucia scrolled down the screen of her phone, the Google results not giving her *anything* that she wanted. It didn't seem to matter how many keywords she put into the search bar, nothing came up except blasts of the same kinds of articles over and over again. Articles that didn't tell her a goddamn thing, really.

Bronx Man Charged with Kidnapping.
Zulla To Face The Judge On Kidnapping Charges.
Man Found Guilty of Kidnapping.
Process to Begin Extradition to Iowa For Robbery Charges On Bronx Man.

The real problem was when Lucia tried to find out *where* in Iowa Renzo had been taken—she was trying to plan a trip to visit him—she couldn't find anything. She was convinced the damn prison registry was broken, or they had spelled his name wrong when he was brought in for the Iowa charges because even on that site, she couldn't find anything. That didn't mean she stopped looking because she *never* stopped looking for him. It felt kind of like she checked the internet less and less with each day that passed for a new update, but that didn't mean she stopped looking.

God.

She had to know where he was now.

California had done its job for her, though. That was the only good thing that she counted in her favor these last couple of months. Oh, she still felt entirely lost and confused. Like she was drifting into the air with no rope to keep her safe and tied down to something on the ground. Like her heart was empty and her soul was missing entirely.

She still felt those things, yes.

They greeted her every morning like the tightness in her chest, and the coldness of the spot in the bed next to her. A constant friend that she didn't particularly like, or want around, but here they were. Day in and day out. It put her to bed with tear stains on her pillow, and an ache in her gut.

California helped, if only a little bit. It kept her busy and getting ready to start school made sure she didn't really have much else to think about except what she needed to do for it. She still felt robotic, in a way. Like she was just going through the motions, but not living.

What was the point?

Her life was somewhere else entirely.

She wasn't as angry, now, but she believed that was only because she wasn't faced with her father every single day. She knew the anger was still there, if only distant in her mind, because when she was faced with the possibility of talking to her father … it came rushing back like a wave determined to take her under and drown her with its poison.

Lucia never realized just how much anger and contempt she could harbor for someone she loved until now. And what a fucking complex that was, really. To love and hate someone at the same time. Still, she wasn't the kind of person to blatantly hurt someone just because she couldn't get in control of her feelings, except she had done that to her father before leaving for California, so she knew putting distance between them was the best option.

That distance was closing now.

By the second.

Lucia still wasn't sure she was ready for it. In fact, that anger was already starting to burn hot and destructive inside her gut all over again. She was going to have to face her brother, who took Renzo away. And her father, who didn't seem to understand all he had done to hurt her. She was going to have to make nice, or *try*, and it was the very last thing she wanted to do, really.

Maybe coming home for Christmas break was a mistake. Not that she had really been given a choice. Her father left a message on her phone— because she still refused to pick up a call from him directly—stating he had bought her ticket, and she would find it in her email. She was to make sure she was on the plane to come home for Christmas … nothing more, and nothing less would be acceptable.

She shouldn't be here at all.

It was too late to back out now.

"What are you trying to find over there?"

Lucia was quick to turn the screen of her phone off and shove it back in her bag at her mother's question. In the driver's seat, Jordyn offered her a small smile and Lucia did her best to return it. She didn't think her smile reached her eyes like it usually would because Jordyn was quick to press her lips together in a thin line before going back to watching the road as she drove.

"You're still angry, then," her mother said softly.

Was it that obvious?

Did that agony in her heart just burn through her eyes?

"I feel like I wasn't given a choice about coming home for Christmas, and I don't feel like this is the best time of the year to make nice with Daddy and John … or anyone, really."

"Lucia, they love you."

"I'm not sure that makes it better. Worse, actually."

Jordyn sighed, and shook her head but never took her eyes off the road in front of her. "Okay, well then let's talk about something different. Not them ... how about you?"

Lucia eyed her mother from the side, not at all sure where Jordyn was trying to go with this conversation. "What about me, Ma?"

"How's prep for starting school?"

"It keeps me from wishing I wouldn't wake up in the morning."

Lucia didn't miss the way her mother's fingers tightened around the steering wheel so much that her knuckles turned white from the pressure. She figured her mother didn't want to think about her daughter depressed and alone in California, dealing with the kind of emotional baggage that no eighteen-year-old should have to deal with ... but she asked.

Hadn't she?

Lucia was trying to tell the truth more often, now.

It was freeing.

Too bad it wouldn't get rid of the contempt that she constantly harbored, now.

"You know," her mother said, her voice barely above a whisper, "even if you don't want to be here with us for Christmas, just know that *we* want you here, Lucia. I know you're angry. I know you feel alone, but we're still here, too. Okay?"

Lucia heard her mother, but she didn't feel very much about her words. She watched the buildings pass them by in the city as they headed for the suburbs going ten over the limit.

"Lucia," her mom said again. "*Okay?*"

She turned to glance at her ma, then. "No, it's not okay."

That was the problem.

She wasn't okay.

This wasn't okay.

It was never going to be *okay*.

Ever.

• • •

Lucia found it was easier to focus on the television, and the drama unfolding on the reality show than it was the person who darkened the entryway to the living room of her parents' home. She'd heard him come in, talk to their mom, and even ... slyly ask about her like it was going to make a difference to whether or not she wanted to talk to him.

It didn't make a difference.

She still didn't want to talk to him.

Her brother also didn't seem like he was going to give her a choice. What great fun this Christmas break was turning out to be, honestly. If her family would just get the hint and leave her to be on her own, then Lucia might find the moments she had to spend with them to be easier to swallow.

Instead, they kept trying to force their presence on her.

Like *now.*

"So hey, do you want to talk to me today, or what?" John asked, leaning in the entryway a little more.

Lucia didn't even look away from the show on the television. She wasn't at all interested in this garbage—it did nothing to fulfill her mind, but it was better than talking to her brother. She was still angry at John. Part of her didn't *want* to be, but if she let go of the anger burning in her chest and the contempt that felt like it was constantly holding her hand, then what else would she have left?

Nothing but herself.

And emptiness.

God knew she would rather be fire-red and ready to fight than sad, quiet, and alone. Lucia didn't expect them to understand, really.

"No," she said flatly.

She didn't miss the way John flinched at her dry tone.

"I tried to call you while you were in California." John cleared his throat. "Every couple of weeks."

Yeah, and she ignored every one of those calls, too.

That should have told him something.

Clearly, it didn't. Or he was just stubborn enough like her father that he was willing to keep trying even if that only made her anger with him ten times worse.

"Maybe my phone doesn't work there," she said, keeping that flat tone all the while.

"I think it does, Lucia."

"Then maybe that's a sign, John."

John sucked in air through his teeth, and quieted for a moment. She stupidly hoped that meant he was going to drop this whole attempt at shitty conversation with her, and go on his way. Maybe when she was feeling up to engaging him on another day, they could try again.

Today was not that fucking day.

Tomorrow didn't look great, either.

"You've been back from California for a couple of weeks, kiddo," John said. "I thought—"

She turned on him, then, her gaze burning with the intensity of the sudden rush of anger that flooded her veins like nothing else. She had never been one to have an anger problem, but it sure seemed like she did now. A single *word* could send her spiraling, really. Like right now.

"Don't ever fucking call me that again, John," Lucia hissed.

He stiffened. "What—kiddo? I've always called you that."

"Not anymore."

God, let it go, John. That's what she wanted to tell him more than anything. If he kept this up, she was going to hurt him the same way she did everyone else who got in her path lately, but especially if their last name was Marcello. It was like she couldn't help herself. They were a constant reminder of the person who had been taken away from her.

John wasn't giving up that easily, it seemed.

Kind-hearted like their mother.

Stubborn like their father.

"How's California? You've been there for a couple of months now." He didn't seem to mind that she just continued staring at him with a cold gaze, all the while, saying nothing at all. Finally, her brother murmured, "You could at least talk to me, Lucy."

Lucia wasn't stupid. She knew he was only using *Lucy* because John was aware she hated that nickname even more than the kiddo one. Not that it mattered. She wasn't falling for that damn bait. She wasn't a fish about to gulp the whole hook down all at once.

"California is hot," she said, unaffected.

There, if he wanted conversation, here it was. She couldn't offer much more, though.

"Yeah, I bet," he murmured.

"I start classes during the second semester. Next month after I go back."

She hadn't been ready to start right when she went to California. She'd visited the school a couple of times, got all the things she was going to need to be comfortable, settled into her new place, and tried to … feel better. None of it worked. Color her surprised.

"You're all settled in, though?" John asked.

"Guess so."

Lucia had to wonder, in those moments, if her brother felt as awkward about this conversation as she did. Could he tell how disinterested she was in even being in the same room as him? Because this was killing her, and not in a way that was going to be good for him. It drove her crazy how just looking at her brother could send her anger spinning—how staring at him in the face, one that was so familiar and used to be comforting to her, could now make her remember every single second of him coming into that apartment to rip her away from Renzo and Diego with a painful clarity.

Did he know what he had done, yet?

Did he appreciate her pain?

She doubted it.

"You were supposed to be my best friend, John," Lucia whispered.

She looked his way again, but this time, she wanted him to see more

173

than her anger. The telltale prickle behind her eyes said far more than she could. A single tear escaped, and it made a track line down her cheek. Quickly, she wiped the wetness away, and let out a hard breath.

How long had it been since she cried?

Oh, yeah.

Last night.

Like every damn night.

"You shouldn't have run off like that," John said simply.

Lucia didn't even know what to say to that because clearly, no, her brother did not understand why she was angry with him still. Some part of him still felt like he was in the right, and she was just going to move on. That was never going to happen. All she could do in reply to that was keep silent, and clench her jaw to keep back the words that threatened to spew out of her mouth.

"I was hoping you might let me apologize, and we could spend some time together while you're visiting," John said, shifting from one foot to the other in the entryway. "But even at Christmas, you ignored me."

That was a joke, right?

What was he going to apologize for?

Something he didn't think was wrong?

God.

They were all hypocrites.

And hell no, she wasn't going to talk to him at Christmas dinner when she had barely even managed to swallow her dinner without feeling like she was choking on every bite because of who else was in the room.

"Perhaps you should take a fucking hint, then," Lucia snapped.

"Lucia." His sharp tone did nothing for her. She refused to speak. Not that it mattered to her brother. He just opted to try a different direction again, asking, "What made you get mixed up with a guy like Renzo, anyway? Didn't I tell you not to mess with boys like that?"

Lucia couldn't help it.

She laughed at that.

A bitter, dark laugh that should have warned her brother. Those words were coming quicker than he was going to be able to handle them. Words that would cut him deep, and ones she wouldn't be able to take back. Not that she was even sure she wanted to take back all the things she had said to him, or anyone else who pushed her just a little too far.

"Like him?" she asked, cocking a brow. "John, you and every other man in our family are no better than him. Except what? We've got money, and you guys wear nice suits and drive expensive cars. So, you've got a last name that gives you respect, and a family legacy that affords you privilege."

Lucia shook her head, refusing to back off even a little bit as she added, "And guys like him? They come from the streets, and hustle every day of their lives just to survive. Did you know he was paying for his sister's private schooling? Nobody else paid for it. He was trying to let her be something when they came from nothing. Where do you think that left her? Or his little brother—his parents fucked off years ago. Where does that leave the boy? Don't worry, I'm sure his sister—who can't go to school anymore—took him, or better yet, maybe a nice foster family picked him up."

John blinked.

Fuck, yeah.

Even Lucia could hear the contempt burning in her voice. Her bitterness was bred so deep now, she was never going to be able to get it out.

Her brother didn't seem to know what to say, and Lucia liked that just fine.

"Fuck you with your *guys like him* shit," she said, fists balling into her lap so tight that her fingernails cut into her palms. Pain was something, though. It meant she was feeling something, and something was better than nothing at the moment. "So, you've got money and a suit, but that's all you've fucking got, too."

It took John entirely too long to come back with something to say.

Lucia wished he wouldn't have bothered.

"You come from the same privilege I do," John said quietly.

"Except I can own it now. Can you?"

"I'm sorry, Lucy. Really, I am. I didn't think that it was all going to lead to him being put away for—"

"Shut up," Lucia forced through her clenched teeth, not even wanting to go *there* with John. Like he honestly gave a fuck that Renzo had been locked away. Like her father, he probably looked at it like a blessing to them. "I bet Daddy had that planned, and you knew about it, too."

"Dad didn't plan anything. I just came after you to bring you home. The rest was circumstance, and shit."

Whatever.

She was done with this conversation.

Lucia turned to stare at the TV again, refusing to give him even one more second of her attention. Problem was, she knew her brother … he was going to keep pushing until she broke, and she just wasn't going to let him do that. There was really only one way to get her brother off a conversation, and that was to turn it on him. To make it *about* him.

There was nothing John hated more than someone asking about him—it was like being diagnosed with bipolar had made her brother defensive from the time his disorder was handed down. He always felt like people were inadvertently judging him just by asking about him. Lucia tried not to make her brother feel like that, but right now, she really just needed him to get the fuck away from her.

"Why don't we talk about you, John?" Lucia asked.

The shift in the room was instant.

She could feel the discomfort radiating from John.

"No, I'm good," he said, crossing his arms.

Yeah, she figured.

Lucia almost laughed, but managed to hold it back. "Then we have nothing else to say here. Daddy and the rest of them are upstairs."

Her brother still didn't move from the entryway.

"So that's it for us, then? You're going to go back to California in a couple of weeks, and you won't even bother with me at all while you're here? Nothing at all?"

"Don't take it personally, John. It's all of them, not just you."

There.

Let him take that however he wanted to take it. She didn't know how else to make it clear to John. Thankfully, he didn't say anything else. He was quick to leave her alone which was what she thought she wanted the most.

Maybe that was her problem …

Maybe she found comfort in loneliness now.

Who knew?

Not her.

Lucia wasn't sure how long she sat alone in the living room before she felt yet another presence in the entryway. Long enough for the reality show to change to something else she wasn't interested in, of course. Story of her life, lately.

She didn't even bother to turn and see who was in the entryway this time. She figured they would get the hint that she wasn't up for conversation if she kept ignoring them, but apparently she hoped for too much. This time, the voice was enough to *instantly* make her angry.

Hell, even with John it had taken a few minutes of conversation before she was ready to kill him with nothing more than her words. Not this time.

"Your brother mentioned that you weren't very … welcoming to him," her father said quietly.

Lucia sucked in a long inhale, and let it out slowly. "Maybe that should be a warning for you as well, Daddy. If you haven't gotten the hint since I came home for this break, I'm not interested in spending time with you, him, or … well, anyone, really. Not really sorry about it, either."

Lucian made a noise under his breath. "I was hoping that you might allow me to extend an olive branch, of sorts."

She didn't know what in the hell he was talking about, or what on earth he could offer her next to Renzo—*impossible now*—that might bring a bit of peace between them. God knew her lines were clearly drawn in the sand where her father was concerned. She wasn't even trying to hide it. The fact that he continued to ignore them sounded like a problem he had to deal with. She wasn't changing how she felt about him any time soon.

"Would you like an olive branch?" her father asked.

"Honestly, Daddy, I don't care what you do."

Let him make what he wanted of that statement.

Lucian sighed. "All right, Lucia. I tried ... not that it changes what I planned to do, anyway." She peered at him from the side, but he wasn't even looking at her, then. "Rose and Diego Zulla. I have their contacts after pulling some information. I thought you may like to have it. Perhaps visit them, even, while you're home. If you're—"

"Yes," Lucia said instantly.

She couldn't even pretend to be disinterested in *that*.

She wondered about Diego *all the time*. She didn't know Rose's number to call her—her contact had always just been labeled as *Rose* in Renzo's phone. Lucia tried looking for the girl's number, but found nothing. Like it had been changed to private after the whole Renzo ordeal. She bet the damn reporters got ahold of it, and wouldn't stop calling Rose for a comment. Not to mention, from the articles Lucia found, Rose had been the one to fight and *win* custody of Diego after he'd been placed in foster care.

Lucian smiled faintly as his gaze turned back on Lucia. He nodded once, and turned to leave her alone once more. Over his shoulder, he said, "I will get you the info, and make sure you have a vehicle to take with you when you're ready to go visit them. Oh, and Lucia?"

"Yeah?"

"This olive branch isn't meant to be an attempt to earn back your forgiveness. And it is not meant to be an apology from me. You're not ready to give me anything, and you're not willing to hear my apologies just yet. I know that—whether you believe it or not, I understand, too. Just so you're aware. I love you, *vita mia*."

That was another problem.

She didn't think he understood at all.

But he was right, too.

She wasn't ready.

Not to forgive.

And not for his apologies.

She might never be.

• • •

"So, you just went back to California?" Rose asked.

Lucia was sure Renzo's sister didn't mean for that question to sound accusatory, and yet, it still did. Or maybe that was just Lucia's guilt making itself known again by hearing things that didn't really exist. Her guilt, on the other hand, was very real. It never really left, even if it did sometimes give her a break occasionally.

It wasn't like she could forget about it, though.

She was free.

Renzo was … not.

What did it matter if he was locked up in New York, in Iowa, or somewhere else they had decided to send him to serve out his sentence? The facts would remain the same at the end of the day. She was here, and he was not. She could watch his little brother jump from the bars of the jungle gym to the puffy snow on the ground, and he could not.

That was the reality.

Her guilt was a killer.

"It was that, or stay here and feel like I couldn't breathe," Lucia murmured.

Rose nodded on the bench, and tightened her coat a little more around her neck like she was trying to keep the wind out. "Yeah, I guess I can understand that. After it first happened, it kind of felt like everything was hopeless. You know what I mean?"

Lucia shrugged. "Probably for a different reason than you, but yeah."

"I bet."

Looking over at Rose, Lucia gave her a small smile. "You got Diego, though. I bet he was happy when you brought him home."

Rose laughed. "I mean … terrified might be a better word. It was like he was convinced someone was going to come and—"

"Take him from you."

"Exactly that, yeah." Rose shrugged. "Sometimes, I think he still believes it, but he just doesn't talk about it now. The counselor told me to try to make everything feel permanent for him. Let him decorate his bedroom. Fill it with things *he* wanted and liked. Let him claim spots in the apartment that feel like his, or whatever. It helped, and then other days, it just feels like those are more things for him to lose if someone comes and takes him away."

Lucia frowned.

She couldn't even hide it.

"I'm sorry—we really messed up, huh?"

Rose looked over at her. "I don't see it like that, no. I know why Ren did what he did, and why you went with him. You have to understand, too, that nothing has ever felt very permanent or stable for us growing up. Diego was not really the exception just because he had Renzo to fall back on. He still moved around a lot. He never got to keep very many things that were supposed to be his. I'm trying to do different for him, now. That's all."

"What about school, and stuff? Does having him make it impossible to—"

"I finish this year anyway," Rose interjected quickly. "At first, I thought I was going to have to quit, but the caseworker attached to our file helped me a lot with different programs. Daycares for low income, and stuff like that. Renzo had paid for my housing up until this month, but I ended up finding a cheaper place that we move into at the end of the month. I'm trying to work Diego into it slowly, so I actually have been paying the rent for two months now, and taking him over there every other day. Each time, he brings something else to his new bedroom."

"But it's still hard."

She heard what Rose didn't say.

Rose nodded. "The money I had tucked away is running out, you know? Everything costs something."

That guilt was back tenfold.

Lucia's bank account had more zeroes that she cared to admit. Her trust fund was a constant source of stability for her. She never had to struggle for anything. If she wanted something, she always had the money to go get it.

"Could I help—"

"Please don't be offended," Rose said quickly before Lucia could even finish her statement, "but we're not a charity case, Lucia."

"I know, I didn't mean it like that. I just ... I'm sorry."

She should have known better.

Rose was just like her brother.

The thing was ... Lucia was smart, too. She knew the name of Rose's school, and that they sold the artwork of their students in a gallery, but especially the pieces that were done by the most talented. Students like *Rose*. She knew this because of her friend that had attended not long ago. And eighty percent of each sale went directly to the artist. It wouldn't take Lucia long at all to find out how many pieces of Rose's work that the school had for sale, or for her to buy every single one of them and have them stored away. If Rose wouldn't let Lucia help, then she would figure out another way.

Simple as that.

"I'll figure it out," Rose said, leaning back on the bench and staring across the park at her brother. "I always do. I promised Ren, you know, so I gotta make it work for Diego."

At just the mention of his name, Lucia's mouth decided to work before her brain could properly think about the question that slipped out far too easily. "Does he call you?"

God, maybe she could get the inmate number attached to his file. Or the facility he was now in ... anything that she couldn't seem to find on her own no matter how hard she tried to look.

Rose shook her head. "Not anymore—he did when he was in New York, you know? And then they moved him, and it stopped. He said that might happen, though. That when he got a chance, he would call again."

Lucia's brow dipped in her confusion. "How long ago was that?"

"A couple months," Rose whispered. "But when he calls again, I'll let him know you're asking for him, and stuff."

What did that mean?

Was he even—

"Lucia! Come play with me!" Diego shouted across the playground.

Lucia didn't even think about it. She got up from the bench, and headed for the little boy who, even after everything, still smiled at her like he loved her, too. Diego turned, and darted up the slide to climb the playground equipment again. While she had a second to do it, Lucia pulled the phone out of her pocket, and turned the screen on.

She typed out a single message to her father.

It simply read, *Thank you.*

It was the best she could give him. For now. The contempt she constantly harbored in her heart now still raged on, though.

Would it ever leave?

Lucia couldn't say.

ABOUT THE AUTHOR

Bethany-Kris is a Canadian author, lover of much, and mother to four sons, two cats, and three dogs. A small town in Eastern Canada where she was born and raised is where she has always called home. With her boys under her feet, a snuggling cat, barking dogs, and a spouse calling over his shoulder, she is nearly always writing something ... when she can find the time.

Find Bethany-Kris at her:

WEBSITE: www.bethanykris.com
BLOG: www.bethanykris.blogspot.ca
FACEBOOK: www.facebook.com/bethanykriswrites
TWITTER: @BethanyKris
INSTAGRAM: www.instagram.com/bethany.kris
PINTEREST: www.pinterest.com/bethanykris

Sign up to Bethany-Kris's New Release Newsletter here: http://eepurl.com/bf9lzD.

OTHER BOOKS

Renzo + Lucia

Privilege
Harbor
Contempt

Andino + Haven

Duty
Vow

John + Siena

Loyalty
Disgrace

Cross + Catherine

Always
Revere
Unruly
The Companion
Naz & Roz

Guzzi Duet

Unraveled, Book One
Entangled, Book Two

DeLuca Duet

Waste of Worth: Part One
Worth of Waste: Part Two

Standalone Titles

Effortless
Inflict
Cozen
Captivated
Dishonored

Donati Bloodlines

Thin Lies
Thin Lines
Thin Lives
Behind the Bloodlines
The Complete Trilogy

Filthy Marcellos

Antony
Lucian
Giovanni
Dante
Legacy
A Very Marcello Christmas
The Complete Collection

Seasons of Betrayal

Where the Sun Hides
Where the Snow Falls
Where the Wind Whispers
Seasons: The Complete Seasons of Betrayal Series

Gun Moll Trilogy

Gun Moll
Gangster Moll
Madame Moll

The Chicago War

Deathless & Divided
Reckless & Ruined
Scarless & Sacred
Breathless & Bloodstained
The Complete Series
Maldives & Mistletoe

The Russian Guns

The Arrangement
The Life
The Score
Demyan & Ana
Shattered
The Jersey Vignettes

Find more on Bethany-Kris's website at www.bethanykris.com